The Dark *of the* Moon

OTHER TITLES BY FIONA VALPY:

The Sky Beneath Us

The Cypress Maze

The Storyteller of Casablanca

The Skylark's Secret

The Dressmaker's Gift

The Beekeeper's Promise

Sea of Memories

Light Through the Vines (previously published as *The French for Love*)

The Recipe for Hope (previously published as *The French for Christmas*)

The Season of Dreams (previously published as *The French for Always*)

PRAISE FOR FIONA VALPY

'An immersive and moving story which will stay with me for a long time . . . I savored every moment.'

—Freya North, bestselling author of *Little Wing*

'A gifted storyteller with a unique voice . . . a beautifully written, uplifting, moving and evocative story that will stay with you! I loved it so much, I didn't want it to end!'

—Santa Montefiore, bestselling author of *Shadows in the Moonlight*

'Love, love, loved it . . . Brilliant story, I was completely immersed in it, so moving and touching too. The research needed must have been hard to do but it brought the war . . . to life.'

—Lesley Pearse, author of *You'll Never See Me Again*

'A novel that will whisk you to another time and place . . . a tender tale of hope, resilience, and new beginnings.'

—Imogen Clark, bestselling author of *Postcards From a Stranger*

'Fiona Valpy has an exquisite talent for creating characters so rounded and delightful that they almost feel like family, and this makes what happens to them feel very personal.'

—Louise Douglas, bestselling author of *The House by the Sea*

'A wonderfully immersive novel set against a vivid and beautifully described . . . setting. I loved it!'

—Victoria Connelly, bestselling author of *The Rose Girls*

'A moreish story of love, war, loss, and finding love again, set against an atmospheric . . . backdrop.'

—Gill Paul, author of *The Second Marriage*

The Dark *of the* Moon

Fiona Valpy

LAKE UNION
PUBLISHING

Published by Lake Union Publishing, Seattle

www.apub.com

EU Product Safety contact:
Amazon Publishing, Amazon Media EU S.à r.l.
38, avenue John F. Kennedy, L-1855 Luxembourg
amazonpublishing-gpsr@amazon.com

ISBN-13: 9781662516870
eISBN: 9781662516887

Cover design by Emma Rogers
Cover images: © Stuart Greenhalgh / Alamy Stock Photo; © Lukasz Szwaj © Lana Veshta © brillenstimmer © yaalan © SusaZoom / Shutterstock; © Otto Stadler © Daniel Viñé Garcia © claudio.arnese / Getty Images

Printed in the United States of America

For Mala.
Thank you for checking my maths.
And for teaching me about factorials!

The sea is calm tonight.
The tide is full, the moon lies fair
Upon the straits; on the French coast the light
Gleams and is gone; the cliffs of England stand,
Glimmering and vast, out in the tranquil bay.
Come to the window, sweet is the night-air!
Only, from the long line of spray
Where the sea meets the moon-blanched land,
Listen! you hear the grating roar
Of pebbles which the waves draw back, and
fling,
At their return, up the high strand,
Begin, and cease, and then again begin,
With tremulous cadence slow, and bring
The eternal note of sadness in.

. . .

And we are here as on a darkling plain
Swept with confused alarms of struggle and
flight,
Where ignorant armies clash by night.

from 'Dover Beach',
Matthew Arnold

Prologue

It was another long night shift at Fighter Command HQ. From their viewpoint on the gantry in the intruder operations room, the duty controller and his new assistant contemplated the sloping table beneath them, painted with an outline map of Britain, France and the Low Countries. The two Women's Auxiliary Air Force officers plotted the movements of any aircraft across the Channel and the North Sea, either outgoing or inbound. Tonight, all was quiet. Bad weather had grounded both the German and British bomber forces, so the table remained clear, uncluttered by any nocturnal threats. But then one of the WAAFs placed a single aircraft on the map, and the controller watched as it inched its lonely way out across the Channel.

'What's that then?' the assistant asked.

'A Special. They go out in all weathers. But you'll only see them fly during the fortnight either side of the full moon.'

'What are they up to?'

'No idea. No one here knows. Official Secrets Act stuff, I suppose, and none of our business. If they told us, they'd have to shoot us. They go out, then a few hours later you'll see them come back. Usually, at least.'

'Sooner them than me, in this weather.' The assistant shuddered, reaching for his mug of tea. In their underground headquarters they were cocooned from the outside, but the meteorological reports were grim. For a moment, he imagined what it must feel like to be piloting that lonely aircraft, flying resolutely onwards over the darkened, stormy sea towards enemy-occupied territory.

They watched as the WAAF officer moved the solitary aircraft another inch closer to the French coast.

'Well, I'll tell you what it is, Group Captain,' the assistant said, as he pushed aside a pile of papers and put his cup back down, settling in for a quiet night. 'It's a mystery. No. More than that, it's a – whatchamacallit? – a ruddy enigma, that's what it is.'

Philly

'. . . And this is your room,' says Kendra, stepping back as she opens the door, allowing me to enter first. As I turn to thank her, I'm struck again by her resemblance to her grandmother and for a moment my mind plays one of its silly tricks, making me think I'm back in the dormitory at school more than seven decades ago and she is Ella, my best friend. I look around, expecting to see the iron bedsteads pushed against the walls and Beatrice, the third of our tight-knit band, sitting on one of them, brushing her copper-coloured hair. The Three Musketeers, they used to call us. Ella was the beautiful one. Bea was the artistic one. And I was the brainy one. But this isn't school, and they are both gone now. I'm the last one of us left.

I give my head a little shake, trying to clear it, pulling myself back to the here and now. The room is bright with French sunlight, the only bed a double one, covered with a pretty *toile de Jouy* quilt. There's a painted chest of drawers with a jug of wildflowers set on it and a wooden stand on which hang two neatly folded white towels. It's just as I'd always pictured it from Ella's descriptions, after that first heady summer she spent here so very long ago. The summer we left school and our lives went in such different directions . . . I wonder whether Kendra feels Ella's spirit here, just as I do. She well knows how much this house on an island just off the west coast of France meant to her grandmother.

I blink, forcing my meandering mind to focus again as the boy clumps up the stairs carrying my suitcase. He's at that awkward stage in his early teens, all elbows and knees, and he bumps his shoulder against the door frame as he enters, as if his brain hasn't quite caught up with how quickly his body has grown. I wince, thinking he must have hurt himself, but the expression on his face doesn't flicker. He uses both hands to lift the case and swing it on to the bed with a bounce. His straight blond hair hangs to his shoulders and the back is matted into a tangle. I suppose trips to the hairdresser must get complicated if even the thought of being touched sends you into a frenzy of panic and horror.

'Careful, Finn,' says Kendra. 'Don't damage Mrs Delaney's things.'

He doesn't reply, but turns to look at me, the first time he's done so directly. Those eyes. They are the same colour as Ella's were, sea-green flecked with gold. But there's a tautness around them, a look of tired anxiety no child should have to carry. Despite the sun and the wind – because surely he must spend some of his time outdoors, or is he one of those youngsters who's glued to a computer screen from dawn to dusk? – his face is untanned. There's a pinched, tense look to his features, but otherwise they're expressionless.

'What happened to your leg?' he asks. It's the first thing he's said to me, social niceties clearly being surplus to requirements.

'I lost it in France, a long time ago,' I say, tapping my walking stick against my prosthesis. The stump of my knee is swollen from today's flight and from walking what seemed like miles, firstly at Gatwick and then when we landed at La Rochelle. The plane had come to rest some distance from the terminal, so I'd had to limp across the expanse of tarmac and then take my place at the back of a long queue for passport control in the early summer heat.

'You've come to the right place to look for it then,' he says. His face, as pale and waxy as the full moon, holds no hint of a smile.

'That was a joke, by the way. Haha.' The tone of his voice is flat, even his laugh lacking inflexion.

'Finn!' The tone of Kendra's voice is sharp; the reprimand makes him wince. 'I thought we agreed you were going to practise good manners.'

'Sorry.' I can see the tension draw tighter around his eyes as he drops his gaze to the floor. I sense he hates being in the wrong, letting his mother down.

'Don't worry, it's a good joke actually,' I say, smiling to reassure him. And of course he's uncannily close to the mark, although it's not my missing leg I've come to look for. It's something else altogether. But I keep that to myself. 'I'll tell you the whole story sometime. But right now I think I'd like to freshen up a little after my travels.'

'Of course, Philly,' Kendra says, relief showing in her expression that I haven't taken umbrage.

I've known about Finn's autism for years. Ella used to talk about him often, and I know she had a particular soft spot for this special great-grandson of hers. I'd seen him at the funeral, but he'd kept himself apart, sitting in a corner with a pair of ear defenders clamped on his head. The noise of chatter in the reception room at that hotel was so loud I thought I wouldn't have minded donning a pair myself. Kendra had come over to talk to me, proffering a plate of sandwiches. And it was there that she'd first issued the invitation to come and spend a couple of weeks with them here at the house on the Île de Ré. She'd written Ella's life story – indeed, she had had some success with the book – and asked whether I'd mind sharing my own experiences. She was developing her career as a writer, she told me, always on the lookout for new ideas. She'd heard a little about me from her grandmother and thought she might write my biography, if I'd agree to it. I said I'd think about it.

A couple more years passed, as they do, and her invitation was repeated in each of the Christmas cards she'd send me.

And then I picked up the phone and asked if I could come and stay in the summer. Because I decided it had been long enough, at last. I can now talk about those times. About the things we'd kept so secret for seventy-five years, now they've been declassified.

So Kendra's invitation was a good excuse to come to the island. And, if I'm being completely honest, I suppose there's a bit of vanity as well, thinking my life story could be worth writing down. She's going to find out that it's a story without an ending, though, full of loose ends that haven't been neatly tied up.

But maybe I have it in me after all, to try one last time. To continue the search I thought I'd given up years ago. One last chance to try to find out what happened. I know it's a fool's errand really. This is the only place I haven't yet been to and looked, and of course, there's a good reason for that. I already know the war graves in the cemeteries here on the island hold no possibilities. I ruled them out long ago, back in the days before every new hope became yet another dead end.

As Kendra and Finn leave me to unpack and rest a little, though, I'm suddenly overwhelmed by a longing to be back in my own home in England. Perhaps I shouldn't have come away. What on earth was I thinking? Two weeks suddenly seems an eternity to be staying in this house with this family of strangers. How am I going to manage, with my missing leg and my wonky mind, and my fragile digestive system that'll never withstand the onslaught of foreign food? What an old fool I am.

I kick off my left shoe and then unstrap the prosthesis from my right knee, gingerly prodding the swollen stump. With a grunt, I lower myself on to the bed and swing my legs up on to the coverlet, exhaling a long sigh of relief.

A breath of sea air stirs the white muslin curtains framing the window, and for a fleeting moment I think I see Ella standing there again. I close my eyes. Yes, I think, coming back to France is a mistake. Continuing the search is nothing but a wild goose chase.

Too many ghosts have followed me here. Too many memories. Faces in the moonlight, their eyes dark with fear. They knew they were risking everything. We all were. But we did it all the same. Because what other choice did we have?

Finn

The Old Lady smells of lavender, flowery but not too sweet – I like it because it's like the drops Mum puts on my pillow to help me sleep and it doesn't make me want to vomit like some ladies' perfumes do. She wears bright-red lipstick that bleeds into the lines around her mouth. Her false leg is pretty cool, and her eyes are bright and wise like a bird's. She told me to call her Philly. 'But your name is Mrs Ophelia Delaney,' I said.

'It is,' she agreed. 'But my friends call me Philly.'

I don't think we are friends really. She's at least 80 years older than me. But it was nice of her to say that. Good Manners. Which we're all trying to have at the moment.

At supper, my Mum and Dad made Polite Conversation, talking about the sailing camp. It was Dad's idea. He's been teaching me to sail a dinghy, which I quite like because when I sail it single-handed it feels like a place where I'm in charge and I can be on my own. Then he read something online about an organisation called Autism Afloat, which tries to get people like me who have an Autistic Spectrum Disorder interested in sailing bigger boats. Before I could point out all the reasons why it was a really bad idea, he'd got in touch with them and suggested they run a summer camp here on the island. He's found some dinghies and a bigger boat, and helped organise accommodation and they are bringing some kids to have this Amazing Experience. And I'll be on that boat too, having the Amazing Experience with all the others. Only I know it's going to be awful. I've been stressing out about it for months.

'It's going to be an amazing experience, isn't it, Finn?' said Mum, continuing the conversation. I knew her question wasn't a real one. She was just saying it for the benefit of the Old Lady, in that tone of voice of hers that goes too high and too bright. She uses it to try and convince me – and herself too, along with anyone else who's listening – when she knows something is probably going to be the opposite. Like going to a new school. Or eating cauliflower, which looks like bits of white brain.

I couldn't really be bothered making Polite Conversation, so I kept on counting the peas on my plate, making sure there was an even number of them before I could start to eat, and hoping yet again that some cataclysmic event would occur to stop the camp from going ahead. The boats being no longer available, perhaps, due to being hijacked by pirates or swamped by a rogue tsunami. Or the planet being struck by a meteorite and all living things being wiped out. It's not impossible. The Canary Island of La Palma is a basaltic shield volcano and it's been shown that these structures have a tendency to experience catastrophic landslides about every 100,000 years. The last one happened about 89,000 years ago, plus or minus 8,000 years. If we assume it's actually plus 8,000 years, then we're about due the next one any day now. There's a hypothesis that if the side of the island does collapse catastrophically, it will cause a mega-tsunami. So I don't really want to be out in a boat when that hits.

There were 42 peas on my plate.

When I looked up from spearing my peas 2 at a time to eat them so the number on my plate would always be even, the Old Lady was watching me, and her eyes were sharp and bright, which made me think once again that she looked like a bird. Maybe one of the white-headed kittiwakes that swoop around the mast when I take the sailing dinghy out. I don't mind sailing on my own or just with Dad. It's the thought of having to do it with lots of other people that freaks me out. I think maybe she could see what I really thought about the Amazing Experience my parents have in store for me. She didn't say anything though, just cut up a tiny piece of chicken and put it in her mouth.

'There's quite a bit for us to do in the week ahead, isn't there, Finn? Putting the final arrangements in place,' said Dad. This was really for the benefit of the Old Lady as well, because he went on, 'So we'll be keeping out of your hair, Philly, while Kendra gets your life story down.'

People say things like that a lot. As if we would be in their hair in the first place. It would be impossible. The Old Lady's hair is straight and white and it's cut short so it fits the shape of her head, just like a kittiwake's feathers.

'The timing's worked out so well,' said Mum. 'And it's good that I can fly back with you, too, on my way to the creative writing course.'

The Old Lady smiled and nodded, but I could see the brightness had gone out of her eyes a little. Maybe she can't be bothered with making Polite Conversation either. I think she was tired, and she kept shifting her weight on her chair, so perhaps her leg was hurting her. After supper, I went straight upstairs to my room and I heard her coming up too, just a few minutes afterwards. Her false leg makes her steps a bit uneven.

Next morning, she looked a bit brighter again when she came downstairs to sit at the breakfast table. She didn't eat much, but she seemed glad to accept the cup of coffee Mum made for her. Then Dad went off to do some of the final arrangements for the sailing camp. He asked me to join him. 'We could get the bikes out of the shed,' he said. 'Cycle over to the harbour?'

I said no thank you, I'd prefer to stay at home and read the book he gave me about sailing. I find making Polite Conversation can sometimes be a good way to get out of doing things you don't want to do. It's a lot less tiring than having a meltdown, anyway. I don't really need to read the book. I know how to sail from using the dinghy, which is just for one or two people. Exactly the same principles apply to sailing the bigger boat, only you need more people. You have to Work As A Team and each member of the crew has to Play Their Part. Exactly the characteristics that autistic people aren't exactly known for, in case Dad hadn't noticed.

I sat on the sofa in the sitting room with the book on my knees while Mum and the Old Lady went into the study so Mum could start listening to her story. 'Let's start at the beginning,' I heard Mum say. And I was actually quite interested to hear the story too, so I left off my ear defenders.

Philly

My family was pretty unconventional for the time, I suppose, although I never realised it when I was young. Even the most eccentric childhoods seem normal when it's all you've ever known.

My mother was Polish, and my father came from a wealthy Scots family who owned a jute mill in Dundee. So money was never a worry, even when he ran off to Argentina with a woman who'd been giving him and my mother tango lessons, and disappeared from our lives. It was the 1930s and the divorce was a terrible scandal. Mother's (Catholic) family had already disowned her when she married my (Protestant) father, and the divorce was absolutely the final straw, so we never saw that side of the family. But Mother didn't let it hold her back. I suppose she'd decided her reputation was already in tatters so she might as well do as she liked. And what she liked was lounging around the house in a silk negligée all day, then going out in the evenings to party, drink vodka martinis and play card games.

Most of the time her Polish roots were subsumed by a wish to appear thoroughly British, although her cut-glass accent would slip and she'd even lapse into speaking her native language when she'd had a few drinks. The one exception to following British customs was at Christmastime, when she'd insist on observing her childhood traditions. We'd fast all day on Christmas Eve while the house filled with the wonderful smells of the twelve dishes she'd prepare for our Wigilia feast, to be eaten that night while we held our Christmas vigil. I loved the vividly coloured *barszcz* with little *uszka* dumplings, the wild mushroom *pierogi* fried in butter, and the poppy seed rolls she made for dessert. Ella and Beatrice, my Scottish friends, would beg their parents to be allowed to come and spend the evening at my house, thrilled by our exotic traditions as well as the opportunity to extend Christmas by a day.

I was sent to boarding school and left largely to my own devices during the holidays, spending my days devouring books in the local library or staying over at Ella's. My two brothers were older. Frank, who was ten years my senior and had a somewhat pompous and superior attitude to match, took over the running of the factory once Father left. I was closer to Teddy, who was nearer to me in age. And when he joined the RAF, based at Turnhouse, just outside Edinburgh, he was the one who got me interested in flying.

Thanks to him, I used to devour the newspaper reports of female aviators like Amy Johnson, the first woman to fly solo from London to Australia and who set many another record in the 1930s. My brothers had been at school in Edinburgh with her husband, Jim Mollison, and although they hadn't been close friends – Jim being a couple of years ahead of my elder brother, Frank – I still considered it counted as a direct link to my idol. Teddy gave me a Schiaparelli bag named after 'Johnnie', as she was nicknamed, and it was by far my most treasured possession. I longed to be like her and become a pilot.

I think I was about fifteen when I first pulled on a pair of jodhpurs and a sheepskin jacket and climbed into a plane with Teddy for him to take me for a spin. I was immediately hooked. It gave me a freedom I'd never known before. He pulled back on the throttle and we soared away out over the sea, flirting with the clouds, leaving behind all the petty mundanities that existed back on solid ground. I loved the logic of it, the laws of physics that made us airborne and kept us aloft, and from that moment on I was determined I'd learn to fly. Mother gave me a pretty generous allowance and I spent every penny of it on lessons. By the time I finished school, I had my pilot's licence along with an offer to study Maths at Cambridge.

But then the war changed everything, turning our lives upside down. It closed some doors but opened others, and so I shelved my plans to go to university and wrote a letter to a woman I'd heard about from Teddy, who was recruiting female pilots into the Air Transport Auxiliary. I desperately wanted to do something useful, especially when I read about Germany invading Poland. Even though my mother had turned her back on her homeland and her family there, my Polish roots ran deep within me, and I realised my pilot's licence would probably be of more practical use than a university degree. Teddy was doing his bit, and I wanted to help where I could as well.

Now that Britain was at war, things moved fast. Almost straight away, I was invited to attend an interview at White Waltham Airfield in Berkshire. And so I did the logical thing and flew down for it in the Tiger Moth I'd borrowed from my flying instructor. I pulled up on the edge of the runway alongside a parked-up Spitfire and climbed out of my plane, clutching my handbag and attempting to smooth down my hair, which was in a sorry state having been squashed into my flying helmet for the journey. An RAF mechanic marched up to me pretty smartly and asked me what the hell I thought I was doing, arriving unannounced and unauthorised like that. I pointed out that it was hardly unannounced, and neither was it unauthorised: I'd radioed the tower and been given permission to land, and I had an appointment to see Miss Pauline Gower.

He scowled at me. 'Oh, you're one of *them*, are you? Bloody women, thinking they can fly planes.'

'I don't *think* I can fly a plane. I can,' I retorted. 'As, in fact, I have just proven. Q.E.D.'

'Queuey . . . what now?'

'Q.E.D. *Quod erat demonstrandum*. It means "that which was to be demonstrated". And now, if you would be so kind as to point me in the direction of Miss Gower's office, I shall leave you to get on with your work, which I'm sure is of far greater importance than wasting time attempting to put a woman in what you mistakenly believe to be her place.'

He scowled again, but waved the spanner he was carrying in the general direction of a group of Nissen huts beside the control tower before turning away and marching off towards the Spitfire, shaking his head and grumbling something that was, fortunately, largely unintelligible.

My 'interview' was a formality. Pauline Gower had seen me land. 'You're very young. But if you can handle a plane, you're in,' she said, after a cursory glance at my licence and a few questions about my age and my schooling. 'Welcome to the ATA, Miss Buchanan. Our ferry pool pilots work to a schedule of thirteen days on and two days off. When can you start?'

And so, a fortnight later, I found myself based in Luton, where I was to undergo Elementary Flying Training School. Even though I already had my licence, every ATA pilot had to go right back to the beginning and learn a new way of flying, without instruments, using maps and plotting a course within sight of the ground below.

Our job as ferry pilots would be to fly planes up and down the country to where they were needed. Sometimes it would be a brand-new model, just off the production line, needing to be delivered to an air base. Other times, especially later as the war heated up, we had to deliver damaged planes back to the factory to be fixed or to the scrapyard if they were beyond mending. Every job was different, but the crates we were flying weren't up to scratch. Even the new planes were usually unfinished, lacking their instruments, which would be fitted by the RAF at the base. So, because we were essentially flying blind, with only a map and compass, we had to navigate by sight along railway lines and rivers. That meant we could only fly during the daytime and were grounded when visibility was poor. Which was often, of course, in the British winter. It was a frustration for me because Teddy had taught me all about using instruments, and I enjoyed the technical aspects almost as much as the sense of liberty I felt as I soared above the clouds and set my course by dead reckoning, relying only on my readings and my instinct.

My exasperation overflowed on the first day I was allowed up in a trainer. The plane I had been assigned to was a 'Maggie' – a Miles Magister low-wing trainer – for a lesson with Captain Weatherly, an elderly former First World War pilot who'd been drafted in out of his retirement to teach us recruits. He sported an impressive white moustache, streaked with yellow from the cigarettes he smoked almost non-stop, even when behind the throttle of a plane. It was so wide that he'd twirled the ends into points that jutted out well beyond the sides of his jowly cheeks. Captain Weatherly was renowned for taking a dim view of women being allowed anywhere near an aircraft, let alone being allowed to fly one, so I don't think either of us faced the prospect of the lesson with much enthusiasm. I climbed into the seat behind him and tried not to breathe in too much of his second-hand cigarette smoke as he barked a few instructions at me. We took off and I began to relax a little, enjoying the sensation of being airborne again after days of theory classes in a poky Nissen hut. It was a beautiful day, the sky clear and visibility good, and I could plot my course with ease, following the railway line beneath us. I amused myself by using the points of the Captain's moustache as an artificial horizon, flying straight and level as instructed. My spirits lifted, and so did the plane as I eased back on the throttle, instinctively climbing higher. Through my headset, I heard the Captain shout a command to reduce height immediately. But I wanted to climb just a little higher, putting the Maggie through her paces. He swivelled round in his seat, fixing me with a baleful glare. I could see him mouthing something at me, since I was ignoring what he'd been shouting through the headset, and I knew that – in between the expletives – he was telling me to obey orders and return the aircraft to the ceiling of three hundred feet he'd specified at the outset. His face had turned a furious dark red, but the blue of the sky above us was just too tempting and I continued my climb. Suddenly, the plane lurched and bucked, and the controls stopped responding to my touch. The pitch of the engine began to increase, rising to a scream, and the nose lifted higher. Panic rose in my chest as I tried to compensate, but to no avail. The Captain had taken back control and begun a slow roll. Nausea rose in my throat, and I swallowed hard as we climbed up and over, making a full loop. At the very top, as I hung there helpless, my straps cutting into my shoulders, I vowed never to disobey instructions again. I'd learned my lesson.

The Captain hadn't finished with me yet, though. He righted the plane, and I was mightily relieved to spot the airfield below us, but then he began a dive. I saw the needle of the air speed indicator swing right, then tremble at the very edge of the dial, and gasped as the ground sped up to meet us. At the last moment, he pulled out of the dive and began another sickening roll. Finally, he cut the throttle, and in the sudden silence I heard him say calmly through my headset, 'She's all yours. Force land on to the field.'

Somehow, I managed to regain control of both myself and the aircraft and executed a bumpy landing. As I climbed shakily out of the cockpit, having brought the Maggie to a halt in front of the hangar, Captain Weatherly reached into the breast pocket of his overalls and lit yet another cigarette. He sucked in a lungful of smoke, then blew it out through his nostrils, reminding me of an angry dragon. 'Well, Missy,' he snorted, 'I hope you've learned your first lesson today. And if you ever disobey orders again, I'll make sure you're put straight back behind a desk for good, where you belong. Do you understand?'

'Yes, sir,' I replied, suitably chastened.

'Bloody disobedient woman.' His tone was caustic. But then the expression in his eyes softened the tiniest bit. He flicked the tip of ash from his cigarette before sticking it back into the corner of his mouth, and just as he was turning away, I thought I caught the faintest smile beneath the awning of his moustache as he made his final assessment of his pupil. 'I'll say one thing for you, though. You do know how to fly a plane.'

After that, in the weeks that followed, I knuckled down and reined in my enthusiasm, and made jolly sure I obeyed the rules, practising endless circuits and bumps – as we called take-offs and landings without stopping – over the fields of Bedfordshire.

Early one grey December morning I was outside the hangar, chewing the fat with the mechanics and waiting for my instructor to appear. I was to practise emergency landings for the first time that day and had spent hours poring over the ferry pilot's 'Bible', a small ring-bound folder containing crib cards with the handling notes for every one of the hundred different types of plane we might be expected to fly. Each entry included the standard settings for the aircraft as well as how to operate the undercarriage manually and what landing speed to use should the hydraulics fail. I was feeling a little anxious, and I patted the knee pocket of my overalls, my fingers tracing the cardboard cover of my 'Bible' for reassurance. But then I forgot to be nervous when a dark-haired young man in a flight suit appeared around the side of the hangar.

By then, I'd grown used to many of the characters who'd been drafted in as ATA instructors. They seemed to be exclusively either ex-First World War pilots like Captain Weatherly (of whom I'd begun to grow rather fond, after our inauspicious start), or men who'd been rejected by the Royal Air Force because they didn't meet the rigorous physical standards required to fly in combat, but who still wanted to do their bit for the war effort. From the outset,

I knew this man was different. Despite the fact that his right arm was in a sling, there was an air of confidence about him. He walked with a spring in his step and wore his RAF cap at a jaunty angle. I stood up a little straighter and ran my fingers through the tangles of my hair, wishing I'd had time to brush it before leaving my digs.

'Flight Lieutenant Ben Delaney,' he said, holding out his good left hand for me to shake. I took it, a little awkwardly, and then forgot to let go for several moments too many. His eyes were as blue as the clearest summer sky, and as he fixed his gaze on me it felt as if the dreary grey clouds above us parted and the sun came out.

'Is this your first time?' he asked me, smiling.

I must have looked a complete idiot as I stood there, blushing. So taken was I by that smile that I could hardly think, let alone stammer a reply. It felt as if he could read my mind as I realised that, yes, this was my first time. The first time I'd fallen in love with someone at first sight.

Seeing my discomfort, he gently prompted me. 'Your first time doing an emergency landing?'

I attempted to pull myself together. 'It is,' I said. 'Sorry, I thought it would be Captain Weatherly or one of the other instructors . . . I wasn't expecting . . . I mean . . .' I clamped my mouth shut, inwardly berating myself. *Shut up, Philly, you sound like a complete imbecile.*

'I know. You weren't expecting a newly qualified Spitfire pilot. Bit of a setback. I'd just completed my training and got my wings. Then the day I finished my stint in an operational training unit, I came off my motorbike. Temporarily out of action due to mild concussion and a broken arm.' He raised his plaster cast in the air. 'But don't worry, between us we have three good arms and one brain that works properly. I think we'll manage. Shall we?' He gestured towards our aircraft.

His unflappable demeanour – even when having to endure flying around above the airfield for half an hour at a time while his panicked pupil frantically operated the hand pump to lower the undercarriage, simulating emergency conditions – and the warmth in those blue eyes of his when he turned to congratulate me after my first successful emergency landing filled me with reassurance. But his obvious skill as a pilot, when he took the controls on our next flight, filled me with awe. With his right arm in its plaster cast, he used his knees to control the stick and reached over with his left hand to adjust the throttle without missing a beat. Even one-handed he flew better than many able-bodied pilots.

In the mess hall afterwards, we talked for hours. That day, I blessed the weather for closing in, so that his duties were curtailed. He told me he was keen to get out on his first front-line duty. 'That stupid accident put me out of action, but once my brain unscrambled itself enough, I thought I might as well volunteer to do some of the more advanced training for the ATA while I'm *hors de combat*. Every cloud has a silver lining, though, doesn't it? Otherwise I wouldn't be sitting here drinking tea with you.'

He told me he'd only volunteered in order to keep up his flying hours, but I soon learned his love of flight equalled my own passion and he'd really just wanted to find a way to take to the skies until he was fit to fly fighter planes again.

In the days that followed, I wasn't the only female trainee to seek him out in the mess hall as we downed endless more cups of lukewarm weak tea, waiting for the weather to clear. But I liked to think his smile was especially broad when he saw me approaching. He made me a better pilot. And he made me want to spend every possible moment in his company. The sessions when his initials – BCD – were jotted in my logbook alongside the entries recording my flying hours and experience were the best days of all.

Once my training was completed, I wasn't sorry to leave Luton, but I was very sorry indeed to say goodbye to Flight Lieutenant Ben Delaney. My heart did loop-the-loops at the sight of him and, although

I tried to dismiss it as a crush, no other man had had that effect on me. So I also felt it breaking a little when the time came to say goodbye.

I was being deployed to the ATA base at White Waltham and he was champing at the bit to see some action, now his arm was out of its sling at last. I'd seen how his eyes lit up when he talked about getting back to his beloved Spitfires. The Maggies and Tiger Moths we used for training must have seemed so dull and clumsy to him. You can tell a lot about a person by the way they handle a plane. I now knew from our training flights that he was as skilled as he was dashing. He could get the best out of whatever machine he flew. And he could get the best out of people too. He somehow made me feel simultaneously more alive and more grounded, and chatting to him in the mess hall made the awfulness of the food and the dreariness of the surroundings evaporate.

Reluctant as I was to say goodbye to him, I knew we were both impatient to put our training into practice in our different ways. I felt a sudden surge of fear, picturing him alone in a Spitfire and facing the enemy in earnest for the first time. If he felt any qualms about the challenges he was about to face, though, he didn't show them.

'Good luck, Ben. I hope we'll meet again someday,' I said as he took his leave. I felt myself blush, realising I'd accidentally addressed him by his first name.

He smiled that calm smile of his and reached for my hand. 'We will, Philly. It's a small world. I'll be watching out for you. Fly safe.' For a moment, I thought he was going to lean closer and kiss me. And every cell in my body longed for him to do so. But he just gave my hand a squeeze instead, then turned smartly on his heel and marched away.

'You too,' I whispered to his retreating back, the surge of hope rising in my chest making the bits of my heart that were breaking apart suddenly snap back together. But then I had to set my emotions to one side and focus on the next chapter of my career as an ATA ferry pilot.

Finn

In 1505, Leonardo da Vinci wrote his Codex on the Flight of Birds. He was fascinated by the thought of making a human flying machine, but when he tried to design one – powered by a man making a pair of wings flap – he underestimated the limitations of human anatomy. A human being could never flap their arms hard enough and fast enough to fly. (Anatomy also proves that angels don't really exist, because if they did, they would need to have a breastbone more than 3 metres deep to support their wings.) Leonardo da Vinci did, however, also consider the anatomy of birds' wings and think it could have something to do with them being able to fly. It's all about the shape of the wing (it's the same thing in sailing too – the sail is just like a big wing) and the effect that has on the air flowing over it. The curved shape forces the air to flow faster over the curved area, and when air moves faster the pressure decreases. Therefore, there is higher air pressure underneath a bird's wing than on top of it, and this creates lift. So even though all Leonardo de Vinci really managed to invent was a hang-glider, he had some of the right ideas.

I was thinking about Leonardo da Vinci and birds as I bounced on the trampoline. I have to take my melatonin at bedtime because otherwise I feel too anxious to get to sleep. But often I wake up before it gets light, especially if I've had a nightmare, and so I go outside in the darkness and jump. It helps me get the bad dreams out of my head and it's the best time to do it, before the sun comes up and makes everything too bright and too busy. We have a big trampoline in the garden back home in Scotland. We've been coming to the house in France in the summer holidays for as long as I can remember – it used to belong to an old friend of my Great-granny Ella, a lady called Caroline, and then when she died a few years ago she sold it to Mum and Dad so we could keep coming. So then we got a trampoline here as well. Jumping takes the pressure off my brain. Not literally, of course, it just makes my thoughts go a bit quieter. They're usually very loud.

After a while, I noticed a light come on in the window of one of the upstairs bedrooms. It wasn't Mum – I knew she was downstairs doing her writing. Then the shutters opened, and the Old Lady looked out. She watched me jumping in the moonlight for a few seconds and then she raised one hand to her head, like a salute, and turned away. So I stopped jumping, because I didn't want to disturb her if she wanted to go back to sleep, and I went back inside to do some maths instead.

The thing about the air pressure and the wings was really discovered by Daniel Bernoulli, who was a Swiss mathematician. He came up with an equation that, in its simplest form, is written like this:

$P + ½ \rho V^2 = \text{constant}$

Where P is Pressure (force exerted divided by area exerted on)

And ρ is density of the fluid or air

And V is velocity of the moving object or fluid

The Bernoulli equation states that an increase in velocity leads to a decrease in pressure. Thus, the higher the velocity of the flow, the lower the pressure. Therefore, air flowing over an aerofoil will decrease in pressure. The pressure loss over the top surface is greater than that of the bottom surface. The result is a net pressure force in the upward direction. This pressure force is lift.

Q.E.D., as Philly said to the mechanic.

I wrote out the equation and laminated it.

I like the language maths problems use. It takes you through a problem one step at a time until you can resolve it. It's logical. Mostly, people aren't logical, they are emotional. Emotions are often illogical on the surface, but if you look at them in a bit more detail, to get to the root of them, you can see that they actually come from a pretty logical origin. Like how our brains are programmed for fight or flight and that goes back to the days when we lived in caves and had to be ready for attacks by sabre-toothed tigers. The ones who didn't either fight or run away got eaten, so their brain wiring died out. We're left with the fight or flight wiring, even if there are no sabre-toothed tigers left now.

It was my fight wiring that got triggered when I had a meltdown about doing the sailing camp, the first time Dad brought it up. Afterwards, he said he couldn't understand why I was getting so emotional about it. He was putting some antiseptic cream on his hand where I'd bitten it. I tried to explain about the La Palma volcano and the mega-tsunami hypothesis, but he wouldn't listen. And that seemed pretty illogical to me.

I wonder whether Mrs Philly Delaney would like to sail the dinghy with me. I have a hypothesis that if she knows how to fly then she should understand how to sail. I don't know if she could manage to climb into it with her false leg, but she seems pretty calm, so I think she'd be good in a crisis, unlike all the other kids who are going to be coming on the camp.

We're not renowned for our calmness in the face of stressful situations, those of us with autism.

Dad says one day it would be nice to get a plane to France, just throw a few things into a suitcase and travel light. But we have to take the car because of needing to bring things like our bikes and the laminating machine and the jars of Marmite. Also, I don't think I'd like going on a plane because of all the other people. A private plane would be cool though. Perhaps Philly could fly it.

I spent the whole morning looking at maths blogs. You can find all sorts of interesting things on them. My favourite one is by Stephen Wolfram. He's developed his own computer language, and also an answer engine called Wolfram Alpha. I went on to it to find out about earthquakes in the Canary Islands, but it said there haven't been any in the last 30 years. There was an eruption of the La Palma stratovolcano on Tuesday, 26 October 1971, though, which just goes to show there could be another one any day now, resulting in a catastrophic landslide.

After lunch (my usual Marmite sandwiches on white bread with the crusts cut off), Mum and Mrs Ophelia Delaney did another session of the Old Lady's life story.

I just sat and listened this time, without even pretending to read the book about sailing.

Philly

Once I've had a rest after lunch, I go down to the room leading off the kitchen that Kendra uses as a makeshift study. I suppose it must once have been used as a formal dining room, although now we eat our meals sitting at the round kitchen table, the doors propped open to the patch of garden beyond, which contains a few ancient fruit trees and that large trampoline Finn was bouncing on in the wee small hours. The sea breeze is pleasant, cooling the summer heat, carrying with it the faint sound of the waves breaking on the beach beyond the dunes.

As I enter, Kendra is typing on her computer. I don't think she notices me standing there in the doorway because she takes off her glasses and rests her chin on her hand for a moment, gazing towards the window. Her expression is one of complete exhaustion. Then she suddenly realises she's being watched and turns to smile at me. As she does so, she is transformed, although the tiredness is still just visible behind her calm blue-green eyes, even as they shine with their customary warmth. She reminds me so much of Ella again, with her honey-blonde hair and heart-shaped face.

'Did you have a good rest?' she asks. 'I hope Finn's bouncing didn't disturb you last night? I can ask him not to, while you're here.'

'No, please don't do that. I'll only hear him if I'm already awake anyway.' It's a polite lie, of course, meant to ease the burden of anxiety that is evident behind those eyes.

'It helps him, you see,' she says. 'He has bad dreams. I think it brings him some relief from the anxiety he feels.' There's a defensive edge to her voice, as if she's expecting criticism.

I nod. 'It can't be easy, having a brain that active. He's a bright boy.'

She sighs. 'He finds transitions hard. Any changes. So even something as simple as waking up can be overwhelming for him. The jumping is a way of dealing with the feelings it triggers.' She hesitates, fiddling with a pen on her desk, setting it perfectly straight alongside the tape recorder and notepad she's using to jot down my story. I sense she's reluctant to talk about Finn to others she thinks may not understand. I suppose it must be something she's come up against a lot. She glances up at me and I nod, recognising her need to talk. I can't do much these days, but at least I can listen.

'Even falling asleep used to be hard for him,' she continues, encouraged. 'It's another transition, you see? He'd fight it, frightened and anxious about giving up control, but now he takes a pill to help him drop off. The minutest of changes can be terrifying for him – the fear of the unknown, I suppose.' She laughs and shakes her head. 'We learned that the hard way, which is the way we learn most things, come to think of it. He hates surprises, you see. So even something that's meant to be fun, like a wrapped gift, can trigger panic. I took him to another child's birthday party when he was about five and they were playing a game of Pass the Parcel. You can just imagine how that went down for him. In the end, we had to ask the hosts if he could take over being in charge of the music rather than playing the game – he liked that, feeling in control of something. Of course, it made him seem even more strange and antisocial to the other kids.'

'Hmm. Well, socialising can be a complete minefield at the best of times,' I say.

'Yes, but for a child it's so important. We've struggled with it for Finn, walking that tightrope between what he can and can't manage. I've pretty much given up now. We've had to learn to change in the context of Finn's life, to be with him in his world instead of making him fit into ours, to create an environment where he doesn't feel he's being punished all the time for simply being himself. Basically, that means being confined to home. So I think we've all become more isolated. Ironically, we're not alone in our isolation, if you see what I mean. So many families live with autism nowadays, desperately in need of help when there is none. You just have to get on with it as best you can.'

'It must be a worry,' I say. 'Thinking about what the future may hold for him?'

For a moment, I think she's going to cry. I worry I've overstepped the mark. But she regains her composure, her expression determined, holding it together, and I guess that must be something she's learned to do out of all-too-frequent necessity. 'Of course. We worry constantly about how he'll cope with things like work and relationships, navigating life . . . And what happens when we're not here. But most of the time we're just trying to get through each day as best we can, dealing with the curveballs that seem to come out of nowhere whenever something affects him. It's relentless.' Her gaze travels to the trampoline in the garden. 'A bit like being on that and never, ever being able to get off.'

I realise Kendra and Dan are as trapped by autism as Finn is. Imprisoned by the fear and the endless second-guessing, the walking on eggshells as they try to navigate their way through the minefield of emotions, the constant questions, the fragility of his brilliant but intricate mind. I see the tears well up in those sea-green eyes of hers, but she blinks them away once more, then readjusts the already perfectly aligned pen, grasping at some semblance of agency and order in a world where such things are scarce.

She's giving her life to help her son. So I reckon giving her my story is the least I can do.

'Are you ready to continue?' I ask, and she smiles and nods, reaching for her pen and notebook. 'Remind me where we got to last time,' I say.

She scans her notes. 'You'd just finished your ATA training . . .'

'Ah yes.' I settle into the chair, easing the perpetual ache in my muscles as I stretch out my good leg, and pick up where we left off.

◆ ◆ ◆

I'll never forget the morning I walked into the mess hall at White Waltham, reporting for my first proper stint. My new uniform felt scratchy and uncomfortable, but I felt so very proud to be wearing it at last. It was a foggy day, so flights were grounded, and the canteen was full of the hissing of the tea urn and the chatter of the pilots, who were lounging around waiting for the cloud to clear. I was attempting to conceal my nerves and appear relaxed and confident as I met my new colleagues, but then my jaw dropped at the sight of none other than my heroine, Amy 'Johnnie' Johnson, sitting there drinking tea alongside a couple of the other girls. She was still the epitome of glamour. By the time she'd joined the ATA she was divorced, had become a journalist and had modelled for the Schiaparelli fashion house, lending her an even greater aura of sophistication. Seeing me standing there, goggle-eyed and awkward on my first day as a new recruit, she got to her feet to say hello, pulling up a chair for me at the table.

'You're Philly Buchanan, aren't you? I met your brother, Teddy, at the Astor Club in London the other day. Small world. It turns out he and your other brother were at school in Edinburgh with my ex-husband. He told me to look out for you.'

I was utterly astounded that my idol knew my name! You'd have thought someone so famous would have been a bit standoffish, but Amy was the opposite. She was natural, warm, and down-to-earth. I've never forgotten her kindness, nor how she and the other girls welcomed me and made me feel an equal. Even though I was a lowly Third Officer, they readily accepted me on the basis that we were all ferry pilots together and would be facing the same duties and dangers.

We were a motley crew. As with most of the trainers at Luton, the men were pilots who were deemed either too old or too unfit to fly in combat. There was a long-standing joke elsewhere in the RAF that the letters ATA stood for 'Ancient and Tattered Airmen' and now that other substandard category was included too: women. The press loved us. They called us the 'Attagirls' and published photographs of the more glamorous among us in the papers. Especially Amy, of course. Volunteers had joined up from across the world, so I rubbed shoulders in the mess with pilots from Canada, South Africa, the Netherlands. One of the girls was from Poland and we used to exchange a few words in her native language. I hadn't had much opportunity to use my Polish in Scotland, of course, but a few phrases soon came back to me.

'*Dziś jest ładna pogoda*,' I'd say to Agnieszka. The weather is nice today. By British standards, it probably was.

And she'd laugh and reply, '*Nie, pogoda jak zwykle okropna.*' No, the weather is awful, as usual.

When I asked her about her homeland, her expression would grow serious, and I could see the sadness in her eyes. Like so many of her fellow Poles, she'd fled when the Nazis invaded her country, coming to England to join the fight under General Sikorski's government-in-exile. Her parents hadn't managed to get out, though, and she was desperately worried for them and the other members of her extended family who'd been left behind. So I'd try to distract her by asking her to speak Polish to me, and was surprised by how much I understood, even if it was a struggle to think up the words with which to reply from the depths of my childhood memories. With practice, though, I began to get a little more fluent.

We all had plenty of time to get to know one another. Because we were so often constrained by the weather, much of our time was spent sitting around in the mess hall waiting to be given clearance to fly. We'd play cards or backgammon, and I enjoyed doing the crossword in the newspaper – the cryptic one – and found I could often solve the final clues that the others couldn't get. That first winter, I chiefly remember the cold and the damp in my digs and having a perpetually dripping nose. But the mess hall was warm with camaraderie, and I made some really good friends.

I was the baby of the group. Amy, being so much older and more experienced than I in every way, took me under her wing from the outset – keeping her promise to Teddy to look out for me, I suppose. Before each sortie, if she was around, she'd always check which type of aircraft I'd been assigned and make sure I'd gone through my handling notes. She knew as much about the particular quirks of each model as any of the flight engineers. They all loved her, of course, even the grumpiest of the ground crew, and had huge respect for her because of all her experience.

After a while, as we worked together and spent many an hour sitting in the mess hall waiting for the weather to clear, Amy became a good friend and I could laugh with her about how starry-eyed I'd been when I met her on that very first day. One afternoon, when I arrived back to the base after delivering a plane to Tangmere, an airfield on the south coast, she announced a group of the girls were going up to town (as we called London) that evening and asked me to join them. 'We'll go to the club, see who's around. Come with us, Philly. It'll do us all good to have a change of scene.' It was springtime and the Blitz hadn't yet begun (little did we know what the Luftwaffe would prove capable of when they unleashed their bombers on the city in the autumn of that year), so popping up to town for the evening was easily done. It felt strange to do my hair and put on a frock for once. I'd grown so used to wearing my air force blue trousers and jacket and pulling on a flying helmet that I'd almost forgotten what it felt like to get dressed up. We crowded into a train carriage for the hour's journey into London. Amy pulled out a tube of scarlet lipstick from her bag and applied it, using the window as a mirror. She saw me watching and handed it to me. 'Here, put on a bit of this,' she said. 'I find it helps no end in distracting attention from my red and runny nose.' I followed suit and when I went to hand it back to her, she waved it away, saying 'Keep it. The colour really suits you.'

The whole lot of us walked arm-in-arm from the station through the blacked-out streets, laughing and chattering, excited to be out on the town for once. We attracted a few turned heads and wolf whistles along the way, too. I felt a bit overwhelmed when we walked into the club, it was so crowded, so hot, so bright. It felt as if the room fell silent for a moment at the sight of Amy Johnson walking in. She had that effect wherever she went. I remembered the newspaper reports of a million people lining the streets of London to cheer her home on her return from her record-breaking flight to Australia. Her beauty and her charisma made her what would nowadays be termed a celebrity, I suppose, but all the attention never went to her head. She just wanted to get on with her job and fly planes.

I was still so young and gauche – just nineteen – and not nearly as worldly as most of the others. But after we found a table and a round of drinks appeared, I began to relax and enjoy myself.

Amy knew everyone, it seemed, and we were soon surrounded by a noisy group of young men, resplendent in their RAF uniforms. More drinks appeared, as if by magic, and the band struck up a dance tune. Several of the girls were whisked off to the dance floor. And then a pilot slipped into the newly vacated chair next to me and I found myself looking into a pair of smiling blue eyes. 'Fancy meeting you here, Philly Buchanan,' he said.

'Ben!' I'm sure my cheeks must have blushed crimson all over again. I'd thought about my handsome instructor often since saying goodbye to him at the end of my training, and whenever I saw a Spitfire when delivering planes to airfields the length and breadth of the country, I couldn't help but check to see whether he might be piloting it.

We talked for hours. He asked about my work and told me what he could about his, although naturally he was bound by secrecy not to divulge any specifics. We all knew from the posters at airfields that *Careless Talk Costs Lives*. I gathered he'd been assigned to a squadron that was preparing to see action over Europe.

And when we weren't talking, we danced. He was as good a dancer as he was a pilot. The only dances I'd been to before then were awkward Scottish reel evenings, yet with him my feet scarcely touched the ground as he guided me around the floor. I was floating on air.

When it was time to leave to catch the last train back to White Waltham, he walked me to the station. He said goodbye, but he didn't walk away, as if he were as reluctant to part as I. Perhaps it was the headiness of falling in love – although it might just have been the gin I'd drunk – but on the spur of the moment I stood on tiptoes and kissed him. And he kissed me back. I wanted that moment to last forever. But then the guard was blowing his whistle, bringing me back down to earth with a bump, and one of the others grabbed my arm and pulled me into the carriage. The door slammed shut behind me and the train began to move. When I looked back, pressing my nose against the window, he was still standing there. And there he stayed, watching the train pull away, until I couldn't see him anymore.

The other girls teased me mercilessly on the journey home. 'Be careful, Philly,' Agnieszka warned. 'Pilots are nothing but heartbreakers. And he's a classic example.'

But Amy just smiled and gave me a hug, saying, 'Pay no attention to them, Philly. They're just jealous that you hooked one of the best-looking pilots. Besides, even if he does turn out to be a dud, we all need to have our hearts broken a few times in life. You might as well start with a good-looking one.' Then she added, 'I told you that red lipstick works like a charm!'

I've worn that colour ever since. Because Amy gave it to me. And it reminds me of that first kiss, and the night I knew that Ben had fallen in love with me, just as I had with him.

Finn

Today Mum decided we should take the Old Lady out to see the sights on the island. I think she was using it as an excuse to make me go outside too because she didn't swallow it when I said I needed to stay at home and read the sailing book again.

Dad was busy talking to some of the parents on the phone about the arrangements for the camp next week. He says it's like trying to herd cats getting everything organised. I asked him when he'd been a Cat Herder but he just laughed. It wasn't a joke, I genuinely wanted to know as I hadn't realised that might be a job until now. Not that I'm a fan of cats. The only animals I like are the donkeys that graze in the field up the road. They're usually quiet and placid, and they tend not to do anything sudden or unexpected, unlike cats and dogs. There are some eating the grass in the old earthworks, too, which are the fortifications surrounding the citadel in Saint-Martin, and Mum said that was one of the places we were going to show Mrs Philly Delaney. So I went upstairs to put on my trainers and get my ear defenders because I like going to the citadel. It's really a high-security prison but everyone pretends it's just a marvellous historical fortress, because they don't like the idea of people who've done such bad crimes having to serve a life sentence in the middle of a tourist spot. I find it quite interesting. There's also Fort Boyard, which is out in the sea, and it was used as a military prison once. But then it was abandoned and only used for a game show on the telly. If the weather's OK, Dad is planning to end the sailing camp with an outing to go and see it. He says it will be the Highlight of the Week.

We drove to Saint-Martin and Mum parked the car, then we walked along the embankment to the citadel. The Old Lady uses a walking stick, which is covered in flowers. It can be collapsed down and carried in her bag too, which is pretty handy.

Apart from the donkeys grazing in the old fortifications, the other reason I like the citadel is I can collect more names. In the olden days, it was used as a place to keep prisoners before they were shipped off to the penal colonies in places like French Guiana, which is in South America, or New Caledonia, which is in the Pacific Ocean. The prisoners must have been made to work on the fortifications or to wait for ages beside the walls for the boats to come and take them away, because the stones have hundreds of names carved into them. I like doing rubbings of the carved names with a pencil and a piece of paper. I do rubbings of headstones in cemeteries too. I'm making a collection. I laminate them and put them in a big folder. My favourite ones so far from the citadel are G.T. GIRAUD 1874 and GRAND 1871 and JOYEO JOSEPH because they were very good carvings, and the rubbings came out really well. It's nice when they have a date. There are some more recent ones too.

I only had time to do one rubbing (DURTAUD ROBERT 7 jul. 1943) when Mum came to tell me it was time to go back to the car. I was wearing my ear defenders because the seagulls can be really loud beside the sea, so I didn't hear her until she came round and stood in front of me and waved. She and the Old Lady had walked all the way to the beach on the other side of the citadel, which is quite a long way for someone with a false leg, even with the flowery walking stick. I wanted to do another rubbing because

I'd found a few more names that I hadn't noticed before. But Mum said it was time to sit down at a café because Philly was a bit tired, and I could have an ice cream if I came straight away.

I had my usual – salted caramel with salted caramel sauce. It's the best and it's a speciality of the island. The salt comes from the salt pans which are further along the north coast. I've sailed there in the dinghy before. The salt pans are also why there are so many donkeys on the island. They were used to carry the baskets of salt that had been raked from the shallow seawater in the pans. The donkeys used to wear pantaloons made of striped material to protect their legs from bites when they worked in the salt pans because the shallow water was the perfect place for mosquitoes and biting flies to breed.

After I'd finished my ice cream and Mum and Mrs Philly Delaney had drunk their coffees, we got back in the car and drove to the other end of the island to visit the lighthouse. The Old Lady's cup had a big print of red lipstick on the rim. We passed the salt pans on the way, but there are no donkeys working there anymore. Nowadays, the salt is transported by tractors.

The lighthouse is at the very end of the road. There aren't too many cars on the island. It's very flat and people mostly use bicycles to get around. There were more bicycles (13, which made me feel a bit wobbly) than cars (8) parked in the car park. 3 more people arrived on bikes while we were buying our tickets, so then there were 16, which made me feel better.

I think the caffeine in the coffee must have given the Old Lady some energy because she insisted on climbing the stairs to the top of the lighthouse. There are 257 steps, but I don't mind it being an odd number because by the time you go back down again you've done 514 steps, so that makes it even. I was pretty impressed that she managed it with her false leg, although she needed to use both her walking stick and the handrail. She was puffing a lot by the time we stepped out on to the viewing platform, but she said it made it worthwhile to see so far out to sea. I put my ear defenders on because the wind was so loud up there and also the kittiwakes and gulls were screeching as they swooped past us. I thought about Bernoulli's equation again and I wondered whether the Old Lady was thinking about flying planes, too, because she stood there for quite a while just gazing out to sea at nothing.

By the time we climbed all the way back down again, it was time to go home and have lunch. Mrs Philly Delaney said she was ready for a Post-Prandial Pause, which meant she wanted to lie down and have a nap. I think we'd worn her out with all that sight-seeing.

As we were driving back to the house, we passed the gates of the cemetery at Le Bois-Plage-en-Ré. The Old Lady's head swivelled round to look at it. She seemed very interested in it, so I said, 'Would you like to go and visit the graves?' I was making Polite Conversation, but also thinking I could do some more rubbings to add to my collection, even though I prefer the ones that were carved by the living prisoners into the citadel walls.

Mum looked a bit exasperated and glanced at her watch. It was already 1 p.m.

'Yes, I'd very much like to do that someday,' Philly said. 'But today I'm a bit too tired. And I think I need to get back to the house.'

When we got home, Dad was supposed to have gone to the shops to buy some things for lunch, but he was still writing emails on his computer. I heard Mum say, 'It was the one thing I asked you to do. And now the shops are closed. What the hell are we going to give her?'

In France, everything shuts at 1 p.m. and doesn't open again until at least 3 p.m. It's because they have a rule about not working too many hours in a week and so everyone goes home for a long lunch. If the government tries to change the rule, everyone goes on strike. Dad says going on strike is the French National Pastime, and that gave me an idea. While Dad was moving his computer and all his folders and pieces of paper off the kitchen table, I told him I was going on strike and not doing the sailing camp. He ran his hands through his hair, so it stuck up all over the place like when we've been out in the dinghy on a windy day. And then he said, 'Nice try, Kiddo, but no dice. You'd have to join a union first. And you're not French.'

I don't like it when he calls me Kiddo. He only does that when he's trying not to lose his temper.

He put the laptop and the pile of folders down on a chair and they slid off and went all over the floor just as Mum was carrying the water jug. She tripped and the water went all over the laptop. I put on my ear defenders and went upstairs to look at my scrapbook of rubbings again because I don't like it when they fight, even if this fight was in hissy whispers because of the Old Lady being in the sitting room.

In the end, we all had Marmite sandwiches for lunch. I ate four because I was pretty hungry, even after the ice cream.

Mum looked pleased. 'I told you the sea air would do you good, Finn,' she said.

'We'd better pack extra sandwiches for the camp next week then,' said Dad. 'There's going to be sea air a-plenty when we're out on the boats all day.'

I'm trying not to think about it.

I've laminated the rubbing of DURTAUD ROBERT (7 jul. 1943) and added him to my collection.

Philly

I'm exhausted again after our morning's sightseeing. After lunch, I excuse myself and go to have a lie-down on my bed for an hour. 'Just a little lie-down,' I say to Kendra, 'before we do the next instalment.' To tell the truth, talking about those times so long ago takes it out of me a bit too. Although I do enjoy thinking about Ben again. It brings him back to me after all these years on my own. Perhaps that's all it is, recalling the stories, reliving the sensations of flying and falling in love – which are, after all, almost identical – but somehow I feel closer to him here on the island. Is he here? How can I find him? Where do I start to look?

Sometimes the grief is still overwhelming, so to distract myself I try to do the crossword on my iPad, daily copies of *The Times* being unavailable out here of course. But the squares swim before my eyes as I begin to doze, drifting on the edge of sleep, and other lost faces from those wartime years float through my mind like clouds across a blue sky.

Amy . . . my brother Teddy . . . Jakub and Janina . . . Antoni . . . Gwido . . . Noor . . . Violette.

And I must have fallen into a proper sleep because I wake with a start and find I've been crying, my throat tight with sadness and my cheeks wet with tears. I lie there for a few moments, trying to calm the gulps of my breath, forcing myself to focus on the peaceful sanctuary of the room with the afternoon light playing through the thin fabric of the drapes.

Once I feel a little steadier, I check my watch, get up and splash my face with cold water, washing away the tear stains. Then I run a brush through my hair and reapply my lipstick, resolutely stretching my mouth into a smile before going downstairs to the study to find Kendra and continue with my story.

'Did you manage to sleep?' she asks. 'Aren't naps a wonderful thing? I had one too.' Under her summer tan, there are dark shadows beneath her eyes. 'I haven't had an unbroken night's sleep for years,' she says, without a trace of self-pity, as she reaches for her notebook. 'Finn was never a good sleeper, even as a baby. Still, I can write at any time of the day or night, which is a blessing.'

I realise she must wake up when Finn does, keeping her son company and watching over him through those dark hours before the dawn when he's up and about.

'It's a lot to cope with,' I reply, wanting to give her more time to talk about her own situation before I re-embark on my life story.

'Dan and I have learned to divvy it up between us. I do the nights so that he can do the days.'

'That's good. The two of you finding a way to make it work.' I let the words hang there, in the beat of silence between us, as she thinks about replying. Will she brush away my gentle invitation to open up a bit, or can she see I really want to know, to hear how hard things are between them? Her need to talk wins out.

'It's caused so much friction between us,' she says quietly. 'Some autistic children don't differentiate between day and night, you see. The second Finn wakes up, he's hyper-alert, as if the volume in his brain is immediately turned up to full blast. When he was tiny, I'd walk for miles around the darkened streets, pushing him in his buggy. Or I'd drive for hours through the darkness with him strapped into his car seat, desperate to try to get him to fall asleep.

Even when he does finally drop off, his brain can still torture him. It's not just bad dreams, he has extreme night terrors. He wakes screaming, inconsolable and unreachable. Before we discovered the trampolining helps, I'd read him stories for hours on end just to give him a little respite from the fear, and so that Dan and I would have a little respite, too, from our desperation. When you watch your child biting at his fingers until they bleed, his hands swollen from being hit against things, hurting himself physically as he tries to fight against the terror in the only ways he can find, you'll do anything to make it stop. We've tried everything . . . medication, changing his diet, more stimulation, less stimulation . . . in the end, adapting our routines to fit in with what works best for him has been the only solution we've been able to find.

'It's not all bad though,' she continues, forcing her tone to become a little more cheerful. I suspect she's pulling herself up in case I'm feeling sorry for her. 'I've learned to welcome the darkness, to stop fighting against being up and about in the middle of the night because it can be a peaceful time. There are wonderful moments, too. Like watching a hedgehog snuffling among fallen leaves in the garden, or listening to the questioning hoot of an owl and hearing its partner reply. Walking on the beach in the moonlight with Finn, the feeling of having the whole world to ourselves. He gives me that. And he's taught me a lot about the peace of simplicity, the beautiful clarity of seeing the world without filters, as it truly is. How often do we really do that?' She laughs. 'Of course, honesty isn't always the easiest option, which I suppose is why we tend to tell hundreds of little white lies to ourselves and others just to get through the day. "*I'm fine*" probably being the most common one. That's something else Finn's taught me – as the parent of an autistic child, I've certainly learned a lot about society's rules and expectations.'

She smiles apologetically, as if to ward off more judgement. Or perhaps it's pity she's more afraid of. I reach out my hand and place it over hers for a moment, reassuring her that I'm still listening. 'And what happens to your and Dan's relationship in all this?'

She shakes her head, shrugs, blinks to hold back the tears I can see pooling in her eyes. 'Maybe one day we'll be able to get it back. For now, we're like ships that pass in the night. Or a relay team, I suppose, handing the baton back and forth. Dan's the one who's made the biggest sacrifices really, giving up his career, managing the money and keeping the home front running in order to give me the time to write. Of course, we were so lucky to have Granny's legacy, which took a lot of the pressure off us financially, and even more so to be able to buy this house in France, thanks to an old friend of Granny's called Caroline, who was the previous owner. She knew how much coming here meant to us as a family, and she kindly sold it to us for a ridiculously low price. We'd never have been able to afford two homes otherwise. Being able to come here in the summer helps us give Finn the best environment possible, and it also helps Dan and me just about hang on to what passes for our own sanity. So we're very thankful for all that.'

She sighs, despite the determined – slightly forced – cheerfulness of her tone. 'Who knows what the future will bring, how Finn's autism will develop? All we can do is hope that, with our support, he'll grow into a young man who can cope a bit better with the world than he does at the moment. We can hope things will get easier. And when that happens – *if* it happens – we can hope there'll still be enough left of our marriage, for there to still be an *Us* for me and Dan.'

'Well, if there's anything I can do while I'm here, please let me know.' My words sound empty to my own ears. I'm just a useless old woman, probably more of a burden than a help.

'You're already helping me by telling me about your life, Philly. And I'm very much enjoying immersing myself in your world. It's not just Finn who benefits from being told stories, you know!'

'Well, in that case, my dear, let us continue. Ah yes, I believe I was busy falling in love with my Ben . . .'

◆ ◆ ◆

After the evening at the club, Ben and I would meet whenever we had the chance. Usually, I'd get the train up to London, but if he was on leave and I was still on duty he'd ride his motorbike to White Waltham so that we could spend time together. Before the night in London, I used to pray for clear skies and good weather so I could go flying. But now I found myself hoping for fog and rain, so that the day's schedule would be put on hold and I could snatch a few hours with him. We'd ride out into the countryside and find a pub where we could shelter from the rain, or huddle on a rug beneath the dripping branches of an oak tree, eating whatever picnic we'd managed to cobble together from our rations. As spring began to think about turning to summer, though, the better weather meant I was kept busy delivering planes all over the country and he had less and less free time too. The fighting was hotting up across the Channel. We both knew what that would mean for him.

I could sense something in him had changed since joining the squadron. It seemed he had both witnessed and inflicted death now and he was a little quieter, sometimes becoming lost in thoughts of his own on our outings. He seemed to hold my hand more tightly as we walked through beech-woods where new leaves were beginning to unfurl or skirted wheat-fields where green shoots pushed their way through the earth. I think I was the only one who saw that occasional flicker of doubt within him. To the other girls, he was still the confident, debonair fighter pilot who'd helped train us, but I felt he was hiding a deeper fear. Each time we parted, I sensed how reluctant he was to let go.

We'd arranged to meet in London one Sunday in May. As soon as I saw him standing on the platform as I alighted from the train, I knew something was wrong. He enveloped me in his arms, but instead of his face lighting up with its usual smile, his expression was serious, his mood preoccupied. It was a glorious day and we wandered through Hyde Park, where the sweet chestnut trees were coming into leaf. It was one of our favourite places to spend time together. The surrounding city streets were filled with piles of sandbags (my older brother, Frank, was busier than ever in Dundee running the jute factory at full capacity to produce the material needed to make them) and the shop windows were blacked out. But in the park's calm green spaces, you could almost forget there was a war on. To fill the silence, I chatted away about the delivery to Scotland of a 'Maggie' I'd made that week. I'd cadged a ride back down south as a stooge in a much larger Wellington bomber and been overawed by the sensation of power. Ben smiled and nodded in all the right places, but I could tell his mind was elsewhere.

Eventually, we made our way to the Lyons Corner House at Marble Arch and ordered a pot of tea and some dry Madeira cake, which was about all there was on the menu that day. I reached across the table and took hold of Ben's hands. 'I know you can't tell me where you're going,' I said, 'but I just want you to know that wherever it is, I'll be flying with you in spirit.'

He lifted my fingers to his lips and kissed them. 'I know that, Philly. Sorry, it's stupid of me. Why is it that the more action I see, the more I doubt myself? And things are really hotting up now – I can't say more than that, but we know what we've seen so far has just been the beginning. With the invasion of France, we're going all in now. Am I going to be good enough to face what comes next?'

'Of course you are. You and the rest of your squadron. Your Spitfires give you the edge, and you're some of the best pilots in the world. Europe needs you. Keep those Jerries away from our cities!'

He tried to smile, but his eyes were sad. 'There's something else I have to say. And I've thought about this a lot. So please, hear me out, Philly.'

He withdrew his hand from mine, and my heart plummeted with the dread of knowing what was coming. I tried to stop him, shaking my head, refusing to listen. But he went on. 'There are tough times ahead, for everyone. And my squadron is going to be fully committed. I don't feel it's fair of me to ask you to take on the strain of being in a relationship with a fighter pilot.' He swallowed hard, as if a lump of that horrible Madeira cake were lodged in his throat, then continued. 'For the time being, I think it's better if we part. Until this is all over. I've properly fallen for you, Philly. I've never met a woman I've wanted to marry, until now. But war is not the time. Especially not in my risky line of work. It wouldn't be fair to you, and I have to focus all my energy into the fight that's ahead of us.'

I sat in stunned silence, hardly able to take in the words he was saying as he went on. 'You're still so young, and I will understand completely if you meet someone else, someone in a nice, steady job who can look after you and provide you with the life you deserve.'

I felt the blood drain from my face, and I thought my heart would burst with anguish. I didn't know it was possible to feel your heart breaking so literally. 'No,' I said. 'I don't care about the risks. I can't bear to lose you simply because you think you're somehow protecting me by walking away.'

He'd dropped his eyes to the crumb-strewn tablecloth, but now he raised them to meet my pleading gaze. The pain I saw written in them silenced me. 'I'm sorry,' he said. 'I just can't, Philly. Please don't make this even more difficult. Let's make it a clean break, shall we. We both know it's better this way.'

For a fleeting second, I thought I saw another expression flit across his face. And it stopped me in my tracks because what I'd seen was sheer, raw terror. I realised then that it wasn't the relationship he was afraid of. It was death. It sat on the shoulder of every fighter pilot like a constant, unwanted incubus, every time they climbed into a plane. I would only be adding to that burden, loading him with an extra responsibility. Young and selfish though I was, I somehow understood that it would be easier for him to face the fight ahead alone, without distractions. That realisation, and the glimpse I'd caught of his deep-seated fear, silenced me.

The skies overhead were bluebell-clear that day as he walked me back to the station, and I tried not to picture them filled with flak and smoke and wheeling machines of war, intent on the kill. We walked side by side, in silence, not touching. I knew that if we spoke, it would only make things harder. And I knew that if we touched, our parting would be impossible.

And so I walked away from him at the station and refused to allow myself to look back. If he'd been standing watching me, it would have been hard. But if he'd already gone, I'm not sure I'd have been able to hold myself together and get on to the train at all.

Little did we know that just a few short weeks later there'd be a desperate scramble to evacuate hundreds of thousands of troops from Dunkirk. Ben's words came back to me as we pored over the newspapers in the mess hall. Spitfires – flying at the very limits of their range – had been reported to have taken part in the operation, providing what cover they could from the air as hundreds of little boats pulled Allied soldiers away from the slaughter on those beaches. I felt sure he'd been there, and I scanned the lists of those killed in action with trepidation, relief flooding through me when I didn't find his name.

Just a few months after that, London was in the throes of the Blitz and those same skies we'd walked beneath in early May saw scenes of devastation far greater than either of us could have imagined on that day. The piles of sandbags in front of the shops and houses would be needed more than ever.

◆ ◆ ◆

In the weeks that followed Dunkirk, I kept an eye out for any mention of Ben's squadron. I knew from the gossip in the mess hall that Spitfires were seeing action in the skies above Holland and France. But he was true to his word about making it a clean break and he didn't contact me. Each night, I simply prayed he'd returned safely from the latest sortie. And then the war threatened us all a great deal closer to home.

At first, the faint scribbles of vapour trails far, far up in the summer skies were the only signs to those of us on the ground below that the Battle of Britain was flaring overhead. Squinting against the glare, you could just make out the diamond glint of a plane, scintillating in the sunlight, engraving white curlicues on to the blue, which would then slowly dissipate in its wake. Being situated inland, very rarely did we witness an actual dogfight, although we heard other aerodromes around the coast were being heavily targeted by German bombers, and RAF crews were being kept on constant readiness. Once, we ferry pilots stood on the field in silence, watching as a plane spiralled down trailing a plume of grey smoke behind it before we heard the impact of its final contact with the earth, the crash muffled by distance. 'A Heinkel, I reckon,' said one of the engineers, spitting into the grass before turning back to finish readying another machine for delivery.

Worrying about Ben and then witnessing that crash affected me profoundly. I couldn't shake off the image of the plane spiralling out of control and my mood seemed to follow the same trajectory, plummeting me into a depression from which I struggled to pull out. I thought I was managing to disguise it, but one morning as I was running through my pre-flight checks beside the runway, Amy came over and stood watching me. I pasted on a smile as I turned to her, about to make some outwardly cheerful remark about the flak-damaged crate I was going to deliver back to the factory in the Midlands, but she put a hand on my arm to stop me.

'You can't let it get to you, Philly,' she said. 'Not a plane crash nor a heartbreak. When we fly, we have to have our minds clear, our focus sharp. Otherwise we put ourselves at risk.'

I began to protest that I was fine, but she smiled a little sadly and shook her head. 'I can see how much all this is getting to you, no matter how hard you try to hide it. You're not yourself. And if you aren't careful, you'll find yourself in a tailspin you can't get out of. I've spent enough long, lonely hours flying over grey seas to know how you're feeling.'

I thought at first she must be talking about her record-breaking flights to the other side of the world, but then I realised she was telling me something else. She was giving me a glimpse into something more, something with which she had struggled within herself too. She understood.

She squeezed my arm, then squared her shoulders and marched off to her next job, but I could still feel the imprint of her fingers through my sleeve, as if she was trying to give me a little of her strength. That simple act of solidarity was a turning point for me. I shook off the clouds of heartbreak and managed to fly straight and true once again.

Keeping busy was a help, and now we Attagirls were certainly being kept busier than ever, ferrying new planes to air bases around the country and delivering more and more damaged craft back to factories for repairs. It was quite eerie flying a bullet-riddled machine, imagining what it must have been like for the pilot to hear the metal pierce, to feel the aircraft lurch with the impact of enemy fire or the bump of flak and have to summon up every ounce of courage to keep flying and get home in one piece. It put my own preoccupations into perspective, and although I took Amy's advice and managed to set aside the sadness of my break-up, I thought about Ben all the time, feeling closer to him in the sky than I did back on solid ground. I wondered whether he ever felt the same way about me, sparing a thought for the young, awkward girl he'd loved once. Perhaps the other girls had been right, and I was just one in a long string of broken-hearted WAAFs and Wrens left dangling in his wake. But I could never forget the glimpses of love and pain and fear that I'd seen in those blue eyes of his. They'd always seemed as completely real as the feelings I'd had for him.

By the end of the summer of 1940, the Luftwaffe must have been growing desperate, realising they couldn't win the battle in the air against our Spitfires and Hurricanes. They'd lost hundreds of planes but carried on throwing everything they had at our island. One afternoon in early September, when I'd made a delivery to an airfield in Kent and was waiting for my lift back to base, I witnessed another dogfight. Three Spitfires harried a German bomber approaching from on high, the far-off rattle of the guns sounding like a child running a stick along iron railings. I watched, open-mouthed, as the sky blossomed with white parachutes, which floated gracefully towards the blue waters below. It would almost have been beautiful had it not been for the fact that these were human lives hanging by a thread, intent on the kill themselves just moments before. The other personnel at the aerodrome scarcely looked up from their work, so accustomed had they become to such sights.

By the time autumn arrived, the Germans had given up on daytime bombing raids. The Battle of Britain was over. But the Luftwaffe deployed a new strategy. They would focus their attention on London and the other big industrial cities of Britain, and they would come at night: the Blitz had begun.

◆ ◆ ◆

Christmas that year was a subdued affair. Rationing was strict and we'd become used to the dull meals the canteen served up, mostly nondescript stews with scraggy bits of meat floating in thin gravy among shreds of cabbage. That special day, though, we tried to keep our spirits up on the base. Dinner was marginally more edible than usual, and was washed down with a special extra beer ration, although I couldn't help longing for my mother's Christmas Eve feasts, the twelve delicious dishes she'd conjure up for us.

Afterwards, we listened in silence to the King's Christmas speech, broadcast from a secret location to keep the royal family safe. We realised how lucky we were. Thousands of Londoners were being forced to spend their Christmas in air raid shelters, and news trickled through of the bombing of Manchester the night before, leaving hundreds dead and thousands injured. The mood in the mess was subdued. But then Amy got to her feet, saying, 'Come on, girls. We can't let it get to us or it'll be a victory for Herr Hitler.' She went over to the wireless and turned the dial until she found a programme of dance music. Then, hamming it up, she marched over to the duty sergeant and said, 'May I have the pleasure?'

We pushed back the tables and chairs and followed her lead, and soon the room grew warm with laughter and chatter again as the Attagirls danced with each other, or with the other pilots and staff who didn't have homes nearby and families to be with. I thought of all those Londoners, making the most of it in air raid shelters and Underground stations, and I hoped that Ben and Teddy – wherever they were – were able to distract themselves with a little festive cheer too. As Agnieszka and I foxtrotted around the room, I remember looking across at Amy, dancing with the canteen cook now. She caught my eye and grinned and nodded, and I felt a surge of gratitude for her friendship and the thoughtful way she had of making everyone feel special.

Amy always had that effect on people: a way of making you feel the world was a better place because she was in it.

The fun of that impromptu Christmas dance was short-lived, though, and by the next day we were back to our duties.

A few days into the new year, Amy and I travelled together up to Blackpool aerodrome, assigned to deliver a couple of Airspeed Oxfords (fondly known as 'Ox-boxes') to airfields in the south. The weather had closed in, so we spent the night in a lodging house, hoping the morning would bring better conditions. So it was that on the fifth of January, a day like any other, we sat in the canteen, trying to warm our hands around cups of lukewarm tea as we rechecked the handling notes about the aircraft and plotted the courses we'd be following, folding the maps so we could more easily cross-reference them with the landmarks we'd be able to see below. I glanced out of the window. It was still a cold, grey day and heavy clouds formed a solid ceiling overhead, although it was just high enough for us to fly.

'Where are you headed?' I asked her.

'Kidlington. Taking an Ox-box to Oxford. Honestly, I know that course so well I could do it in my sleep. I'm so fed up with this grim weather. Think I might fly over the top and see if I can find a glimpse of sunshine up there.'

I thought of the times I'd flown with Teddy before the war, breaking through the cloud cover and soaring into the sunlight, in a world of our own. Up there, we could bask in the warmth coming through the Perspex canopy, thawing out our fingers, which would be frozen even in our flying gloves, enjoying the dazzle of the sunshine after the damp, grey gloom down below. It was tempting. But I knew both the planes Amy and I would be flying that day were new builds, so they wouldn't yet be fitted with their radios and their navigation gear. I laughed, getting to my feet and collecting my things. 'Well, it goes without saying but you're a better pilot than I am, Amy Johnson! I think I'll stay low and stick to following the rivers and the railways.'

One of the WAAFs popped her head round the door, waving a meteorology report. 'If you're going to get out today, you'd best go now. The window's going to close later.'

The two of us walked out to the field together and Amy waved me off. 'Fly safe, Philly. See you on the other side,' she said, patting the underbelly of the plane.

That was the last time I saw her. By the time I finally returned to White Waltham after making my delivery, the whole base was in mourning. Because our Amy was missing.

It was a mystery. In the days that followed, the newspaper reports said that eyewitnesses on a ship had seen her plane come out of the clouds and dive into the sea over the Thames Estuary. It was surmised that she'd got lost in the bad weather that had closed in, run out of fuel and ditched her aircraft. And although we heard that a lifeboat had been launched, they hadn't been able to save her. One crewman had dived in and tried to get to her, but the January waters were freezing, and he'd succumbed to hypothermia and subsequently died. Her body couldn't be found, although they did find pieces of wreckage from the plane. *There is no possibility that Amy Johnson could have survived when her plane came down*, the reports said.

It was the not knowing that was the worst, not being able to bury her properly, not having a place we could go to remember her and pay our respects. I couldn't make sense of it. She was not just one of the best among us ATA ferry pilots, she was one of the most experienced aviators in the world. If she had gone over the top, she was perfectly capable of working out her route by dead reckoning. Her trip should have taken only about an hour. And if she had somehow lost her way, she'd have known to drop down below the cloud base and pick up the route again, stopping off to refuel, if need be, at one of the other airfields we knew so well.

Then the unofficial story came trickling through, passed along by word of mouth. One of the girls had a friend whose sweetheart was in the Navy . . . The rumours were that a plane had been seen over the Thames Estuary, coming out of the clouds, in the wrong place at the wrong time. The warship patrolling below had sent its routine radio signal: Identify, Friend or Foe. When there was no response, it had sent it again. And when there was still no response to a third and more urgent signal – how could there have been, when the Ox-boxes we were delivering hadn't yet had their own radios fitted? – they'd opened fire.

Amy's overnight bag washed ashore a couple of days later. But her body was never found.

Finn

The basic formula for dead reckoning is Distance = Speed x Time. So, for example, if a plane has flown at 200 knots air speed for 2 hours it has flown 400 nautical miles through the air. But then there are lots of other factors that can make it more complicated. Like the wind. Or the weight of the plane, which can be affected by how much fuel it's carrying so it changes over time. Or the density of the air. And air speed is not the same as ground speed, which is why when you fly across the Atlantic from west to east it usually takes a shorter time than flying the other way because the jet stream helps push you along. Amy Johnson would have had to use dead reckoning for flying above the clouds. But maybe she didn't do the right calculations. And if she made an error then that could have meant that her next calculation was wrong too. That's probably why she had to drop down to see where she was, and she found she was in the wrong place entirely.

When we were standing on top of the lighthouse, the wind was very strong. The kittiwakes were swooping and banking hard to steer against it. If Leonardo da Vinci had been there, he might have written about that in his Codex on the Flight of Birds. The Old Lady was watching the birds too. She was probably thinking about flying the planes. And maybe about Amy Johnson.

Mum wasn't watching the birds, because she was too busy stressing about the time and looking at her watch a lot.

Nowadays, planes have computers to work out all the navigational stuff, so it would be a lot easier to fly by dead reckoning. If Amy Johnson had had a computer – even one just the size of Dad's laptop – or at least a working radio, she wouldn't have been shot down.

Philly

Although I've only been here a few days, I'm detecting even more of a growing tension between Kendra and Dan. They try and hide it from me, but this sailing camp he's trying to organise seems to be at the root of it. Although of course looking after Finn takes an awful lot of doing and must be a constant worry for them.

I can see how frustrating it must be, never being able to solve their son's autism. We humans are programmed for problem-solving. Our brains are wired that way. There's huge satisfaction to be gained from facing a challenge and resolving it, that's why I love doing my daily crossword puzzles. Come to think of it, I suppose that's why I always found my career in cryptography so fulfilling. But for Kendra and Dan, there is no resolution. They try everything, hoping for a breakthrough that never comes. And so I think they try to find other ways to be in control: tidying the house; serving up the perfect lunch; Kendra's meticulously researched writing; Dan's immaculately organised sailing camp.

I feel for them. They've both put their lives on hold, as Kendra said. I suppose her writing is a good solution, giving her an income as well as the flexibility to help with Finn, while Dan manages the money and the day-to-day care of his son. They've both sacrificed a lot though. I can see how much they love their son, how desperately they're trying to help him navigate his way through a world that must seem to him so confusing and chaotic. I notice the moments of fleeting suspension, just a heartbeat or two, when they would naturally reach out to touch their boy, to hug him or ruffle his hair or give him a pat on the back, and they have to hold back, folding their arms instead, suppressing the instinct. I see how he never touches anyone, and how he can't bear to be touched. It must have been even harder for them when he was a baby – at least now he's old enough to do most things for himself. But how must it feel to have every sense on high alert in every waking moment? To have no way of filtering the merciless bombardment of sights and sounds and smells the world throws at you? It must be unrelentingly exhausting for him. But it's exhausting for his parents too. It shows in their faces in unguarded moments.

'Did you sleep well?' Kendra asks me at breakfast the next morning.

'Insofar as it goes,' I reply. 'It's one of the curses of old age, not sleeping through the night.'

She laughs. 'I think it can be a curse at any age. Dan and I know all about sleepless nights. And, as you know, Finn has his own routine too. He sleeps deeply at first, now we've got him on the melatonin to help him actually get to sleep at all. But if he wakes, even in the wee small hours before the dawn, he needs to move. As you've seen, the trampolining seems to help him. It's a distraction, I suppose, from a brain that's on hyperdrive all his waking hours. He prefers being outside in the dark to the daylight. Less visual stimulation makes things a bit calmer for him. So we let him go outside and jump. It gives us a few more hours before the day begins.' Her neutral tone is forced, a little wary. Then she adds, more defensively, 'I suppose you probably think that's bad parenting. But we've given up trying to parent Finn conventionally.'

'I don't think anything of the sort,' I reply evenly. 'I'm sure an unconventional approach is entirely appropriate when Finn is an unconventional child. There's nothing wrong with moonlight trampolining. If it weren't for my missing leg, I'd probably be tempted to have a go myself – it looks rather liberating.'

She looks relieved. 'Sorry,' she says. 'It's just that Dan and I are so used to the disapproving looks we get when we can't control our child in public. People always seem to assume we're terrible parents. As if we didn't already feel inadequate enough as it is. The trouble is, Finn looks normal to people, until suddenly he isn't – it's like walking on eggshells every waking moment. But we've learned over the years to take the path of least resistance, for our own sanity as well as his – it's less important to fulfil society's expectations of you than it is to maintain a relationship with your child where you can help him.'

I hear the tremor in her voice, see again the exhaustion that lies behind her eyes in spite of her resolutely cheerful demeanour. 'It can't be easy,' I say levelly.

I feel bad that my presence here is another burden for Kendra and Dan. She insists it's no trouble at all having me to stay, but I can see the extra effort they're going to on my behalf. The over-rich cheeses and fancy pâtés they feel they have to buy for me play havoc with my digestion and give me terrible heartburn. To be honest, I prefer the Marmite sandwiches. Finn and I have that in common.

I just hope she's getting enough out of writing down my story to make all that extra effort worth her while.

'Shall we continue?' I say, nodding at her tape recorder and the notebooks she uses to jot down my story.

She looks grateful. 'Yes, thank you, Philly. Whenever you're ready . . .'

◆ ◆ ◆

I had loved my job as a ferry pilot, but Amy's disappearance shook me to the core. We all missed her most dreadfully. The world had been a better place for having her in it. It certainly felt like a worse place without her. The possibility that she'd been killed by friendly fire made it so much harder to bear. I began having terrible nightmares, dreaming that the planes I was flying were being shot down in flames, my heart thumping with the sensation of plummeting out of control, hearing the sound of screeching metal as the aircraft was torn apart around me. Amy's face would flash before me, smiling just as she'd done on that last morning at the Blackpool aerodrome. She seemed to be trying to tell me something, but at first I couldn't make out the words. Then her smile turned to a look of terror, and I realised she was begging me to come and find her. I'd jolt awake, tears running down my cheeks and my chest constricting with helplessness.

I was exhausted by day, afraid to go to sleep by night in case the dreams came back.

I was struggling to do my job as well, and not just because of the lack of sleep. I'd be flying some aircraft or other and suddenly I would find that I couldn't breathe, overwhelmed by a sense of panic that came out of nowhere. After one of these attacks of panic, I managed to regain control of my breathing only to find I'd pushed the joystick forward and put the plane into a nosedive, heading straight towards a cluster of houses beside the railway line I'd been following. I pulled back, just managing to regain height in time to prevent a terrible accident. It left me shaken, doubting myself. I never let it happen again, erring on the side of caution in all my deliveries, focusing all my attention on keeping my breathing under control, as well as whichever plane I was handling. But the joy I'd once had for flying had become obscured by doubts and fears, grey clouds of depression and grief blanketing the elation of soaring into the blue. I'm sure some of the other girls were struggling too, although we never shared how we were feeling with one another. Compared with what people across the Channel in Europe were confronted with, day in, day out, the dangers we faced were nothing really.

About a year later, I was killing time in the mess on another damp January day, trying to distract myself by doing the crossword as usual, when Agnieszka brandished the newspaper she'd been reading at me from across the table. 'Here's a challenge for you, Philly,' she said. 'The *Telegraph*'s going to run a puzzle-solving competition. They're setting one to be done under test conditions up in town. Some chap's offering £100 to be donated to charity, supporting the Services, if anyone can solve it in under twelve minutes. You should go and do it.' She pushed the paper over to me, tapping a finger on the relevant section. Like mine, her nails held faint traces of engine oil from whichever machine she'd been tinkering with in the hangar earlier.

I read the article. Apparently, disgruntled *Telegraph* readers had been complaining that the puzzles they were printing were growing too easy, and so this challenge was being set to prove them wrong. I checked the date they'd set for the test. I'd be off duty that day. And it might make a nice change, going up to town again. For the past year, since Amy's death, I hadn't joined in the other girls' outings, despite their repeated efforts to cheer me up with invitations to join them for a jaunt to the club or a show. I decided to put my name down.

Agnieszka was off duty too that day, so we went up to town together and made our way to Fleet Street. 'Show them how it's done,' she said, waving me through the doors of the *Telegraph* offices before I could change my mind and chicken out. 'The honour of the Attagirls rests upon your shoulders! *Powodzenia!* Good luck!'

I joined the queue of about twenty-five people lining the corridor. Eventually, we were shown into a large room, not unlike a school exam hall, where desks had been set up. At each place, a single sheet of paper lay face down with a stubby pencil placed on top of it. A man stood at the front of the room with a stopwatch.

'On the paper before you is printed a crossword puzzle,' he said, once everyone had shuffled in and found a place to sit. 'You will have a maximum of twelve minutes in which to complete it.

Before we begin, please write your name and address on the back of the sheet.'

The silence in the room was broken only by the scratching of pencils on paper.

'All ready?' he asked. 'Then I shall count down five seconds and you may turn the sheet over and begin. Five, four, three, two, one . . .'

My mind was completely focused as I worked on solving the clues, enjoying slotting the answers into the blank squares. Some were easy enough. SILENCER. BOGIE. AGENDA. Others were more cryptic. I hesitated momentarily over NEWARK – 'Is this town ready for a flood?' – then filled in the last of the blanks to make 21 down SENNIGHT. Done! I looked up from my work. A couple of the others seemed to have finished already and I exchanged a faint smile with the man diagonally across from me as he, too, set down his pencil.

'And stop! Time's up.' The invigilator clicked his stopwatch. 'Right, that's the test over. Please leave your paper on the table so that your answers can be checked. A few of you seem to have completed the puzzle. Whether anyone has managed to do so correctly, and whether the donation can therefore be made to charity, will be announced in tomorrow's paper.'

I went to meet Agnieszka in a nearby café. 'Well?' she asked. 'How did you get on?'

I shrugged. 'It was easy enough. I did it within the twelve minutes.'

She laughed. 'I knew you would, you're such a brain-box. What a lark!' She loved dropping in colloquial English expressions wherever she could practise using them.

I thought nothing more of it until, a couple of weeks later, a rather strange missive dropped through the letterbox of my digs. It said that, as a result of my successful solving of the test crossword in under twelve minutes, I was invited to report to an address in London the following Monday afternoon. I should bring my kit-bag and be prepared for a reassignment of my duties. Beneath the signature were printed two even more intriguing words: Military Intelligence.

I sat on the top deck of the bus from Paddington as it jolted its way through the bomb-torn streets to Green Park. The Ritz wore its cladding of sandbags with an air of stolid defiance. As I got off, a pair of smartly dressed women coming out of the door brushed past me in a cloud of perfume and cigarette smoke. I shouldered my kit-bag and crossed the road, checking the address on the letter for the umpteenth time to make sure I was in the right place. The doorway of the building was nondescript, but it seemed I was expected and I was ushered in, told to leave my bag at the front desk, and shown along a labyrinthine series of corridors and stairwells to a small office on the third floor.

I knocked and entered the room, where a smiling major I presumed to be from the Army Intelligence Corps sat behind a polished table with a pile of folders before him. He checked the name on the top one, then extended a hand for me to shake. 'Miss Buchanan. Please take a seat.' I noticed he didn't offer his own name.

My interview must have lasted about an hour, I suppose. He'd clearly done his homework. He asked me about the *Telegraph* crossword and whether I enjoyed doing such puzzles. He enquired about my schooling in Scotland, about the offer of a place at Cambridge University and about my duties in the ATA. He asked about my parents and my brothers. Then he asked which languages I spoke.

'Polish – although I understand more than I can actually speak. Schoolgirl French and German. But none of them exactly fluently,' I replied apologetically. I had no idea what I was being tested for, but I didn't want to disappoint the major. He seemed a kindly man.

And my competitive streak had kicked in at the sight of those other folders in the pile beneath mine.

'Splendid, splendid,' he said, smiling and nodding, making a note on a pad of lined paper. 'To be honest, we really need someone who can speak mathematics more than any other language. Arithmetic was never my strong point. It's all Greek to me!'

There was no opportunity for me to ask any questions of my own. It appeared the interview was over and that I had been successful. There was no explanation, no offer made for me to accept or reject. He simply stood up, shook my hand again and gave me a movement order, along with a rail warrant to be swapped at Euston Station for a ticket. 'Get the train to Bletchley. Ask for directions to Bletchley Park. They'll take things from there.'

In a bit of a daze, I collected my bag from the desk downstairs and stepped out into the afternoon drizzle to find the bus that would take me to Euston. The station was crowded and chaotic as people milled around trying to find trains. The timetable was always disrupted, for all sorts of reasons including air raids, blackouts, and troop movements. But I managed to get my ticket and push my way through the throng to the platform pointed out by a helpful guard, where a train was just pulling in. I even found a seat, stowing my kit-bag in the overhead luggage rack and sinking into it thankfully to try to assimilate all that had just happened over the course of the day. I felt a pang of regret at leaving the ATA and my friends back at the base. I hadn't even had a chance to say my goodbyes. But I was excited, too, and not a little intrigued to see where this new assignment might take me.

Another girl scrambled on at the last minute, just as the guard was blowing his whistle outside the carriage window, and the corporal who'd taken the seat opposite mine got up and offered it to her. She plonked herself down, smiling her thanks and breathing a big sigh of relief. She noticed the movement order I was holding as I wanted to scan it again to be sure of the name of the place typed on it.

'Where are you headed?' she asked, nodding towards it.

'A place called Bletchley,' I replied. I supposed it would do no harm to tell her that – she'd see where I got off the train in any case.

'Me too! That's a coincidence. It's all been a bit of a blur today, I must say. Do you know anything about this Bletchley Park place?'

I shook my head. 'No idea. I just had an interview, then was handed this and told to get myself to Euston.'

'Same here,' she said. 'It's all very cloak and dagger, isn't it. Thrilling! My name's Jessica, by the way, but everyone calls me Jess.'

'Ophelia,' I replied, as the train gave a lurch and the posters advertising Bovril and War Savings Stamps slowly began to move past on the other side of the window, 'but everyone calls me Philly. And you're Scottish too?' Her accent had a faint lilt to it, so we quickly settled down and began chatting. She'd been born in France, to British parents, she told me, and had been working in the French Consulate in Edinburgh when war broke out. She'd moved to London and joined the ATS, but the other day she'd received a letter inviting her to come for today's interview and precipitous reassignment to Military Intelligence.

We felt like old friends by the time we reached Bletchley Station, where we heaved our bags down from the rack and clambered from the train on to the darkened platform. Night had fallen and it was pitch black. We asked the stationmaster the way to Bletchley Park and he pointed us towards a track between two high fences. We lugged our bags along it until we came to a guarded gatehouse.

The corporal manning it looked over our movement orders without a word. Then he handed them back to us and nodded, unsmiling, saying, 'Welcome to the lunatic asylum, ladies. Wait there. Someone will be along for you shortly,' before disappearing back into his hut.

After a disorienting car ride along winding country lanes, we arrived at our billet – from what we could make out in the darkness, a small cottage among some trees. Jess and I were both dead on our feet. 'The coach will pick you up at seven thirty sharp tomorrow morning,' said the driver. 'Make sure you don't miss it. You don't want to be late on your first day.' Then he drove off, leaving us to tap on the door of the cottage. The moon had emerged through a break in the clouds, making the leaves of a holly bush, standing like a sentry beside the gate, shine like black lacquer. Otherwise, the darkness was featureless, adding to the sense that we'd somehow left the world behind, landing in this place that was so completely mysterious and unknown. In the silence beyond, a fox barked a series of sudden, high-pitched yips, making me jump.

Then the door opened, casting a slanting rectangle of light on to the path, and we were greeted by our hosts, a friendly couple called Mr and Mrs Webb. They ushered us inside, exclaiming over the journey we must have had from London, and gave us slices of toast and dripping, washed down with cups of tea, before showing us upstairs to our bedroom.

I was used to being in digs, and to making do with beds in dingy boarding houses or even sleeping on an occasional mess hall floor at aerodromes around the country, but I think Jess was a bit thrown by the sight of the single bed in our room.

'We'll go top to tail,' I said, dumping my bag down on the bare floorboards. 'You can have the end with the headboard.'

I was so tired I honestly couldn't have cared less where I slept. The room was small, tucked under the sloping eaves of the roof, but the sheets were clean, the pillows soft, and there were warm blankets for us to wrap ourselves in. And so, at the end of that long, strange day, I resigned myself to this new accommodation, setting the alarm on my travel clock before falling into the deepest of sleeps.

Finn

Dad had to go to the harbour to talk to the man about the boats and Mum said she would go with him as she could just pop to the shops, and would Philly and I be OK if we were left to our Own Devices? We both said we'd be fine. The Old Lady's Device is an ancient iPad – it must be about 5 years old at least – and my Device was my laptop.

It was lovely and quiet, and we were both sitting on the terrace because it wasn't too hot yet and Mum said I needed the fresh air. I looked at what Philly was doing, and it was a crossword. She saw me looking and asked what I was doing so I showed her my Sudoku. It was a Difficult one. I prefer logic to words, because words can be slippery things, with confusing meanings. She nodded. 'Good problem-solving.' Then she said, 'You like doing puzzles, don't you? Well I've got another one for you.' She picked up a pencil and some paper that Mum had left lying on the porch table and she wrote out an equation like this:

$(12+144+20+3\sqrt{4})/7 + (5 \times 11) = 9^2 + 0$

I looked at it for a while. I could see it was correct, but I didn't know why it was a puzzle, it just looked like a straightforward bit of maths to me. 'I'll give you a clue,' she said. 'It's actually a limerick. But you have to know the old-fashioned names for some of the numbers.' She pointed to each of the operands in the equation in turn and recited this rhyme:

> 'A dozen, a gross, and a score
> Plus three times the square root of four
> Divided by seven
> Plus five times eleven
> Is nine squared and not a bit more.'

'Haha!' I said. 'That's funny. I like it. Can I keep it?'

'Of course.' She handed the paper to me. 'Are you going to laminate it?'

'Yes,' I said.

Then we turned back to our Devices again to finish our own puzzles. We both finished them quite quickly and Mum and Dad still weren't back. I remembered the way she'd looked at the cemetery when we were driving past it the other day, and that I'd thought I could do some more rubbings there. So I said, very politely, 'Would you like to go to the cemetery to look at the gravestones? You said you wanted to do that someday.'

'Do you think we have time?' she said.

'Well, it's only just about a mile along the road. If you can walk two miles on your false leg, then I think you can do it, there and back. If we walk at three miles per hour, we can go there and back in about an hour and a half, allowing a little bit of time to look at gravestones. I think Mum and Dad will take at least that long.'

'I suppose it will give us even more fresh air,' she said. Her red-lipsticked lips curved upwards in a nice smile. 'But we should leave a note for your parents.'

I went to get a piece of paper and a pen from Mum's study. Once I'd laminated it, we left the note in the middle of the kitchen table, so they'd be sure to see it when they got back with the shopping.

I took some extra sheets of paper and a pencil so I could do some more rubbings in the cemetery. She went to get her walking stick and then we set off up the lane between the vines, passing the field with the beehives and the donkeys. The whole island is very flat, and the track is sandy but firm, so it wasn't hard for Philly to walk. I made sure I matched my steps to hers so I stayed beside her all the way. She asked lots of questions about the vines and the village of Le Bois-Plage-en-Ré. I told her it's where there's a big market, with stalls outside and an indoor marketplace too, as well as a long sandy beach, so it's quite a popular place.

We walked in single file when we got into the village. Some of the streets are very narrow in places and sometimes there's dog poo to be avoided as well. She kept pointing things out like the hollyhocks that grew outside the houses, and the church tower, and there was more traffic and more people around in the streets and that all got a bit tiring, so I put my ear defenders on. I made sure we didn't go through the market because it's way too hectic and noisy and usually full of tourists who crowd your personal space and are too busy buying jars of salt and bars of lavender soap and sun hats to notice if they're going to stand on your toes or bump into you. Then finally we got to the cemetery, and I lifted the latch on the green wooden gate, and we went in.

I like the cemetery. It's surrounded by high stone walls and has 2 tall yew trees standing like sentries on either side of the gate. There was no one else in it apart from the usual Old Man who was raking the gravel between the graves. Some of the graves are very ancient and they have daisies growing out of cracks in the stones. Others are bigger family tombs called mausoleums, with several names on them, that look like mini churches or little houses. They're quite fancy and they often have flowers placed on them. The flowers are mostly plastic ones but there were a few real ones too, which were mostly dead.

Philly walked slowly along the path, peering at the gravestones. She seemed to be searching for something. 'Are you looking for anything in particular?' I asked, being polite. But I really was interested to know what it was she wanted to find in the cemetery because she had seemed pretty keen to visit it. I still wondered whether it might be her missing leg, even though she'd just laughed when I made my joke about it on the day she arrived.

'Yes,' she said. 'There are war graves here, did you know that? I want to see them.'

I did know, because of course I'd been there before. When Mum and Dad go to the market to do some shopping, I usually ask if I can wait in the cemetery where it's quiet and I can do some rubbings. Sometimes they make me come to the market with them because it's good for me to learn Life Skills and they think it's a bit macabre for me to be hanging out in the cemetery. But it's usually peaceful and sunny inside the walls and the Old Man is often there so he can keep an eye on me if there's any trouble. Mum and Dad recognised him the first time we came in here, so they knew he wasn't a Stranger. He lives in the smallholding we passed on the way up the lane from the house, where he keeps his bees and the three ancient donkeys, which graze beneath a big walnut tree. He doesn't talk to me when I go into the cemetery, he just keeps raking the gravel and tidying up the dead flowers on the graves.

'Some of the war graves are over there,' I said, pointing to the far corner beside the wall. 'There's a propeller from an aeroplane too, which you will probably find very interesting.'

She seemed to perk up a lot when I said that, and she marched down the path pretty speedily for someone with a false leg.

There are 9 war graves in this section. Some have names on them but some of them are for unknown servicemen. Philly was very interested in one that said:

AN AIRMAN
OF THE
1939 – 1945 WAR
17TH JUNE 1940
KNOWN UNTO GOD

It stands in between 2 others, which are for A SAILOR and A SOLDIER of the war. Interestingly, they all have the same date on them. This is because they were all on a ship called the RMS *Lancastria*, which was being used to evacuate servicemen and also civilians after the big evacuation from Dunkirk. I looked it up online. It was moored near Saint-Nazaire and had more than 5,000 people on it waiting to be taken back to Britain. It was bombed by a German plane and sunk, and it is believed that over 4,000 people were lost. It's the United Kingdom's biggest ever maritime tragedy and it was the single biggest loss of British military personnel during the Second World War. Not many people know that. Bodies washed up on the beaches all along this coast. Some of them washed up on the island and those are the ones that are buried here.

Philly spent a few minutes looking at the gravestone for AN AIRMAN and came back to it after she'd wandered around to look at the names on the other war graves.

'Are you looking for *someone* in particular?' I asked, repeating my earlier question but changing it a bit because I felt we were getting a bit closer to whatever it was she was searching for. I was taking a rubbing of T/4186951 SERJEANT D M JONES who was a soldier in the Royal Army Service Corps.

'I am,' she said. 'But this can't be him. The date's wrong.' I told her about the sinking of the *Lancastria* and she nodded.

'The propeller is pretty cool, isn't it?' I said.

'It is indeed. Looks like it could have been from a downed Spitfire or Hurricane. I suppose it must have washed up on one of the beaches here too.'

'There's another airman buried over there,' I said, pointing to another section of the war graves. 'He was from New Zealand. The date's the sixteenth of October 1942. I don't suppose that helps?'

She shook her head. 'I saw that. But no, not the right details.'

'Maybe we can visit some other cemeteries on the island to see if the person you're looking for is there instead?' I said. I quite liked the idea of it being a puzzle that we needed to solve.

She didn't answer. She just stood there looking at the gravestones and her mouth was turning downwards so I think she must have been feeling a bit sad and tired. Then she looked at her watch and said, 'Heavens alive, we've been here ages. We must be getting back, or your parents will think I've abducted you.' So we walked back to the gate. The Old Man raised his head to look at us as we passed by and he nodded at me, so I think he recognised me, but he didn't say anything, he just went back to his raking again.

It was hot and Philly was limping quite a lot by the time we got back to the house. Mum and Dad were trying to be polite, but I could tell they were a bit annoyed that we hadn't been there when they'd got back. Lunch was already on the table.

Afterwards, we all went to our rooms for a Post-Prandial Pause, and I laminated SERJEANT D M JONES and put him in my scrapbook. I lay on my bed and did another Sudoku. This time it was a Fiendish one. I liked the calm, happy feeling I got when I finished it.

Philly

We were all silent on the bus ride to our new workplace at Bletchley Park on that first morning. At the time, I put it down to the early morning start on the part of those who were old hands and to nerves for us new arrivals.

We pulled in through the gates, passing the guard house where Jess and I had presented ourselves the night before. The guard's grim greeting – 'Welcome to the lunatic asylum' – rang in my ears, serving only to heighten my sense of uneasiness. But the other workers looked like a very ordinary and remarkably sane bunch of people, so I drew comfort from that. Most walked off towards some rather ugly-looking huts, but an officer with a clipboard herded those of us who were new around to the front of the main building. It was an extraordinary-looking edifice, a sprawling hotchpotch of an English country house comprised of a muddle of red brick and white stone. It seemed to have been designed with no particular eye for cohesion – Tudor timbering jostled for position between Gothic turrets and Baroque gables. An ornamental lake sat in front of the building, the water reflecting the grey of the January sky. A chill wind made me shiver and I folded my arms across the front of my ATA tunic, trying to protect myself from the cold as well as whatever it was that awaited us. The officer showed us in through the arched main door of the house, leading us to an entrance hall and telling us to take a seat.

When my name was called, I made my way down a long corridor to a room that had been commandeered as an office. An army captain sat behind a mahogany desk on which were placed some papers and a military pistol. He didn't return my smile, just pointed to a chair, where I perched somewhat nervously, eyeing the gun. He pushed the papers across to me. 'Read that and sign it,' he said.

Printed across the top of the first sheet, beneath the royal coat of arms, were the words Official Secrets Act. By the time I'd finished reading it, I was fully aware of the fact that if I discussed or disclosed anything I saw or heard in my new workplace I'd be liable to receive a hefty jail sentence at the very least.

'Do you understand?' asked the captain, driving the point home. His tone was matter of fact. 'Anything you read or hear around these parts is not to be discussed outside the department to which you'll be assigned. Absolutely nothing is to be disclosed until thirty years after this war ends, not even to family members. An act of treason is an offence that carries the death penalty.'

I realised the pistol on the desk only served to reinforce the message. No wonder everyone on the bus had been silent.

'I understand,' I said. I signed my name at the bottom of the document.

The captain stood, saying, 'Welcome to the Government Code and Cypher School, Miss Buchanan.' He showed me out of the room, pointing me back down the hallway. I sat down on one of the chairs lining the wall and waited. Jess emerged from a different office, but I guessed she'd been signing those same papers. She raised her eyebrows and drew down the corners of her mouth in a comical expression of astonishment. I gave her a sympathetic smile, but we didn't speak. At last, the officer with the clipboard returned and told us to follow him.

I was assigned to Hut 8. Judging by the smell of fresh paint, the huts had been built recently and hastily. They were of flimsy construction, tin-roofed and with walls and doors painted regulation MoD green. It was scarcely warmer inside than out and blackout blinds were pulled down, covering every window so there was no natural light. A friendly-looking girl in a Wren's uniform got up from her chair when I entered the room, standing there rather awkwardly as I hadn't a clue what was expected of me. 'Hello,' she said. 'You must be the new cribber? Here, I'll show you the ropes.'

Her name was Beryl, she told me. She'd been working at Bletchley Park for six months and was usually in the Machine Room, although she'd been standing in as a cribber for a few weeks as they were short-handed. Despite her cheery and helpful introduction, I was still none the wiser as to what a cribber was and what I was actually supposed to be doing. She handed me a typewritten manual, saying, 'You can start off by reading the Prof's *Treatise on the Enigma* when you have the time. It'll tell you all you need to know about what we do here. But first, I'll give you the guided tour.'

She showed me round, eventually opening a door leading off from the corridor. It was as spartan as the other rooms in the hut, with a couple of desks set on a slant in the centre and a large filing cabinet pushed into one corner. 'This is the new crib girl,' she said to the two men who stood beside the cast-iron radiator, tin mugs of tea in their hands.

'Hugh Alexander, pleased to meet you. Welcome to Hut 8, Miss Buchanan. This is Alan.'

And so it was that I met my new boss, Alan Turing – also known as the Prof – and became one of the Bletchley Park codebreakers.

◆ ◆ ◆

By the time I joined Hut 8, the codebreakers had already developed a machine that could be used to help break the Enigma code, which the German military used for their most critical messages. Secret radio stations across Europe would intercept the messages, transmitted in Morse code, and relay them to the Registration Room at Bletchley Park. There, they were logged and then passed on to the codebreaking teams. The machines Beryl had referred to – known as bombes – were only effective up to a certain point in decrypting these complicated codes. Before the bombes could be configured to try to discover that day's Enigma settings, sheets known as menus had to be drawn up.

And that's where the cribbers came in. We had to narrow down the possible permutations, then draw up the menus showing probable combinations, which would be passed to the Wrens to set up the machines. The messages would be run through the bombes, their drums spinning and clattering, until a likely setting was discovered. Then the machine would fall silent, its rotors stopping, and the result passed to Mr Turing and his team of cryptanalysts. Once the correct settings were ascertained, they'd be sent over to the Decoding Room, where the day's Enigma intercepts could be run through Typex machines to decode them back into German, which could then be translated. The final messages, in English, were then sent up to the British High Command in London, keeping Mr Churchill apprised of Adolf Hitler's every move. I learned most of this from Beryl, who was friendly and talkative within the safe confines of our hut.

I soon settled in and kept my head down, focusing on the job as I tried to work out any discernible patterns within the columns of figures on the table before me. There was little to go on, but slowly I began to spot clues here and there. If the message was a weather report or some daily news from the front, for example, it could be possible to tease out certain commonly used words or phrases. I derived a good deal of satisfaction from compiling the day's menu and passing it over to the Machine Room, knowing we were one step closer to breaking that day's cipher.

The work was relentless. Every day the Germans changed the settings they were using to transmit messages and every day we had to re-decipher the codes to try to keep up. We worked around the clock in shifts, eight until four, four to midnight, midnight to eight.

After a few weeks, I was set to work the graveyard shift, from midnight to eight, literally left 'minding the Baby'. The 'Baby' in question was a specially designed machine that could be used to reverse engineer a cipher. It was another of the shortcuts we'd devised to try to speed up the process. We'd worked out that the Germans always spelled out numbers in full when transmitting them. So we took the number one – *eins* – and used the Baby to work out all the different ways this frequently used four-letter word could be coded. It narrowed things down, even though there were still more than 17,000 ways that one word could be encoded. My job was to make regular checks and reset the Baby to start another run when a cycle was completed. The results were typed out into a table we called the *Eins* catalogue.

It was quiet in the hut that night, and I was struggling to stay awake when I heard the door open and then soft footsteps in the corridor. I jumped up and went to see who it was.

'Oh, hello, Alan.'

'Sorry, Philly, I hope I didn't startle you. I couldn't sleep – was mulling over a problem I'd been working on earlier. Thought I might as well come in and carry on.'

The Prof's hair was uncombed, his face pale and drawn beneath the stark overhead light. There were dark smudges under his eyes, betraying the strain placed on him by the pressures of his work.

'I'll make us a cup of tea, shall I, before you start?'

He smiled, setting down his attaché case and hanging his coat on the stand in the corner. 'Thanks. That would be great.'

I carried two steaming tin cups through, setting one on the corner of his desk, careful not to disturb the muddle of papers spread out in front of him. He must have seen my interested glance at the problem he was working on because he pushed it across so I could cast an eye over it. More out of generosity of spirit than any actual need for my help with it, I suspected. Although his manner was always quite shy and awkward, I knew what a brilliant mind he had, and I learned a lot from watching him work whenever I had the opportunity.

His intellect was dazzling, and as I followed his workings I saw how he could leap to a solution, seemingly instinctively. I was more of a plodder, preferring to work things through methodically, being thorough and checking my working at every stage. I reached for a blank sheet of paper and a pencil, writing down the steps he'd followed to get them clear in my head.

When I glanced up, he was watching me closely. 'You remind me of the Polish mathematicians I met in France,' he said. 'They used the same approach.'

'Well, I am half Polish,' I replied with a smile, 'so maybe it's a cultural thing. Who were these mathematicians you met?'

'There were three of them. Fortunately for us, they'd been working on decoding Enigma for some years before the war broke out. They'd made huge progress. When Germany invaded Poland, they were whisked away to Paris by the French intelligence service, who saw how useful their work could be. It was the French who set up the meeting between us. Dilly and I went over for it. And if it weren't for what they so generously handed over to me at that meeting, we wouldn't have been able to develop the bombe so quickly. They'd already made a basic prototype, you see, called it a *bomba*, which is where we got the name. Without their help, we wouldn't be anywhere near where we are today in terms of breaking Enigma.'

'Where are the Polish mathematicians now?' I asked. 'Did you bring them to England?'

He laughed, a little hollowly. 'No, the powers that be decided it was better to leave them where they were. The top brass here dithered about bringing them over and so the French, who knew what an asset they had, kept ahold of them. As far as I know, they're hiding away somewhere in Vichy France, which is probably about as safe as they can get when the rest of the country's now occupied by the Nazis.'

He picked up the sheets of paper we'd been poring over and tapped them on the desk, squaring them up, before tucking them away into a folder. I wanted to ask him more, but sensed he already felt he'd said enough, and his gesture was dismissive, so I went back to my table in the next room where the Baby was just finishing its next cycle. But I was intrigued by – and just a little proud of – the fact that it had been Polish mathematicians who'd helped us get to where we were.

The telegram from my brother Frank was waiting for me when I got back to my digs that morning, having completed my shift. The bus dropped me off by the gate and I trudged wearily up the path, looking forward to the breakfast Mrs Webb would have set out in the kitchen for me and then a few hours of blissful sleep in the bed that Jess would have vacated as she was currently on day shifts. Mrs

Webb was hovering in the hallway when I went in. 'Sorry, Philly love,' she said. 'This has just arrived for you. I'm afraid it may be bad news.'

A cold dread gripped me. We all knew what those telegrams meant.

Teddy's death hit me hard. I think it reopened the wounds I was carrying from losing Amy and added a few new, even deeper ones as well.

His Spitfire had been hit in a dogfight over the Channel. He'd managed to fly back to the base, but the plane was badly damaged, and he'd crash-landed. They said he was killed on impact.

I got compassionate leave to go home for the funeral. It was a long, exhausting journey on slow-moving trains all the way back to Dundee. I'd been numb until that point, unable to believe we'd lost him. But as we rattled across the Tay Bridge, the waters grey and choppy far below, I was suddenly overwhelmed with the panic I used to feel after Amy's disappearance, struggling to breathe as my chest constricted with fear and grief. The squaddie sitting across from me asked, 'Are you all right there, lassie?' His familiar, broad accent and kindly concern broke the dam of my tears and I started to sob.

He helped me off the train and carried my bag all the way to Frank's door, even though Broughty Ferry was well out of his way, making sure I was in safe hands before heading off to see the 'wife and twa bairns' he'd told me about on the journey up from Edinburgh.

I scarcely recognised my mother. I hadn't seen her or Frank for two years, but they both looked as though they'd aged by more than a dozen. I suppose I must have done too. The war did that to people. Mother had given up her apartment in Edinburgh when the war broke out and moved back to be with Frank and his family.

I thought I wouldn't make it through the funeral. It was just too much to bear, seeing Teddy's coffin driven up to the church in the hearse, holding up my mother as her knees buckled so she wouldn't collapse to the ground. She had insisted on a full Catholic mass, finding some comfort in the religion of her childhood, I suppose, and who were we to disagree? We aren't supposed to outlive our children. But that war took so many children, leaving a generation of devastated parents in its wake, as well as all the other damage it did.

I didn't register who was sitting behind us in the church, even when we walked out between the pews lined with mourners, the sea of faces blurred by my tears. Our family was well known in the city because of the factory, and many, many people had turned out to pay their respects. But as I stood beside the grave, the bitter easterly wind drying my eyes, I glanced across and saw a man standing a little apart from the rest of the crowd. He looked familiar, in his air force uniform. One of Teddy's colleagues from his squadron, I thought at first. Then I blinked, looking again. And it was the sight of Ben standing there, his gaze steadying me, his eyes telling me how much he still loved me, that helped me through the awful, unbearable moment when the first spadeful of earth hit the coffin in which my beloved brother lay.

He came back with us to the house, offering my mother his arm, holding my hand on the other side. After the funeral tea, he asked me to go for a walk with him beside the firth. The sun was trying to break through the clouds here and there, and the waters sparkled like a thousand diamond teardrops in the stiff breeze.

'I had to come, Philly. Your brother was one of the best among us. And I knew how hard you'd be hit.'

I walked beside hm in silence, unable to speak, as all the emotions of the day washed over me in waves.

'I've never stopped thinking about you, you know,' he went on. 'There's never been anyone else. And Teddy's death has shown me what an idiot I've been, giving you up like that . . . because I was so afraid of losing you that I . . . well, I lost you.'

He stopped in his tracks and turned to face me. '*Have* I lost you, Philly? Have you given up on me? Is there someone else now?' His eyes searched my face, his expression betraying desperation and wretchedness.

'There's no one else.' Chance would be a fine thing, I thought, picturing my work at Bletchley Park, the all-consuming hours, the relentless shifts. On my precious days off, I simply slept. But his words made my pulse quicken, as hope stirred within me.

An answering spark of hope flickered in his eyes. 'Where are you working these days?' he asked.

'In Buckinghamshire,' I replied, deliberately keeping it vague. 'Doing some administrative work.' Making it sound as dull as possible was a good way of discouraging further questions, I'd found. 'And you? Still flying Spits?'

'I have been,' he said. 'But I'm being deployed to a new base. Going to be on Lizzies.'

'That'll take some getting used to, I imagine,' I said.

Flying Lysanders – or 'Lizzies', as they were affectionately known – after Spitfires would be like driving a London bus after being behind the wheel of a sports car. They were solid aircraft, their lumpy, rounded lines somehow bringing to mind an elephant or a hippo. Spitfires were the fastest aircraft we had, whereas Lysanders were the slowest. They could remain airborne at speeds well below a hundred knots without stalling, which made them ideal for reconnaissance sorties. I'd delivered one or two in my days as a ferry pilot and enjoyed the sensation of being so high up in the cockpit, feeling as if I was sitting on a throne with the whole kingdom spread out beneath me.

He laughed. 'It certainly will.'

'Will you be on recon missions?'

'Something like that.' He glanced out across the water towards Fife on the far shore.

So we're both being evasive, I thought. Enough said.

'Do you think I could come and see you sometimes, if we ever manage to get some leave at the same time, that is?'

'I'd like that, Ben.' I knew the chances of us both having a day off when we could meet were probably slim to none.

'And I'll write to you, if I may?'

'I'd like that too. Very much.'

I'd thought I could never again feel anything other than an unbearable grief on the day of Teddy's funeral, that terrible, ghastly day when we had to commit my brother's body to the ground. But Ben took me in his arms and held me tight, standing there beside the silver water with the seabirds crying overhead as a sudden ray of evening light pierced the clouds. And he made me see that it just might be possible to go on living after all.

Finn

I asked Philly what the difference was between a code and a cipher.

'A code replaces words with other words. A cipher replaces each letter of a word to make it unintelligible.'

So when Mum and Dad were talking about me changing schools, but instead of saying the word 'school' they said 'shirt', they were using a code. It wasn't a very good one, though. I broke it straight away. They should have used a cipher. I hated my old school, it was too bright and too loud, and it smelled of chips and a brand of floor polish that made me feel sick, but the new one I went to next was even worse. It was bad enough in the classroom, which was full of all sorts of smells, but when it was lunchtime we had to go to the dining hall, which was incredibly noisy and smelled even worse. I managed to queue up and get a plate of macaroni cheese. I said to the dinner lady, 'No carrots, thank you.'

'You have to have a few. They'll make your hair curl,' she said.

I didn't want my hair to curl. It's hard enough to brush it already and the tugs hurt so much they make me want to yell.

'Here you go,' she said, dumping a spoonful on to the plate. 'See, I've only given you five, my dear.' Those 5 pieces of carrot were probably what tipped me over the edge. I felt the sick coming up into my mouth, but I swallowed it back down because I knew I was supposed to try and Fit In.

I carried my tray to one of the tables where there was nobody sitting but then some other kids came and sat down on both sides of me and that made me feel even more panicky. I picked up my fork and ate one piece of macaroni. And then I threw up all over my plate and the plate of the girl next to me and a bit went on her hand too which made her scream and then I screamed even louder.

Once things had calmed down a bit, the teacher told me to go to the toilets and clean myself up. I went into the girls' toilet by mistake. After that – which was only my first day at that school – I got bullied a lot for being weird and a Mentalist, which is what the other kids called me. They called me a lot of other things too, but Mum and Dad said we don't say those words. We don't, but those kids did.

In the end, I stopped talking completely in case I said something else that made everyone laugh at me and call me those names. That's why I'm home-schooled now, and Dad is my teacher. He says it's not as if he has anything better to do. I think that might be sarcasm, but I don't know because it's hard to tell when people are being sarcastic. People should just say what they mean. There's a special school I can go to in a couple of years' time. I don't know if that will be better, but at least I'll be with other Mentalists and so they won't be able to pick on me for being weird.

Thinking about school made me feel a bit anxious so I thought I would do some maths to calm my brain down. I decided to go through the workings for the number of possible combinations for the Enigma cipher machine.

First you have to work out the number of rotor configurations:

The most basic model had slots for 3 rotors, with a choice of 5 available.

So the first slot would have a choice of 5 rotors, the second slot a choice of 4 and the third slot a choice of 3. So that means there are 5 x 4 x 3 = 60 ways to configure the 5 rotors.

Next you have to work out the number of possible starting settings:

Each rotor has 26 letters of the alphabet on it. So with 3 rotors and 26 possible starting positions for each rotor there are 26 x 26 x 26 = 17,576 choices for the starting settings.

The Germans added a plugboard to scramble up the letters even more. So next you have to work out the number of possible combinations yielded by the plugboard:

Since there are 26 letters of the alphabet, there are (26 x 25 x 24 . . . all the way down to 1) ways to arrange the letters. That's called 26 Factorial, which is written as 26! The plugboard could only make 10 pairs of letters, so it meant they could only scramble 10 + 10 = 20 letters of the alphabet, with 6! left over that must be divided out.

Furthermore, there are 10 pairs of letters, and it does not matter what order the pairs are in, so also divide by 10! Since the order of the letters in the pair does not matter, also divide by 2^{10}.

So now we can work out the number of combinations yielded by the plugboard:

$26! / (6! \times 10! \times 2^{10}) = 150{,}738{,}274{,}937{,}250$

Finally, we need to put together the three components – the rotor configurations, the starting settings and the plugboard combinations:

Hence the number of ways to set up a military-grade German Enigma machine is 60 x 17,576 x 150,738,274,937,250 = 158,962,555,217,826,360,000

That's $1.5896255521782636 \times 10^{20}$.

No wonder they needed Philly's crib sheets.

I laminated my workings and showed them to her, and she nodded. Then she told me the Germans had increased the number of possible rotor combinations on their Enigma machines even more and at that point the British had to invent another even bigger machine to try to decode the ciphers. It was called Colossus and it was the world's first supercomputer, even if there's more computing power in her old iPad nowadays. It was Top Secret so no one knew about it either, until recently. The Americans claimed they'd made the first one in the 1960s. But it was really Colossus and the British who got there first. It was destroyed after the war, to keep the secret.

Philly told me some other cool things about Bletchley Park and the Enigma code. One was that the code had a major flaw, which the cryptologists in her hut discovered. This was that a letter could never be encoded as itself, which gave the codebreakers a piece of information they could use to help decrypt the messages by a process of elimination. It was a Major Breakthrough.

She also told me the food was really terrible at Bletchley Park. Marmite sandwiches would have been welcome. Because she had to sign the Official Secrets Act, she can only talk about these things now.

They're showing a film called *The Imitation Game* at an open-air cinema in Sainte-Marie. We're going to go tomorrow night. Usually, I don't like going out to watch movies because there are too many people talking and I don't like sitting next to Strangers whose elbows take up too much of the armrest and who eat noisy things like crisps, and sweets with rustly wrappings. But I want to go and see *The Imitation Game* with Philly because it's about the work she did at Bletchley Park. I can sit in between her and Mum.

Philly

Last night we went to watch a film about the codebreakers at Bletchley Park. I sat on a camping chair on the grass at the local football field, and I thought I might never get up again, I was so stiff by the end of it. Dan and Kendra had to haul me back on to my feet in a most undignified manner, which we all laughed off.

The film was nonsense in places, really. Artistic licence, I suppose. The overall picture was fairly true to life, but it was riddled with misrepresentations. There never was a Polish spy. In fact, the opposite was true – we owe a greater debt of gratitude to the Poles than has ever truly been acknowledged. And Alan was far more approachable and well liked by all of us who worked with him. It did take me back, though. The darkened huts, lit only by the glare of the electric lights . . . the terrible food . . . the all-consuming routine of work, broken only by the Wednesday morning gas mask drills, and the camaraderie with Alan and the others in the hut.

Finn was full of questions afterwards, as we sat drinking cups of hot chocolate on the porch back at the house. The evening breeze blowing from the sea had a cool edge to it, so I was grateful for the hot drink. A full moon hung above the dunes, bathing them in its wash of white-gold light. It would have been a good night for flying.

The boy reminds me of Alan. Maybe that's why the memories are so vivid here on the island. Maybe that's why I see the faces again, so vividly in my dreams, and my grief has become so much sharper. The passing of the years dulled it, but talking to Kendra about my life is a whetstone honing the edges again. I want to keep going, though. It's like retracing my steps, so that perhaps I can find the turnings I missed, new ways forward in the endless search for those who were lost . . .

◆ ◆ ◆

When I arrived home after the funeral, having spent a few more days of leave in Dundee, there was a letter from Ben waiting for me in the hall. I took it upstairs to read in the bedroom, kicking off my shoes and swivelling my legs on to the bed. It had been another long day of travelling in crowded trains and I was wrung out with the sadness of losing Teddy. His absence had felt all the more real after I visited his grave once more before I left, to plant some winter-flowering white heather that I'd dug up from the garden of our family home. At least I'd been able to do that. It brought me a little respite from the pain of losing him, knowing he was at peace now. How I wished I could have done the same for Amy.

I rested my head against the pillow for a moment, closing my eyes to squeeze back the tears. Then I tore open the envelope and read Ben's letter.

Dearest Philly,

It's so hard to go on, isn't it, after losing Teddy? My heart bleeds for you, having to get back to a place that's so far from home, having to focus on work and the everyday things without him in the world. It's hit me hard, coming back here, so I can only imagine how much harder it will be for you. I hope that knowing each of us is here – even though we can't be together yet – will help a little to see us through the dark days. We have to keep believing there's light at the end of the tunnel of this war and keep doing everything we can to hasten its end.

A strange thing happened when I got back to my billet. I pulled a book out of the small bookcase in the living room here, thinking it would be a good distraction. I can't even remember what the title of it was, because I was thinking of you, of our walk beside the firth, of how relieved I was to hear you feel the same way about me as I do about you. But then this piece of paper fell out from between the pages. The words written on it seem to be the right ones at the right time. They express exactly what I feel for you, in a way that I never could. I'm enclosing them with this letter, so you will read them and know.

I love you, Philly.

Yours, always,

Ben

I unfolded the sheet of paper, smoothing out the creases. On it was a handwritten poem. It had no title, nor any author's name, and the words were simple. But, as he'd said in his letter, they were indeed exactly the right words at the right time.

As I read them, I cried again. But this time my tears were a potent mixture of longing and joy, falling like spring rain that carries the hope of a summer to come.

The light of the sun
On the water by day
Is a pathway that leads me to you.
The dark of the moon
In the night that we face
Holds the promise that helps us get through.
You don't need to be with me
For me to know
That our two hearts will always be one.
For the days without number
I'll always be yours,
By the dark of the moon and
The light of the sun.

◆ ◆ ◆

Shortly after my night-time conversation in Hut 8 with the Prof, I was moved from cribs to join the cryptanalysis team in his office, working day shifts again. My job still involved trying to decipher the day's Enigma settings but now I was concentrating on the more probable variations produced by the outputs from the bombe, a few steps along the process from where I'd been working before. Then, one afternoon, just as I was finishing my shift, Alan asked me to call in at the Cottage on my way home.

I was surprised. I knew the Head of the Cryptology Department's office was housed in one of the cottages in the stable yard, alongside the Mansion, as we called the big house, and Alan would regularly say he was going over there for meetings with his boss, the same 'Dilly' he'd mentioned in passing when he'd told me about the meeting with the Poles. But I'd never had the opportunity to see inside the place for myself.

I was shown through to a small room at the back of the house, where the air was thick with the odour of tobacco smoke. 'Mr Knox,' said the girl who had answered the door, dressed in a twinset and pearls. 'I have Miss Buchanan for you.'

A pale, bespectacled gentleman took the pipe from his mouth and waved it vaguely towards me, ushering me in. 'Thank you, Mavis. Please have a seat, Miss Buchanan. I'm very pleased to meet you.' Although I didn't know it at the time, Dilly Knox was ill with cancer when I first met him and only occasionally made the journey to the Cottage at Bletchley Park from his home, where he continued his work breaking the trickiest enemy codes. I suppose he must have come in specially for this meeting that day, and the girl I met must have been one of the team of crack cryptanalysts whom he had personally trained.

He settled himself behind his desk and took a few puffs on his pipe, exhaling another cloud into the air of the already smoke-laden room. 'Alan speaks very highly of you. And he tells me you have a Polish mother back in Scotland.'

I nodded, still unsure as to why I was there.

'He also tells me you are aware of the Polish mathematicians who helped us get to where we are with Enigma, is that correct?'

'Well, yes, but I only know the barest of facts.' I wasn't sure what I should say, and that pistol sitting on the desk when I'd signed the Official Secrets Act was still etched on to my memory.

He must have guessed what I was thinking because he smiled and said, 'It's all right, Miss Buchanan, within these four walls we can speak freely. But nothing I tell you today must ever be discussed with anyone else, not even your colleagues in Hut 8. Do you understand?'

I nodded again. He was softly spoken, and the tone of his voice was mild, but I could sense the gravity of this conversation.

He went on to tell me that the team of Polish cryptographers, whom he'd met in 1939 just as war was breaking out in Europe, had been moved by the French Intelligence – the *Deuxième Bureau* – to a château in the unoccupied Vichy zone in the south of France, where they were carrying on their work.

'My contact in the Bureau tells me there are now about a dozen of them there,' he said. 'And they continue to provide us with some of the most important information about what the Nazis are up to. I'm keen to maintain the relationship we have with them because they're such crucial allies in the fight to break the German codes. As you'll be aware from your work in Hut 8, our enemies constantly keep us on our toes, frequently changing their cipher systems. The Polish team are some of the very best in the world at understanding German tactics and coming up with new ways to decipher the radio traffic.'

I listened in silence, still unsure as to why he was telling me all this.

'The Head of the *Deuxième Bureau* is keen to keep them in France. He's gone to great lengths to secure a place for them at a base, a château code-named Cadix. We don't wish to rock that boat. However, at this juncture, not only do we want to let them know how much we value their work, and the fact that they risk their lives every single day in order to further the Allied cause, but I personally want them to know we haven't forgotten them. I have some materials I'd like to get to them,' he said. 'A few things that might help them in their work. Remind them that they have friends over on this side of the Channel too.'

I was still silent, although I was beginning to suspect I could see where I might come in. My stomach began to flutter with nerves.

As if he'd read my mind again, Dilly Knox continued, 'So I need a courier. Someone who is entirely trustworthy. Someone who speaks their language. And I don't just mean Polish. I mean a mathematician, like them. A cryptanalyst who can talk to them about the progress we've made here with our codebreaking and can, in turn, understand anything they may care to share in terms of the techniques they've developed there.' He peered short-sightedly at me over the top of his round-rimmed glasses, squinting through the smoke-filled atmosphere. 'You, Miss Buchanan, fit the bill.'

I met his gaze calmly, although my mind was clattering like one of our machines with what he'd divulged, circuits firing and thoughts whirring as I made sense of what was being asked of me.

'How would I get these materials to them?' I asked, focusing on the practicalities.

'We have a method in place for inserting agents into Vichy France,' he replied. 'But firstly I have to ask, do you know what's being asked of you? Do you think you could undertake such a mission? Do you understand the risks involved?'

'I do.' My heart drummed out a beat faster and louder in my ears than any teleprinter. Conflicting emotions surged through me. It wasn't just fear at the thought of what I was being asked to do. It was excitement too. I was thrilled to think I might meet the Polish mathematicians, that the materials I'd be bringing them might help them in their work just as they had helped us with ours earlier in the game. And I was fascinated to find out what they were doing in their French château, under the very noses of the Germans. From newspaper reports I'd read, I knew the Vichy government in the southern third of the country was nominally French, but really operated as a puppet regime, complying with every hateful Nazi edict the Germans issued from Paris.

I realised my hands were shaking, so I clasped them in my lap to steady myself. I didn't want Dilly Knox to mistake my excitement for cowardice. Alan had told me it was Polish intelligence that had given him such a head start in breaking Enigma. What if the information I brought back could help us take another leap forward, foreshortening the war still more? It would be worth the risk. There was no doubt in my mind about accepting the challenge.

'Very well. In that case, I'll put everything in place. I'll have to liaise with our French counterparts, but once we're ready, I'll let you know.' He got to his feet and reached his hand across the desk to shake mine. 'The Poles taught me a word: *Dziękuję*. Thank you. For all you are doing. Even though no one can ever know.'

And with that I was dismissed. I went back to my digs and tried to carry on as usual, chatting to Mrs Webb about safe topics like the weather as I helped her peel potatoes for supper at the kitchen sink.

'You look a bit peaky, dearie,' she said. 'Are you all right?' She'd been very solicitous ever since I'd come back from Scotland after Teddy's funeral, looking after me, offering me little extra bits and pieces to eat from the rations and a hot-water bottle for my bed, even though the nights were less chilly now. 'Not bad news in that letter today, I hope?'

Whenever a letter from Ben arrived, she'd leave it on the shelf in the hall beside the telephone, so it'd be the first thing I'd see when I got home.

I patted the latest letter in my pocket, smiling at her reassuringly. 'No, all's well. I'm fine, thanks, just tired.'

Jess was setting the table. Our shifts had synchronised again, which meant we enjoyed each other's company in the evenings, sitting playing card games and chatting about safely anodyne topics, such as the best places in Edinburgh to buy shoes. She swivelled round and shot me a searching look, sensing something more perhaps. I shook my head very slightly, letting her know it wasn't something I could discuss, like so much of what we did.

Mrs Webb picked up a tea-towel and used it to open the door of the stove, lifting out the casserole she'd prepared. 'They must work you girls ever so hard over at that place, doing all that filing and typing and whatnot,' she said.

Jess and I exchanged grins, while our landlady fished in a drawer for a spoon with which to stir the watery stew before popping it back into the oven to finish cooking, in the vain hope that the tough and stringy meat might soften a little. We were aware that there were various rumours circulating in the local community about what went on at the Manor, as it was known. These included the theory that it was either a home for knocked-up Wrens or that it really was a lunatic asylum, given the eccentric assortment of staff who came and went on their bicycles and buses every day.

I smiled again and nodded, careful to give nothing away. 'I think I just need a bit of fresh air,' I said. 'I'll pop out for a walk – be back in time for supper.'

I let myself out, shutting the gate behind me, and walked along the lane a way. It was May and the hedgerows were alive with wildflowers, bees buzzing busily from bloom to bloom, collecting nectar in the late-afternoon sunshine. There was something very reassuring about the normality of it all, in the peace of the English countryside.

This is what we're all fighting for, I thought as I walked. This freedom. All the simple, beautiful, everyday things became heightened when I set them against the very real risks I'd be facing. When I thought about the big picture – was I really about to be dropped into enemy France to smuggle materials to a team of Polish spies? – I felt completely overwhelmed. It was too much to contemplate. So instead I concentrated on the bees hurrying to make the most of the last of the day's sunshine, and on the bluebells nodding their heads above constellations of starry white woodruff, on the first green spikes of wheat pushing through the brown earth in the field beside the road, and on the sounds of the birdsong and the scent of new-cut grass. I walked on, putting one foot in front of the other, telling myself that was all I had to do. When I reached the end of the lane, I perched on the wooden stile and took Ben's letter from my pocket.

Darling Philly, he'd written,

I hope you're keeping all right. I know how heartsore you still must be, missing Teddy, but I know, too, you'll be throwing yourself into your work and getting on with doing your bit to help end this war.

As you'll have fathomed, I can't say much about what I'm doing these days, suffice it to say my friend Lizzie is a reliable old bird and together we're doing our bit as well.

That's what keeps me going, the thought that one day it will be over, and you and I can be together at last. We do what we can to fight the good fight, don't we, my love, hastening the day when there will be nothing to keep us apart, when we can wake each morning in each other's arms, in a world where we are safe and at peace.

It will be all the sweeter for knowing we played our roles with every ounce of courage we have. The risks may be great. But the rewards are worth it. And never forget:

For the days without number

I'll always be yours,

By the dark of the moon and

The light of the sun.

Ben

As I folded it and pushed it back into its envelope, a shape at the edge of the field caught my eye. It was a vixen, slinking along the hedgerow, carrying the limp corpse of a rabbit in her jaws. She paused, noticing me sitting there watching her, eyeing me with an inscrutable gaze. Then, from the shelter of the hawthorns, a pair of cubs appeared. She led them away into the shadows. Time for their supper too, I supposed, as I got to my feet and turned to walk back to the Webbs', feeling a little calmer than I had done earlier.

Ben's words brought him closer. He had no idea that they had arrived just when I needed them most. The sight of his letter sitting in the hall had made my resolve waver at first. How could I risk my life when it held the promise of spending my days with him? Then, when I'd read it, his words had spurred me on. Without knowing it, he'd said exactly the right thing at the right time again, giving me the courage to face whatever lay ahead.

But that night, as the foxes yipped and chattered somewhere out there in the darkness, I have to confess that I hardly slept a wink.

Finn

The day after we went to watch the film, Philly said she would like to go back to visit the military graves in the cemetery. She said she only had a few days left and there was something she wanted to do there before it was time for her to go home. She asked if there was a flower shop nearby and Mum said there was a stall in the covered market. Mum also said she would drive us this time and Philly said she would be very grateful for a lift because the walk was a bit much and she had been quite tired after we went the last time. I think her leg was hurting again, because she was using her flowery walking stick, even just to come downstairs for breakfast.

I decided I'd go into the covered market with them this time because it was still too early for the tourists and I didn't need to worry about getting pushed or having my toes trodden on. I wore my ear defenders though, and I covered my nose when we walked past the fish stall near the entrance. The flower stall is in the middle of the big hall. It smells nicer. There was some lavender, so I stood close to it and sniffed it to take away the other odours.

Philly took a bit of time looking at everything on the stall, but then she saw a pot of white heather for sale, and she said it was exactly what she wanted. It cost 15 Euros, which is quite a lot of money, but she didn't mind. The lady wanted to wrap it in a sheet of cellophane, but Philly said, '*Non, merci.*' I carried it to the cemetery for her because she was using her stick and didn't have both hands free. It was quite heavy.

We took the pot of heather over to where the war graves are, and Philly asked me to put it down on the gravel in front of the headstone for AN AIRMAN. Then she and Mum stood there for a while, looking at the graves and the information board, which commemorates two commandos who were part of a raid using canoes that were launched from a submarine to attack the Germans on the evening of 12 December, 1942. The board says their names were Corporal George SHEARD RM and Marine David MOFFATT. Their canoe sunk and they were both drowned. The canoe washed up on a beach and so did the body of David Moffatt, but no one knows what the Germans did with him. He might be buried somewhere on the island. George Sheard's body was never found.

While they were looking at the board, I decided to do another rubbing. The Old Man was in the cemetery, as usual, and he'd stopped what he was doing and leaned on his rake to watch us as we put the pot of heather in front of the war graves. I walked over to look at the headstones where he was working. He'd already raked the gravel in that area and now he was setting pots of plastic flowers back upright on a big stone slab belonging to FAMILLE BERTAUD. Then he turned to pull daisies from the cracks of a smaller headstone next to it. I looked at the name, but it just said INCONNU. That means UNKNOWN. I wondered if maybe it could have been Marine David Moffatt, but then surely they would have known that because the information board said his body had been identified.

The old man's hands are as lumpy as Philly's. When he'd finished pulling out the daisies and moved on to the next grave, I knelt down and did a rubbing of EUGENE BERTAUD 1916–2002 which was the most recent name on the FAMILLE BERTAUD slab. Then I did one of INCONNU too. When I looked up, the Old Man was watching me, and I thought I might be in trouble. It happens a lot that I'm in trouble and I don't know why. But instead he just nodded and went back to his raking. I folded up the pieces of paper and put them in my pocket.

Then Mum came over and said it was time to go because she and Philly had some more work to do, and the clock was ticking. There was no clock in the cemetery, but I think she meant her writing course is coming up quite soon and Philly won't be staying with us much longer so there's not much more time to get her story down.

Philly

A week after my meeting with Dilly Knox, I received a message saying that I was to be ready to travel the next day. I was to come in as usual for my morning shift but bring a small bag with the minimum of personal items I'd need for my trip. At 2 p.m., I should report to the Cottage.

Every day, after bolting down lunch in the dining room (the food was absolutely abysmal, so it wasn't worth lingering over), I would usually snatch a few minutes sitting on the grass by the lake, raising my face to the May sunshine as I tried to soak up as much daylight as possible before returning to my desk. But that day, I went back to the Hut and collected my things, trying to keep down the gristly stew, boiled potatoes and watery cabbage I'd just consumed. My stomach was churning, and I wasn't sure whether it was the dismal meal or my nerves that were making it all the worse.

Dilly greeted me, looking paler than ever. I realised then that he was unwell. He seemed to have visibly lost weight even in just a week. His eyes were sunken in his face, his skin papery and dry, stretched taut across the bones in his hand, which felt fragile when he extended it to shake mine. Previously, I'd put his pallor down to the strain of his job, coupled with the long hours he worked incarcerated behind his desk with the blackout blinds pulled down, the way the rest of us did. He would never sit by the lake, I'd supposed: his job was all-consuming.

'Good afternoon,' he said. 'You have your things with you?'

I held up the overnight bag I'd packed. I knew I'd be away longer than just one day, but the message had stressed the need to bring only the bare essentials and I was used to travelling light after my stint as a ferry pilot. He nodded approvingly. 'Very good. There's not much space in the plane and there will be a few other bits of cargo to fit in.'

He showed me one of the items that would be coming with me, sitting in a wooden crate on the floor next to his desk. 'You know what this is?'

I nodded. It was a small machine that looked very similar to the 'Baby' I'd once been responsible for minding. Now, I realised, I had been promoted from minding it to delivering it.

'This version has a few minor adaptations,' Dilly explained, 'to help our friends with their work.' Once he'd shown them to me, he closed the lid of the box and fastened it with a stout padlock, handing me the key. 'Whatever happens, don't let it fall into the hands of the enemy. It would be far better to destroy it than to allow that to happen. Do you understand?'

I nodded again, swallowing hard. Eating any lunch at all had definitely been a mistake.

There were some boxes of paper too, the squared kind we used for decoding, along with some bundles of pencils and some packs of punched cards. He also gave me a copy of the *Eins* catalogue, saying, 'They probably don't need this, but it's all part of our gesture of goodwill. Where they are, in Vichy France, supplies will be hard to come by, so I imagine the rest of this will all be of use. Among others at the château, you'll meet a man named Marian. Please give him this from me, with my compliments.' He handed over a pouch of pipe tobacco, which I tucked into my bag. 'Keep your wits about you and see what you can learn from them. If they give you anything to bring back with you, make sure you deliver it straight back here to the Cottage, won't you? If I'm not here, you can entrust it to Mavis.'

There was a knock at the door. 'The driver's here,' said the girl. She gave me a smile and a nod, and I wondered how much she knew about where I was going. Possibly more than I did myself, I imagined.

Once the boxes had been loaded into the boot of the car, the driver held the door open for me. It was a beauty, a maroon-coloured Packard 6, and I felt like royalty being driven in it. We swept out of Bletchley Park on to the country lane beyond and were soon bowling southwards, towards my destination. 'Have you been to Tangmere before?' asked the driver, glancing at me in his rear-view mirror.

'Yes. Once. I delivered a plane there.' I remembered the approach to the small airfield, swooping over the South Downs to land the Oxford I'd been flying, pulling up beside an array of Spitfires that stood at the ready along the runway.

We made careful small talk about the weather and how pleasant it was to be driving through the countryside on a sunny May afternoon. 'Beats my usual runs up to London,' the driver said. But mostly we were careful to avoid talking about anything our jobs usually involved, conscious of the need for discretion.

At last, we reached the small village of Tangmere, a cluster of ordinary-looking red-brick cottages, and pulled up in front of a guard house, just before the gates of the airfield. An officer in RAF uniform came over and I showed him my papers.

'Pull over and unload in front of that cottage there, please,' he said to the driver.

I got out of the car, stretching to ease the stiffness from my legs, before being shown inside. Tangmere Cottage, tucked behind an ivy-clad wall, would be my base for the next few days. And then it would be time for me to leave, to deliver the Baby to the south of France and rendezvous with the French and Polish intelligence teams.

◆ ◆ ◆

I met my 'minder' the next morning in what must once have been a sitting room in the cottage. Now it had been turned into an Ops Room, with two telephones on a desk in front of a large map of France on the wall. Red pins were stuck into it in places, more densely in some patches than in others. The man I met introduced himself as Major Tony Bertram and explained he'd be briefing me with everything I'd need to know to prepare for the mission ahead.

I was to be flown to the south of France, to a secret landing site, where local Resistance fighters would meet me. They'd help carry the cargo and take me to a local château where my reception committee would be waiting. Although my French was pretty rudimentary, I knew my Polish and the ability to understand the work of the cryptographers were more important. I was quite excited at the thought of staying in a French château.

I'd remain there until the return flight could be arranged. 'That will depend on the situation on the ground,' Major Bertram said, 'as well as the moon.' He gestured to the map on the wall behind him. 'This shows the latest intel we have on the areas most heavily affected by flak. The pilots need to fly low, through the safest corridor possible, navigating by moonlight while avoiding detection by the Germans and using landmarks to find the way. I believe you were once a ferry pilot, Miss Buchanan? Then you will know how it goes. In this case, though, they fly by night and only during the two weeks either side of the full moon. We don't fly during the dark of the moon.'

I looked at him in surprise. His words reminded me of the poem Ben had sent me. The cogs in my brain whirred, then clicked into place. 'What aircraft do the pilots use?' I asked.

'Lysanders. Lizzies can fly low enough and slow enough to land on the makeshift airstrips that the Resistance identify for us, unmarked fields and meadows mostly, so the Germans don't suspect what's going on when we drop in agents.'

'And when you say drop . . . ?'

He smiled. 'Don't worry, you won't have to use a parachute. It simply involves climbing down a ladder once you're on the ground. The pilot won't hang around, though. It's a speedy turnaround. We've adapted the planes to make it quicker. You'll get the chance to have a practice before you leave, once the Lizzie arrives. The Special Duties boys are based further north but fly into Tangmere when there's a job on. You'll be in good hands. They're the best of the best.'

I couldn't be absolutely certain, but I had a growing suspicion I now knew what Ben was doing. Hope surged within me. What if he turned out to be the pilot flying me to France? I'd love to see the look on his face. But I realised that even if I was correct in supposing him to be a member of the Special Duties squadron, the odds of his having been assigned to this particular mission were fairly long. So I tried not to let my imagination run away with me and to stay focused on the job in hand.

'Just one other thing,' said Major Bertram. 'We'll need to have a code for you, for sending word when we're coming to get you. We usually ask our agents to learn a short rhyme or a poem, something memorable so you don't need it written down anywhere. I can lend you a book of poetry, if you like, so you can choose one to learn.'

'That won't be necessary,' I said. 'I already have one that I know off by heart.' I pulled the folded sheet of paper from my pocket with the poem Ben had sent me. The major glanced at it and nodded.

'That will do very well,' he said. 'Do you know how a poem code works, Miss Buchanan?'

I'd read about them at Bletchley Park. 'Yes. You'll use a particular word or line to create a cipher. And as I'll know which words you're using from the poem, because you'll send me that in numerical form, I'll be able to decode the message you'll send me. I'm assuming you use double transposition codes?'

He laughed. 'We do. I should have known you wouldn't need much instruction on this aspect of the mission.'

'When will I be off?'

'That depends a bit on the weather. We're coming up for the start of a moon phase tomorrow, but we need a clear night over the target area. I'll check first thing in the morning once we have a better picture. But we'll only really know when that phone rings.' He pointed to one of the phones on the desk. 'If it's no-go, we'll get the message "*C'est* off". Ideally, though, we want to get you there as soon as possible, because the plan is to extract you again before the end of this moon phase. If the weather doesn't play ball, you'll be stuck there for a couple more weeks until we can get back to you during the next fortnight either side of the following full moon. Now, if you've no further questions, you have the rest of the day at your leisure. You might like to go for a walk. The Downs are quite lovely at this time of year.'

He pointed me in the direction of a track that would lead up on to the escarpment. The path was tucked into a narrow fold in the hills, heady with the smell of wild garlic that grew in exuberant abundance beneath a canopy of oak branches. After nearly an hour's climb, I emerged on to the top. It was a beautiful day, the sky overhead untainted by vapour trails or clouds, and the sunshine sparkling on the blue sea. I was reminded again of the words of the poem Ben had sent me . . . The poem that had now become the lifeline to bring me home again.

The light of the sun
On the water by day
Is a pathway that leads me to you.

And as I stood there, catching my breath, gazing out across the green fields to the coastline beyond, I thought of the next lines:

The dark of the moon
In the night that we face
Holds the promise that helps us get through.

It made complete sense now. I was more convinced than ever that I'd guessed correctly. At last I knew why a crack Spitfire pilot – the best of the best – had been assigned to fly slow, cumbersome Lysanders, taking on some of the most dangerous war work of all.

Finn

We only ever see one side of the moon. This is because it takes exactly as long for the moon to make one rotation on its axis as it does for it to complete its orbit of the Earth. Dad says it's a bit like a dancer circling, but always facing their partner. He did a bit of a dance in the kitchen with Mum to show me, while we were studying the moon and space. It made Mum laugh and then he hugged her. They don't hug very often these days, because Dad is too busy with home-schooling me and with organising the sailing camp, even though it's the summer holidays, and Mum is too busy with her writing. So the moon never turns its back to the Earth, and this is called Synchronous Tidal Locking.

Some people call the side we never see 'the Dark Side of the Moon'. But that's only because they're looking at it from one point of view. It's more correct to call it 'the Far Side', because it does receive sunlight too. It can shine sometimes, just like the side facing us. To be able to see it, though, depends on where you're standing. I suppose you could say the same about a lot of things.

The moon is also responsible for the tides in the oceans on Planet Earth because of its gravitational pull. At the moment, with the moon almost full, there are spring tides, which means they are both higher and lower than at other times in the month. Today, Dad decided we should go out in the dinghy because it would be good practice for me before the sailing camp and he wanted to double-check some of the places he plans on taking the other autistic kids when they are here. We waited for it to be low tide so we could go out at slack water and then the incoming spring tide would help push us back in when we were returning.

We sailed to where the salt pans are, just beyond the lagoon in the marshes. The sun and the wind make the shallow seawater in the pans evaporate and then the salt can be collected. This is where, in the olden days, the donkeys would have worn their stripy trousers and carried baskets on their backs to take the salt to market. By the time we got there, the sun was lower in the sky, and I had to pull my cap down so my eyes wouldn't be dazzled by it as it reflected on the water, even though I was wearing my sunglasses too. I really do prefer the night-time.

I thought about the old man in the cemetery and the donkeys he keeps in his orchard. It must have been hard for them, working in the heat with all the flies nipping at their legs and the salt getting into the bites and making them sting. I wondered whether that would hurt even more than being stung by a jellyfish. A big white Moon Jelly floated past the boat just when I was thinking that, but they don't sting. Once, though, I found a small brown-ish jellyfish on the beach and I picked it up. That really hurt, like being burnt if you accidentally touch an electric fence, which I have also done, and I had a bright-red line on my wrist for days. Dad had to wash it in seawater and scrape my skin to get the filaments off. Autistic people don't like being touched at the best of times and that definitely wasn't the best of times. A lot of people came over to see what was going on and someone called the police, so Dad had to explain to the policeman that I really was his son, and he wasn't a Stranger trying to hurt me.

The piles of salt around the pans looked like heaps of snow, but of course snow would melt immediately in the summer heat.

There wasn't too much wind, just a steady breeze, and we made it there and back in good time.

Dad said he was very pleased with how I'd handled the dinghy. When we were putting it away, he pointed out the bigger boat that we'll be sailing as a Team when the sailing course starts next week. The other kids and their parents will be arriving this weekend. They're going to stay in some holiday apartments in Saint-Martin, up the hill from the harbour. At least we don't have to stay there as well, but Dad says we do have to have supper with everyone every evening and be Sociable. Being Sociable is another thing autistic kids are definitely not good at, like Working as a Team, but he seems to have forgotten that as well.

When we got back, Mum was busy typing up her notes about Philly's life. She'll be off on her writing course next week and Philly will be going home.

I took my laptop out to the porch, where Philly was sitting doing her crossword.

'How was the sailing?' she asked.

'We went to the salt pans. I saw a jellyfish,' I told her. 'The tide's coming in now and it'll be quite a high one tonight because the moon's still nearly full.'

She nodded. 'Maybe we could walk down to the beach after supper to look at it. I'd like that.'

'OK,' I said. Usually, I don't enjoy going to all the effort of walking through the dunes, getting sand in my shoes, and the sun can be way too hot. But as it would be at night and she only has a few days left I thought it would be Polite to go with her, and she might tell me some more about flying planes in the war and coming to France on a secret mission. As well as how she lost her leg.

I'm really not looking forward to next week at all. I started feeling anxious about it again, so I quickly did another Sudoku to calm my brain down. Then I looked across at Philly and she was watching me.

'Finished already?' she asked. 'You're very good at puzzles, aren't you, Finn?'

'Yes, I am. Can you tell me about poem codes, please? They sound quite interesting.'

'Oh,' she said. 'So you were listening when I was talking to your mother about them, were you?'

'Yes. You said you used the poem Ben sent you when you went on your secret mission to France. So how do they work?'

'I'll show you if you bring me a piece of paper and a pencil.'

'Shall we use the one Ben gave you?'

'No,' she said. 'That one was given to me. I shall give you one of your own.'

I sat next to her on the porch sofa and breathed in her smell of lavender while she drew a grid running across the page, two squares deep. 'Before we started using poem codes, agents being sent to France would often take a copy of a particular book with them. The codebreakers back at home would have a copy – not just of the same book but exactly the same edition. Then the agent could send back a series of page numbers, line numbers and word numbers to create a message that could be understood at the other end. Of course, the danger was that if the agent was captured the Germans would then also have a copy of the book and they began to cotton on pretty quickly to what we were doing. Do you know, the average life expectancy of an SOE radio operator in the field could be as short as just six weeks, and that was partly due to the ease with which the Germans began to be able to intercept and decipher those messages. So we needed to come up with a better system. In fact, we were always needing to come up with better systems – that's part of the work of a cryptographer, continually refining and improving coding systems as the enemy tries to break them. We came up with the idea of poem codes. Poems could be memorised, so there was no need to carry books around.'

She googled something on her iPad and showed me it was a poem called *Dover Beach*, by a man called Matthew Arnold. 'This one can be yours,' she said. 'It's a favourite of mine, and it seems rather appropriate for a boy who lives on an island and loves being out at night-time. We'll take this line, which is quite easy to memorise: *The tide is full, the moon lies fair upon the straits*. Do you think you could learn that off by heart?'

I repeated it straight back to her, along with the rest of the first part of the poem. I'm very good at remembering things even when I've only seen them once.

'Impressive,' she said, and her eyebrows went up towards her white hair. 'You'd have made a very good recruit.'

Then she tapped the grid she'd drawn with the end of the pencil that has the little rubber attached. 'Next, we need to encode the letters. We write the words we'll be using across the top, one letter in each square. Let's take the words "*moon lies fair*". Here, you do it.'

She handed me the pencil and I wrote out the letters.

'Good. Now we need to write in the code numbers beneath the letters. So the "A" is 1, the next letter alphabetically is "E" so that's 2. Write those in underneath the letters on the grid and carry on. That's it, you're getting the hang of it now.'

Once I'd finished coding the letters, she took the pencil back from me. 'Very good,' she said. 'So now we use the numbers we've encoded as our transposition key. We write them out across the top of a new grid in the same order, like this . . . And then we can write the message we need to send in columns beneath the key like this, padding the extra spaces with "X"s . . .'

I looked at the new grid. It looked like this:

7	9	10	8	6	4	2	12	3	1	5	11
M	A	R	M	I	T	E	L	O	W	S	E
N	D	S	U	P	P	L	I	E	S	X	X

'There are actually some more jars of Marmite in the cupboard where the spaghetti is kept, you know,' I said.

'Well, that's a good thing. But you see how the basic premise works, in principle? We would transmit the coded message in groups of four letters, starting WSEL because they're under numbers 1 and 2 in our key. See if you can write out the whole coded message.'

She handed me the pencil again and I wrote out:

WSEL OETP SXIP MNMU ADRS EXLI

She nodded, looking at the work we'd done.

'It's not perfect. Any enemy cryptanalyst with an ounce of intelligence might be able to work it out fairly easily, given enough time. So the next step is to make it more complicated. We make another grid and re-transpose the message. That's called a double transposition code, you see? And then we send that coding in groups of five letters. We also need to tell those on the receiving end which keywords we're using – in the case of your poem it would be line two, words six, seven and eight. You could easily send that information as a cipher at the start of the message.'

She showed me how to do the double transposition and we worked on writing out a few messages that would probably have stumped even the cleverest Nazis, according to Philly.

'So to decipher the message at the other end, you'd need to know the grid layout, with the keywords and the right number of rows, and work it backwards?' I said.

'Exactly. That's one of the jobs the cryptographers at Bletchley Park were doing, day in, day out. Poem codes were a pretty effective way of sending messages from the field, especially if the agent only used the poem once. Even more so if the poem wasn't a well-known one, or if it was something made-up.'

I took the pencil from her and wrote another coded message on the paper, using the simplest way of coding she'd shown me at the beginning.

She looked at it for a moment, then smiled and said, 'You're very welcome, Finn.'

'Are you going to tell Mum some more of your story now?' I asked.

'Would you like to hear some more?' she said.

'Yes. I want to know how you got on when you went on that secret mission to France. Was that when you lost your leg?'

She laughed. 'All in good time, my young friend. But in that case, let's go and see if Kendra's ready.'

I collected up the coding we'd done, so I could laminate it later on, and we went inside to find Mum.

Philly

I passed the day waiting in the cottage, sitting in the Rec Room, listening to the sounds of activity from the airstrip. I was wearing some new clothes that had been set out on my bed when I'd returned from my walk the day before. They were nondescript – a brown jacket, a beige blouse and skirt, underwear and stockings, and a pair of leather walking boots that looked as if they'd been well worn in. None of the items had any labels and I realised this must be to disguise the fact that I was British if I were to be caught. That brought home to me with force just what I was getting into. Although there were unlikely to be German soldiers in the area, the Vichy government was a collaborationist regime with its own agents, and I was well aware what would happen if I were to be arrested.

Major Bertram had arrived after breakfast that morning, with the news that it looked as if we were on for tonight. He led me through to the Operations Room and handed me a few more items that might be of use in the days ahead: a map of the area around the little town of Uzès, printed on thin material that could be stuffed into a hidden pocket in the lining of my jacket; some French money; a bar of French chocolate; and a packet of Gauloises cigarettes along with a silver lighter.

'I don't smoke,' I said.

Without a word, the captain unscrewed the base of the lighter to reveal a concealed compass. I nodded, understanding.

'Your cover name for this operation will be Eveline,' he said. 'It will be used by those whom you meet in France. As I'm sure you'll understand, Miss Buchanan, the need for discretion is essential.'

After lunch, which I struggled to eat even though it was the best meal I'd had in a long time, I sat in my borrowed clothes – clothes belonging to Eveline, I kept reminding myself, trying to get accustomed to my alias – in an armchair in the sitting room, attempting to read a book. But the sounds of Spitfires taking off and landing were a constant distraction. I shut my eyes for a few moments, daydreaming, wishing I was up there flying with Teddy, or Amy, or Ben, in skies free of the deadly threat of enemy planes.

The low thrum of a different engine brought me back down to earth with a bump. This was no quicksilver fighter. It was something altogether slower and heavier. I knew the sound heralded the arrival of my ride.

A few minutes later, a pilot walked into the room. Secretly, I'd still been hoping it might be Ben, even though I knew the odds were against it. But it wasn't him. 'Wing Commander Jim Elliot,' he said. 'I'm your pilot for tonight. Is everything ready here? In that case, come across to the airfield and I'll show you the ropes.'

The Lysander stood in front of a hangar, where the boxes from Bletchley sat in a small pile, ready for loading. I recognised the bulbous lines of the plane, but this one differed a little from the Lizzies I'd seen before. A sizeable extra fuel tank had been added to the undercarriage, and a ladder was welded to the left side, allowing easy access to the rear compartment.

Commander Elliot pointed to the ladder. 'Give it a go,' he said. 'Get familiar with it. You'll need to be able to disembark quickly when we get to the other end.'

I hitched up my skirt and nipped up with ease, clambering into the back. Then I did it in reverse, making sure I'd got the feel of it, sensing each rung through the thick soles of my boots.

Once the boxes were loaded, there was very little room in the passenger compartment. I'd have to sit on a jump seat with my back to the pilot, my legs folded to one side. I calculated the distance we had to travel – call it a round thousand miles, allowing for detours to avoid the main cities in Nazi-occupied France – and the air speed. I reckoned it would take us a good three to four hours, depending on the route. It wasn't going to be the most comfortable flight I'd ever had.

When everything was ready, we went back to the cottage to wait for nightfall.

Over mugs of cocoa (another unexpected luxury) in the Rec Room, Major Bertram gave me my final instructions. 'Someone will be back to collect you from France when the conditions are up to it. We'll get a message to you via the contacts who'll be meeting you at the other end. We've been lucky with the weather window of late, so all being well you'll be back in ten days' time. That's the plan at the moment, anyway.'

Commander Elliot gave a hollow-sounding laugh. 'Plans? What are they?' he said. He must have noticed the flicker of doubt in my eyes because he quickly reassured me. 'Don't you worry though, we'll be back for you.' Then he drained the dregs of his cup and looked at his watch. 'Right-oh, time to get going.'

I followed him in silence back on to the airfield, deserted now but for the Lizzie sitting by the hangar. He did his final checks around the plane and then gestured to me to climb the ladder and take my seat. I squeezed in beside the wooden crate containing the Baby. I remembered Dilly Knox's warning: *Whatever happens, don't let it fall into the hands of the enemy. It would be far better to destroy it than to allow that to happen.*

The pilot clambered into the cockpit. Before putting on his headphones, he swivelled round in his seat and tapped me on the shoulder, reaching between the dense criss-cross of metal struts supporting the internal fuel tank. 'All OK?'

I nodded, but the fear must have been evident on my face because he said, 'It'll be fine. Tonight's a perfect night for flying.'

Then he turned his attention to his controls. A mechanic removed the chocks from beneath us and stepped back to salute. The engine coughed into action and the plane's big propeller began to turn, slowly at first as we taxied to the runway, then gathering speed, the noise of the engine building to a deafening roar. I could feel the power as we surged forwards and the Lizzie left the ground, her comportment no longer ungainly but graceful as she climbed into her element, lifting into the night sky. And as we banked, turning out towards the Channel, the glow of the waxing gibbous moon filled the cabin and lit the way ahead.

I was too tense to try to sleep, but after several hours of flying the low thrum of the engine lulled me into a sort of trance. From my cramped, backwards-facing perch, I'd watched the Channel disappear behind us, the moonlight painting gold streaks across the dark water. And then we were flying over land again and I thought of the people on the ground below, the German soldiers and the French who'd lost their country to the enemy invaders. Our course switched abruptly at a couple of points, and I knew the pilot was following a carefully mapped corridor to try to avoid known areas of flak around the main cities. The silken threads of rivers drew us southwards, shining silver against the darkened earth.

At last, Commander Elliot tapped me on the shoulder again, then pointed towards the ground ahead of us. I swivelled as best I could on my seat to look. In the darkness below, faint even from our low altitude, were four tiny pinpricks of torchlight.

Three of them formed an inverted L-shape. The fourth, off to one side, flashed a call sign in Morse code. The pilot circled, slowing the plane until I thought it must surely stall, but the Lizzie's engine continued to thrum, as it had done since leaving Tangmere. Over the intercom, I heard the pilot ask for the second coded call sign to make sure our reception committee on the ground hadn't been compromised. I craned my neck to try to see the lights again, but now the pilot had lined up for landing and so they were directly ahead of us, invisible to me. All I could see were indistinct, moonlit shadows etched on to the undulating field.

We touched down and I was jerked backwards quite violently against the seat as the plane's speed was abruptly checked. Outside the window, I could see the dim beam of torchlight marking the end of the landing strip, held aloft by one of the *maquisards* who awaited us. The pilot made a sharp U-turn and taxied back towards the first two lights, where he turned again, wasting not a single second in preparing for take-off.

As soon as we drew to a stop, one of the men holding a torch scrambled up the ladder as I opened the hatch. A heady wave of scent met me, the warm night air thick with it. We'd evidently landed in a field of lavender and the Lizzie's wheels must have ploughed through the silver stems, releasing their dusty perfume.

I passed out the boxes, as quickly as I could, somehow finding the strength to heave them into the outstretched arms of the man so he could pass them down to the waiting group below. There were several more people, I realised, as my eyes grew accustomed to the shadows, and everyone lent a hand. Then the man climbed back down the ladder, gesturing for me to follow. As I clambered out of the plane, I took a deep breath of the lavender-laden air, grateful to fill my lungs with something other than the fuel fumes from the cramped cabin of the plane. But this was no time to appreciate the night air and the surroundings. As soon as I let go of the ladder, three people stepped forward, hurrying to take my place in the plane. As there were only two seats in the rear compartment, one had to sit on the floor. Some smaller parcels were handed up – more packets of French cigarettes and chocolate, I imagined, to be used to lend credibility to the next agents to fly in – and then those of us on the ground stepped back. The torch-bearers resumed their positions, and the pilot gunned the engine. I checked my watch as the Lizzie rose into the air, banking as the pilot turned for home again. The whole landing, unloading and reloading of the aircraft had taken less than five minutes.

The torches were switched off, the man at the end of the makeshift runway sprinting back to join us. The group gathered up the boxes and parcels I'd brought, and I picked up my bag. 'Quickly, Mademoiselle, we must move fast in case the plane was seen,' hissed one of the *maquisards*, in thickly accented English. He was carrying the wooden crate containing the Baby.

I stumbled behind him, following the furrows towards the edge of the field where a wooded copse offered some cover. With every step, the ghostly grey stems beneath my boots released another cloud of perfume, which would have been beautiful and calming under different circumstances, I suppose. My heart was hammering in my chest, though, as we reached the trees. One of the men put his finger to his lips and we stood there for a few moments, waiting until the distant sound of the plane's engine had faded away entirely. The pounding in my ears subsided as, at last, I felt I could breathe again, and the silence slowly filled with the sounds of the night, the chirping of crickets and the soft hoot of an owl.

'OK, it's good. *Allons-y*,' said a man dressed in the black robes of a Jesuit priest, who appeared to be the leader. He beckoned us to follow him, and we set off along a small country lane, keeping close to the cover of the hedgerow. We must have walked a good mile or so, joining a larger road, until a small town came into view on the hilltop ahead. The moon hung directly above the pale finger of a steeple, and I could just about make out a cluster of stone turrets surrounding it in the dim light. At the point where the road began to climb, we turned off, heading away from the town down a dusty track. At its end, it opened out into a courtyard overlooked by a huddle of buildings with shuttered windows.

'*Bienvenue au Château Cadix*,' said the priest, using the code name for the base where the French intelligence service hid its Polish comrades.

He led me to an inconspicuous door off one side of the courtyard, knocking softly twice, then three times more. Then the door swung open, and I was ushered inside, into darkness. The door clicked shut behind us and someone flicked a switch, the sudden blaze of electric light dazzling me. I blinked, feeling disorientated, utterly wrung out after the journey. We appeared to be in a kitchen, its dark-beamed ceiling hung with gleaming copper pans. A woman standing beside a blackened cooking range smiled across at me before turning her attention to the kettle that steamed on the stove, pouring boiling water into a coffee pot. And then a man who'd been sitting at a scrubbed pine table with a bottle and glasses before him got to his feet and extended his hand. '*Cześć, towarzyszko*,' he said in Polish. '*Witamy we Francji*.' Hello, comrade. Welcome to France.

Finn

Last night we went for our walk on the beach to see the high tide. My supper was churning around in my stomach, making me feel sick, because I'd been thinking about the people arriving for the sailing camp the next day. I knew I wasn't going to sleep well. The moon looked huge as it began to rise but, as we know, that's just the Moon Illusion. It's all in our heads. The moon appears bigger when it's near the horizon. It's nothing to do with the atmosphere or refraction of the light rays, it's just a quirk of the way our minds work. No one really knows why. It's an unsolved mystery, which I don't like, but sometimes we have to accept that we don't really understand everything that goes on in our minds. The Brain can be even more complicated than Outer Space.

As we walked along the beach, the sea was calm and still because it was the Stand of the Tide. That meant the sea had reached its highest point on the sand and for just a little while it was slack water, before the tide started to ebb again. We stood still too, looking out towards the horizon. The moon was rising fast and shrinking back to its more usual size in the night sky.

'It's like the ocean is holding its breath,' Mum whispered. Even though that's not a real thing, I knew what she meant. It was lovely and quiet.

And then, in the middle of the path of light cast by the moon on to the water, a black head popped up. It seemed to be looking at us.

'Look, a Selkie,' said Philly. 'Do you know the legend about the Seal-People, Finn? They are said to come ashore and shed their skins, walking around like people. They can only return to the sea if they can get their skin back though – if someone steals it away, the Selkie is trapped in human form, feeling as if they don't belong.'

'I know that story. It isn't true though,' I said quickly. Dad once read it to me from a book. I'd thought it explained a lot – maybe I was really a Selkie and that's why I wasn't a normal human being, because I definitely wasn't feeling comfortable in my skin at school at the time. So the next day I looked in the big wardrobe in Mum and Dad's room, in case my real skin was hidden there. I didn't find it, although I did find my Christmas present, which was the laminating machine, so it wasn't a Surprise and I wasn't anxious when it was time to open it that year. I was quite upset about not finding the sealskin, though. That's when Mum told me the thing about Selkies wasn't really true.

The seal ducked back under the water and disappeared, leaving only a whorl of expanding ripples in its wake. Philly nodded. 'I know, it's just a fable. But like all fables, it's a story we can relate to. I suppose that's the point – there's too much beautiful truth in the world to waste your life living a lie. It's said that all creatures on land have their counterparts in the ocean and that seals are the counterparts of humans. I think that's just us flattering ourselves, though. Sometimes people can be about as evolved as Sea Squirts. Maybe it's worth remembering that we're all just animals, really, although some of us are doing a better job of pretending to be human than others.'

I thought about this for a while. As we stood watching the water settle and become calm again, it felt like my stomach had settled a bit as well. I decided that Philly is a very wise Old Lady.

Then we turned and walked back along the beach, alongside the line of shells and seaweed that had been left behind by the high tide.

◆ ◆ ◆

This afternoon we had to go to the apartment complex to meet the other kids who are here for the sailing course. There are 4 of them plus me, and we each have our own Responsible Adult who's in charge of us. Plus there's a sailing instructor from Autism Afloat. His name is Iain and he's actually pretty cool. He once sailed around the world single-handed, so he knows what he's doing. Even if no one else really does.

When we went to the holiday apartments, I thought about what Dad said about being a Cat Herder. No one was where they were supposed to be at the right time, so we had to hang around for ages. Dad was talking to the instructor, and I began counting the coloured mosaic tiles that make a picture of the island on the wall beside the door of the apartment block. I got up to 504 by the time a boy and his Mum arrived. Dad did the introductions. The boy was 2 years older than me but about twice as big in all directions. His Mum talked a lot, but he said nothing. He just sat down on the ground and started to rock backwards and forwards. The others arrived at last (there were 1,345 tiles in the mosaic in total, so it was an odd number, which wasn't good), and we all walked down to the harbour to look at the boats.

Dad had prepared a speech. 'Welcome everyone, to our first ever Autism Afloat sailing camp,' he said. 'As some of you who have already had a chance to go sailing will know, boating is a fun and social activity.' He went on to talk about how good it was for our well-being, being out on the water, even if it can be a challenge, too.

'I hope you will get a lot out of the week, and go home feeling more confident, having used the particular individual strengths you have, and having mastered new skills,' he went on. 'Because you all have a lot of strengths. We know you are good at problem-solving as well as having excellent levels of concentration. And we know each one of you has the potential to become a committed and knowledgeable sailor, developing the specialised skills required. To help us with this, we are so lucky to have Iain, our excellent instructor, who has gained a lot of experience with the Autism Afloat team back in the UK.

'Before I hand over to him, I just want to say I know it must all feel a bit daunting right now, being in a new place and with new challenges ahead of us, but please be assured, we will be taking it one step at a time. I know some of you will be feeling anxious. But to minimise that, it's all the more important we stick to the routine we've set out for the coming week, and we keep to the rules. You have my assurance, and Iain's too, that we are committed to following the timetable we've put in place, which you've already had a chance to see, so you know how the camp will be structured. It will help us all if everyone can try to be on time and keep to the instructions. So I'll hand you over to Iain to get our sailing camp started, with a bit of an introduction and a very important talk about safety.'

While the sailing instructor started talking about what we'd be doing each day in the week ahead, the larger boy was sitting on the ground again, doing his rocking and watching a snail that was creeping across the path. At the beginning of the Very Important Talk about Safety, he stood up and stamped on the snail, which made one of the girls start to scream. I pulled my ear defenders out of my rucksack and put them on, even though Dad had told me not to bring them because we had to be Sociable. The talk ended pretty quickly after that, and Dad said everyone should go back to their apartments and settle in and we'd meet back here at the boats at 10 a.m. the next day, which would be Acclimatisation Day, and we'd have the Important Safety Talk then instead.

I was glad to get home. I think Dad was too. He went straight into the kitchen and took a beer out of the fridge and drank it down in about 3 gulps. When Mum asked him how the briefing had gone, he said it was a bloody shambles and he must be completely crazy to have ever thought he could organise this damn sailing course. 'It's only the acclimatisation day tomorrow and we're already behind schedule, now we have to add on the safety briefing then too. It doesn't bode well, does it?'

He said some other words as well, but they are the Words We Do Not Say. At least, not usually.

Mum hugged him and said, 'It will do the kids so much good, though. And it will be good for Finn. How did he get on, meeting the others?'

I was sitting on the porch with Philly. I'd taken off my ear defenders, because we were just doing our puzzles on our own devices as usual, but I reached down to get them and put them on again because sometimes it's just easier not to hear what people are saying when they're talking about you. When I looked up, she was watching me with her bright, birdlike eyes. She didn't say anything, she just raised her eyebrows and pressed her red-lipsticked lips together tightly, then went back to doing her crossword again.

I was waiting for her to finish because I wanted to ask her about the secret mission to France and staying at the château with the Polish cryptographers. But it was time for supper, so I waited until afterwards and then I asked Mum if I could read the latest bit of Philly's life that she'd written up today. Mum said she was very pleased that I wanted to read it. She handed me the printed pages and then she did our sign, which is when we hold up our right hands and spread the fingers out wide, like a starfish. Most starfish have 5 arms, but some have 6 or 7, sometimes more. There's even one kind called the Antarctic wolftrap starfish that can have over 50. Anyway, Mum and I do the sign instead of her hugging me, because I don't like being touched. I took the pages up to my room and read them when I was in bed. It was good to think about Philly's secret mission and the team of Polish agents decoding the Germans' messages, instead of thinking about the sailing camp tomorrow.

Even so, I did not sleep very well.

Philly

It must have been the strong black coffee I'd drunk so late at night, sitting around the table with my new-found Polish comrades, or it may have been the excitement and adrenaline of finally being in France, because I scarcely slept a wink on my first night at the château. I got up early and made my way down the curve of the stone staircase, attempting to retrace the dimly remembered route from the night before and find my way back to the kitchen. But on my way the sound of voices from a half-open door leading off the hallway drew me in. I tapped, a little uncertainly, and a voice called '*Proszę wejść!* Come in!'

Tall wooden shutters screened the bay windows of the high-ceilinged room, but the early-morning sunshine slanted in through the slats, casting fingers of light across the curlicues of an Aubusson rug covering the floor. Marian Rejewski, the man Dilly Knox had told me was one of the chief cryptanalysts, got up from behind one of three desks positioned in the centre of the room. 'Eveline, please, have a seat.' We were already on first-name terms, Dilly's present of the pouch of tobacco having proven a good ice-breaker on my arrival, although I'd still had to remind myself to use my cover name when I was being introduced to some of the team. 'We are just looking at the gifts you've so kindly brought us.'

The Baby had been taken out of its crate and sat on the desk between us. At a second desk, another man, whom I'd not yet met, was unwrapping a packet of squared paper with evident delight. He reached out a hand to shake mine. 'Henryk Zygalski, pleased to meet you,' he said.

His name was vaguely familiar to me, but it took me a moment to work out why. 'Zygalski?' I said. 'Like the Zygalski sheets we used to use for solving the daily Enigma keys?'

He looked surprised, grinning broadly. 'You are familiar with those in Britain? Yes, I was the one who came up with the idea. We used to have to make our own, but cutting out every square by hand was inefficient and far too time-consuming. When we met Alan Turing in Paris, he took the idea back with him and had machine-cut sheets made. He sent us a set, which we used until the damn Germans changed the enciphering method again.'

I nodded, feeling a little overawed at being in such company. The brain power of these men was legendary among those of us in the know. It was also dawning on me that, despite the difficulties and risks involved, it was no wonder that my bosses at Bletchley Park were so keen to keep the lines of communication open with this Polish team.

Just then, a woman put her head around the door and said, 'There you are! They've kidnapped you already, I see, before you've even had your breakfast.' She wore her hair in a plaited crown and was dressed in a loose cotton skirt and cardigan. She turned to scold the men. 'Where are your manners? You'll wear our guest out, as if she wasn't already exhausted enough after her journey here last night.'

I took to her immediately. Her name was Janina Krakowska, she explained as she led me to the kitchen, and she was here with her husband, Jakub. He was a radio operator, intercepting German messages and passing them on for decoding, and she was another mathematician who worked on codebreaking with the team of cryptanalysts I'd just met. As she bustled around the kitchen, making coffee and toasting slices of bread, I noticed the curve of her belly, rounded like the edge of the new moon, holding the promise of fullness. 'I'm four months pregnant,' she told me with a shy smile, tucking a stray strand of her blonde hair back into its braid. 'Even in the middle of a war, life goes on. Of course, it makes me miss my family back in Poland all the more. I wish I could be with them. Or, at least, I wish they could be here with me. Our country has been torn apart, yet again, by the invaders.'

'Aren't you worried about being captured by the Germans?' I asked. I could hardly bear to think what their fate would be if their activities were to be discovered by the authorities.

'Of course,' she said matter-of-factly. 'But we are well taken care of by the French Secret Service, who pretend to work with the Vichy regime but remain loyal to de Gaulle. They keep us hidden here in plain sight. Apart from those in the Resistance with whom we work, people in the local community think we are simply a bunch of rather eccentric labourers, brought here from somewhere in the east to contribute to the war effort by cutting wood and working in the fields. As long as this part of the country remains under control of a nominally French government, we are left to get on with it. After all, Europe is full of people like us, exiles who've been displaced, uprooted from their homelands. As far as anyone knows, we are just a handful of refugees among the hundreds of thousands who are on the move every day, looking for a safe place to stay.'

She poured me a cup of coffee and set butter and jam on the table before me. 'Now eat,' she said. 'And then we will go and join Marian, Henryk and the others and you can tell us more about the latest advances in codebreaking in Britain. I'm interested to know how you're tackling the extra rotors the Nazis have implemented in the naval Enigma machines. We've been trying to find new ways to hack the daily settings, but it's tough without the means at our disposal to build a more sophisticated *bomba*.'

I felt more relaxed in her company than I had done for days – in fact, ever since my mission to France had been proposed. Dilly Knox had been right. In more senses than one, the Poles and I spoke the same language.

We spent the morning working in the study with the others. Janina showed me how she decoded some of the radio intercepts, which her husband received on a transmitter hidden in the attic of the château. The Germans and the Vichy French were using a variety of coding methods – not just the Enigma machines – and messages transmitted by both police forces were relatively easy to decrypt. They made chilling reading. Most were lists of numbers that, Janina explained, detailed people who'd been rounded up and sent to work camps. 'See here,' she said. 'They've been grouped in categories: Jewish, Romany, Jehovah's Witnesses, Political Suspects, Handicapped . . . Anyone the Nazis choose. We pass these figures on to the British and French intelligence services. It's vital that we tell the story of what's really happening. The horror of what's going on across Europe is unremitting. I know my own relations back in Poland will by now have been sent to the camps. I can't bear to imagine how they are coping in such terrible places.'

An expression of pain flickered across her features and, instinctively, she put her hands on her belly, protectively cradling the slight bump. What would the future hold for her unborn child, I wondered. I could see the strain she was under, and I dreaded to think what might happen if the group at the château were to be denounced by some suspicious local policeman.

'Couldn't you come to Britain?' I asked. 'I could try to ask the people who brought me here to get you out. You and your baby would be safer there.'

She smiled sadly, shaking her head. 'France is the best place to intercept these messages. And the French have been good to us. We have to trust them to keep us safe. I'm grateful for your offer, but the British haven't ever offered us the chance to leave. It's made more complicated, too, by the fact that Russia is a British ally. What they've done to our country is really just as bad as what the Germans did, invading from the east just a couple of weeks after the Nazis invaded from the west. Poland has been torn in two, racked by those enemies, our people brutalised and murdered by both sides.'

I nodded, understanding. 'But Britain is not your enemy,' I said. 'We're on your side. General Sikorski's set up his command in London. Isn't that a declaration of friendship?'

She shrugged. 'Like I said, it's complicated. We've discussed trying to go, of course, but as long as this part of the country remains a *zone libre*, we feel we should stay. It's relatively safe, and the work we do here is so important. Being Polish means we're used to living with an enemy on the doorstep. We have our ears to the ground here, so to speak, and we must continue to be the voices of those who've been silenced.' The tremble of her lips belied the strength of her words.

I reached across and gave her hand a squeeze, struggling to find any words to express how brave I thought she was. She took a deep breath, regathering her composure, and we turned our attention back to the sheets of paper on the desk in front of us. I redoubled my efforts to take in as much as I could, committing most of what she told me to memory and making a few short, coded notes where necessary, so I could debrief the Bletchley cryptanalysts on my return. Even with the limited resources they had access to here, the Polish team had come up with new ways to tackle the range of ever-changing German codes with which we were faced every day.

While the mornings were spent at work in the study, in the afternoons, unless significant radio traffic was coming in, we had a bit more free time. Janina had scratched out a herb bed in a corner of the courtyard, where she grew feathery fronds of fennel and dill, as well as pretty white-flowered caraway for its seeds. Even that early in the summer, the ground was baked hard, but she tended and watered her patch of garden daily, nurturing her little crop, which would enhance the taste of the scant rations with flavours of her homeland. 'These herbs won't survive through the summer,' she said. 'When it gets too hot, they'll shoot up and then die. So I'll pick everything in a couple of weeks' time and dry the leaves, but I'll keep back some of the seeds to grow more later.'

We would also walk in the fields and woods surrounding the château, foraging for ingredients to help supplement the evening meal. Each day, without fail, Janina would tie on a red headscarf to cover her blonde hair, and we'd go down the lane and climb over a gate into a neighbouring field. I couldn't identify the crop growing there at first – robust, waist-high stems sprouting broad leaves, each with the beginnings of a fat bud at the top. 'They're sunflowers,' Janina told me. 'Just imagine the sight at the height of summer! Each stem carrying a flower fringed with gold like a lion's mane, their faces turning to follow the sun as it travels across the sky every day.'

We'd skirt around the edge of the field, which was surrounded by oak woods, giving it a safe, secluded feel, to the far corner where a huge, solitary sweet chestnut tree stood, and we'd sit there in its shade for a few minutes. Leaning against its rough bark, I'd tilt my head back to look up through the branches, spots of sunlight dancing through the leaves. The waxy flowers reminded me of the trees in Hyde Park, where I'd walked with Ben. 'One day,' I told

Janina, 'I hope you will come to London. We'll go for a walk in a park there and I'll take you for tea at The Ritz.'

She laughed. 'I'd love that – The Ritz Hotel . . . Imagine me going there!' She brushed the dust off her skirt, once again cradling the gentle swell of her belly, then reached up to take hold of a low branch to help haul herself back on to her feet. 'Oof,' she said. 'This little one is growing bigger by the minute. Come, let's see what we can find growing in our larder today.'

She was an expert at identifying edible fungi and we gathered handfuls of chanterelles and Penny Bun mushrooms, inhaling their savoury, earthy smell as we plucked them from the ground at the edge of the woodland. We picked more herbs, and salad leaves too – wild thyme, marjoram, chervil and dandelions.

I was surprised to see her stoop to gather a posy of wildflowers as we walked back with our baskets full. She laughed at the expression on my face. 'You think I'm being frivolous! But this is just as important as the nourishment we gather for our bodies. There's a saying that goes, if you have a loaf of bread, sell half and buy a lily. It's important to nourish the soul as well, and remember that there is still beauty even in these times of darkness and cruelty. These flowers remind me of the ones we used to have on the table back home, in the days when my country was free.'

I recalled the evening I'd walked along the lane back in Bletchley, when the hedgerows were full of bluebells and the vixen and her cubs had appeared. I remembered thinking that this was what we were fighting for. So I, too, picked a bunch of ox-eye daisies and cornflowers and when we got back to the château I put them in a jug and placed them on the chest of drawers in my bedroom. Janina was right – they might be just a few wildflowers, but they represented far more. When I woke in the middle of the night – the faces of Amy and Teddy often still haunted my uneasy dreams – the faint glow of the white petals in the darkness gave me reassurance and comfort.

The days passed and soon I realised I'd been in France for a week. The only visitor to the château had been the priest who'd led me there on the night I arrived. He'd appear occasionally and I surmised he was passing messages back and forth between the cryptographers and the *maquisards*. There'd been no word of my return to England, though. I realised how fortunate I was to have that escape route to safety when my friends here did not, so I tried not to let my mounting anxiety show. The weather had been fine, warm and sunny during the day with fresher nights under clear skies, when the full moon shone bright gold among a swathe of silver stars. I prayed the clear conditions would last into the week ahead, when surely they'd come back for me. Otherwise, I'd have to wait another full fortnight while this moon wasted and died away and a new one grew in its place to become bright enough for the Lysanders to be able to fly by its light again.

Even though I tried to conceal my increasing sense of tension, I'm sure Janina knew how I was feeling. One morning, after breakfast, she announced we were going to go to the market in town. I assumed I'd have to remain in the château, hidden away, but she shook her head, knotting her red scarf beneath her chin. 'It's OK. The square will be busy on market day, so you won't stand out as a stranger. And they are used to us going there regularly like everyone else, so if we don't they may think it a bit strange. Don't worry, you won't need to do any talking – if anyone asks, I'll say you're my cousin, passing through on your way to Toulouse to be with family there. Your name is Eveline, remember. But your French accent sounds so British that it would give you away, so don't talk to anyone and we'll be fine!'

I was nervous, but at the same time curious to see more of the town, whose elegant towers perched tantalisingly on the hilltop in the distance. And the distraction of the market would be a very welcome one.

Having been cocooned within the château and its environs, it was a thrill to walk along the road winding up the steep hill, joining a stream of others as we made our way along boulevards shaded by spreading plane trees to the Place aux Herbes in the centre of Uzès. I couldn't help wondering whether pairs of eyes were watching us from behind the shuttered windows of the houses we passed, and if they were, were they friendly ones or did they belong to those who might denounce us?

I tried not to look self-conscious, sticking close to Janina, who seemed far more relaxed than I felt, smiling easily and occasionally raising a hand in greeting to some of the stallholders. We bought some potatoes and a large vegetable shaped like a lumpy football, which Janina called *seler*. I later discovered it was celeriac, although this wasn't something I'd ever been familiar with back home. We also purchased a jar of honey, and some scarlet tomatoes – far larger ones than any I'd ever seen before. There was no meat at the butcher's stall, but he let us have a bag of bones for making stock. 'We'll make a delicious soup with these and the *seler*,' Janina explained. 'With a few pickles chopped into it, and plenty of fresh dill from the courtyard, you'll see what a feast it can be.'

I noticed, though, that she discreetly handed the butcher a slip of folded paper when he gave her the soup bones. So her regular trip to this market was about more than simply buying provisions. The network of *maquisards* must be operating here, I realised. I wondered what might be in that message, and how word might be delivered when the time came for me to be extracted, but I knew better than to ask any questions.

Once we'd finished our shopping, we walked down from the top of the town to wander along the esplanade, making the most of the opportunity to gaze out at the views across the wide valley beneath us before we had to return to the confines of the château. I craned my neck to gaze up at the elegant, soaring towers of the town above us, fine examples of architecture from centuries past, wishing I had more freedom to be a tourist and explore in more detail. But the sun was climbing in the sky, our shadows shrinking before its growing intensity, and it was soon time to walk back down the hill carrying our laden baskets. The air seemed to have grown heavy and humid suddenly, pressing down on us as we went, and I couldn't help glancing anxiously towards the west. From the viewpoint of the esplanade, I'd noticed dark clouds were gathering there. The weather was changing.

Everyone was assembled in the kitchen that evening, where the dishes we'd cooked were simmering on the stove, filling the room with the smells of the celeriac soup and a rabbit stew with a rich gravy of herbs and red wine. Over the past week, I'd got to know the group better. The leaders of the group were high-ranking Polish army officers: Antoni was a General, Gwido a Lieutenant Colonel and Maksymilian a Major. Marian Rejewski and Henryk Zygalski were civilians who'd been co-opted into the Polish cipher bureau and there were about ten others, all skilled codebreakers, radio technicians and translators. Within the confines of the château they used each other's Polish names, although they'd been given French covers, which they used whenever they ventured beyond the safety of its walls. Janina's husband, Jakub, was a man of few words, his complexion as pale as his white-blond hair from the hours he spent hunched over a radio set in the hot, airless attic. The strain of passing on those abhorrent messages for decoding showed in the preoccupied lines of his face. But his eyes lit up with love as his wife set the huge copper pot of soup on the table and stooped to kiss him on the cheek before taking her place next to him.

The room was filled with laughter as the soup was being served, the men relaxing a little at the end of another long week in exile from their homeland. I remember Antoni joking in Polish about how these days even the French were reduced to eating the sorts of vegetables they used only to deem suitable for feeding to cattle and Eastern Europeans. I was passing my bowl to Henryk so he could fill it with soup from the vast copper pan that Janina had placed in the centre of the table, when the kitchen door opened and a stranger walked in. I froze. Was this the moment when we would all be arrested? My presence at the table would surely make it far worse for them all if I were discovered to be British. But Marian looked up from his soup plate and smiled.

'Good evening, Bolek! You're just in time to join us for dinner. Allow me to introduce you, too, to our charming guest, Eveline. You were so kind as to facilitate her travel to be with us for these few days.'

He turned to me. 'Bolek is French, so you'll have to bear with his terrible Polish.'

'*Enchanté, mademoiselle,*' said the man, with a slight bow in my direction. Then he said, in English, 'We are very pleased to welcome you to Cadix. It was good of Dilly to spare you.' I realised then that this must be the head of the French intelligence service, the man who'd brought the Polish team here, and Bolek must be a cover name too.

Henryk produced some bottles of wine – liberated from the cellar, he said – and poured generous glasses for each of us. '*Na zdrowie!*' he said. 'Cheers! Here's to another week of sticking it to the Germans!' As we raised our glasses in a toast, an ominous rumble of thunder sounded from outside. The storm was upon us. There'd be no flying tonight.

The drinking went on long into the night. A bottle of vodka was conjured up as we were clearing away the plates and hours after I'd excused myself and gone up to my room, I could still hear the faint strains of rowdy singing filtering up from the kitchen. They needed to let off a bit of steam from time to time, I supposed.

Despite the festive atmosphere, their work put enormous strain on them and the threat of discovery was a constant danger, lurking out there in the darkness just beyond the château's thick walls where the storm was gathering in force. Lightning flickered suddenly through the slats of my shutters, followed almost immediately by an ear-splitting thunder-crack. Despite the heat, I pulled the covers over my head and prayed it would blow over quickly.

The skies remained overcast for the next couple of days, the air still hot and heavy in spite of the storm, and my despair mounted as the window for my extraction started to close. But then one morning, as we were clearing the breakfast table, Jakub appeared in the kitchen and handed me a slip of paper. On it was written the coded message I'd been waiting for, using my poem. It only took moments to decipher it. *Be ready*, it said. I threw it into the stove and watched the flames consume it, feeling a mixture of relief in knowing they'd soon be coming for me and guilt at the thought of having to leave behind the friends I'd made here.

The next afternoon, as Janina and I walked to the chestnut tree in the corner of the sunflower field as usual, the clouds began to break, and a widening ribbon of blue sky appeared above us. When we reached the tree, I spotted something silver against the dark trunk. A few stems of lavender had been bound together with a strand of blue wool and tucked into a crack in the bark.

Janina reached to take it down. 'Tonight you will leave,' she said. 'This is the sign.' She handed me the little bunch of flowers. 'You will come back to this tree at midnight and wait. Be careful to stay concealed. Someone will come to the corner of the field over by the oaks. They will flash a torch five times. Do not make yourself known until you see that signal. Then you'll know it's safe to go with them. If for any reason they don't appear, or if they don't give the correct signal, you must stay hidden here until one of us comes to find you. Do you understand?'

I nodded, unable to speak as a surge of conflicting emotions flooded through me: relief, mixed with fear for the friends I'd made here and sadness that I'd be leaving them in such danger. As I clutched the lavender, I hugged her tight and for a moment we stood there like that, the scent of the flowers enfolding us. Then she drew away, wiping a tear from her eye as she said, 'We'd better go back. You have packing to do. And we must prepare a few things to go in the plane with you.'

As we walked back to the château, I picked some more wildflowers, gathering an armful of scarlet poppies and white cow parsley into a billowing bunch. I handed them to her at the door. 'Here,' I said. 'The colours of the Polish flag. And the poppies match your scarf – a reminder that you have friends in Britain who are working with you, even at a distance. Get a message out to us if you change your mind about staying here.' Then I left her to go upstairs and pack my bag.

An hour later, I stood back to survey my room, making sure I'd left nothing behind. There was a soft tap at the door and I called, 'Come in.'

Marian Rejewski stood there. 'Are you ready to leave us, Eveline?' he asked.

I gestured to my bag. 'All packed,' I replied.

'I have one more message for you to take back with you,' he said. 'It's urgent. But not to be written down. Please can you make sure it gets through to the highest levels of command?'

I nodded, and listened carefully to what he had to say.

◆ ◆ ◆

Just before midnight, I slipped out of the side door of the château and hurried down the lane to the sunflower field, being careful to keep to the cover alongside the trees. The waning moon was an almost perfect semi-circle among the ragged wisps of cloud. I offered up a quick prayer to anyone who might be listening that the sky would remain clear enough for the plane to get through.

For what felt like an eternity, I stood alone in the tree's dark shadow, careful to remain hidden, keeping my eyes glued on the far corner of the field. Then, at last, a dimmed torch flashed there five times. I stepped forward into the moonlight beside the sunflowers and saw a figure approach.

'Follow me,' said the *maquisard*, taking my bag from me before I could protest that I could carry it perfectly well myself, and setting off through the trees. The pace was brisk. He threaded his way confidently through the woodland in the darkness, with me stumbling over every root and rock behind him. Adrenaline carried me forwards because I knew the plane wouldn't wait. At last, we reached the edge of a clearing where I breathed in the familiar perfume of the lavender field. The silver-grey furrows stretched away from us down a long, gentle slope, making a perfect runway.

'Wait here,' the man said. 'Then come to the plane as soon as it lands.'

I nodded, knowing how crucial that speed would be.

The night was warm, and I was sweating in my woollen jacket and skirt after the scramble through the woods. Nothing moved in the darkness. The air was filled with the orchestra of crickets, but then all of a sudden they fell silent, as if some invisible conductor had let fall their baton, bringing the symphony to an end. I strained my ears to listen. And then I heard it: the low rumble of the Lysander's engine. It grew louder, then louder still, a roar that surely must be heard for miles around, summoning every enemy policeman in the vicinity to come running. My heart was pounding with equal measures of fear and hope as the plane appeared in the moonlight and circled the field. Might Ben be the pilot this time?

At one end of the field, four shadowy figures appeared, and one flashed a code with a torch. Then two of them stepped into their positions and a third sprinted down the gentle slope, forming the inverted 'L' shape to guide the pilot in to land.

I held my breath. A perfect touchdown, and then the plane was rushing towards me up the field. The scent of crushed lavender filled the air as it turned before coming to a halt, and I ran from my hiding place, clutching my bag to my chest. I craned my neck to look up at the pilot, but when he turned his head to watch the cargo being offloaded, I could see straight away it wasn't Ben. As I returned his thumbs-up sign, I swallowed the lump in my throat that was equal parts disappointment and relief.

As soon as the three descending passengers' feet touched the ground, I was climbing the ladder, followed by two more people who'd emerged from the shadows to follow me on to the plane. Even as I was fastening the straps of the seat belt, this time taking the seat at the rear of the compartment where the Baby had sat on my outward journey, the plane was beginning to move again, gathering speed then lifting into the air. It felt slow, the weight of the Lizzie surely too cumbersome to be able to fly, but then, miraculously, we'd cleared the trees and were climbing towards the half-moon above us, which lit the way home.

I gathered myself, taking stock of my fellow passengers. A woman sat in the cramped seat opposite mine and a man was on the floor, his knees curled into his chest, their luggage stuffed in around them. They grinned at me. '*Oh là là,*' said the woman, fanning herself with her hand. '*Quelle aventure!*'

We managed to communicate, in my broken French and their broken English. They were part of a new Resistance network, they told me, coming to Britain to be trained in the use of radios. The man was a teacher, the woman a student at the university in Marseille. I didn't tell them much about what I'd been doing in France, conscious that the fewer people who knew of the whereabouts of the Polish cryptographers, the better. I simply said I'd been delivering some materials and they nodded and smiled, saying, '*Merci.*'

The two of them slept a little as we flew northwards through the night, but I stayed awake, watching as the pilot navigated the corridor of darkness, avoiding the main cities again. When the Channel appeared – a glint of silver at the edge of the darkened land – I breathed a big sigh of relief and reached over to shake the others awake so they could watch England come into view and be ready for our landing.

The first light of a glorious sunrise was just striking Dover's white cliffs as the pilot veered left, towards the Downs. And then I was able to pick out the first familiar landmarks – the curve of the coastline towards the point of Selsey Bill and the Isle of Wight in the distance beyond that – and we began to descend towards Tangmere.

Major Bertram was waiting as I climbed down the ladder. 'Welcome home, Eveline!' he said. 'Mission successful. Well done. And you can now return to being Miss Buchanan once more.'

I turned to say goodbye to my two fellow travellers, but they were already being led to a waiting car.

'Come with me to the cottage,' said the Major. 'There's a bath waiting for you, and some breakfast. Then you can get some sleep, and this afternoon we'll take you back to your people at Bletchley. I know they're eager to hear from you.'

Never had a soak in a hot bath been so welcome. Never had bacon and eggs tasted so good. And never had a bed felt so comforting, as I slipped between the cotton sheets in one of the upstairs bedrooms at Tangmere Cottage. I thought of Janina and the others in the château, imagining them going about their work, and offered up a little prayer for their safety. Beneath my pillow, just before I fell into a deep, replenishing sleep, I placed the little bunch of lavender stems tied with blue yarn, which I'd kept tucked into the breast pocket of my jacket all the way home.

Finn

Before we came on our holidays to France, when we were studying The Moon and Space, I did a project with Dad about 5 Things That Could Happen If The Moon Were Destroyed. These are the things:

Tides would be almost non-existent. During Full Moons and New Moons, which occur when the sun, Earth and moon are all aligned, we have spring tides, which are the largest differences between high and low tide. When they're at right angles, which happens during a Half Moon phase, we have neap tides, which are the smallest differences. It's the moon that exerts the greatest forces on the oceans, so if we had no moon, we would only have small neap tides all the time.

The length of the day would be constant. The moon exerts a tiny frictional force on Earth as it spins, and this is slowing it down, making our days get longer. A few billion years ago, a day on Earth was only about 10 hours long. Little by little, the moon has been slowing down the Earth's rotation and now our days have grown to be 24 hours long. In another 4 million years, we won't need leap days anymore as the rotation rate will have slowed enough to even out the need to add an extra day to our calendar every 4 years. That wouldn't happen without the moon.

There would be no more eclipses. Eclipses require 3 objects to be in alignment: the Sun, a planet and its moon.

The stars would look much brighter in the night sky. Obviously, the Sun is the brightest object in the sky. The moon is the second brightest, 14,000 times brighter than the next-brightest object in the sky (which is Venus). The light from the moon washes out many stars. Without it, the night sky would be much darker and so we'd be able to see loads more stars.

Debris could fall to Earth, but it wouldn't necessarily exterminate life. If the moon were to be smashed up by an asteroid (and you wouldn't need a very big one, just a medium-sized one about 1 kilometre in diameter would do the job), the debris would spread out in all directions and some of it would hit the Earth. If the moon were to be hit in just the right way by the asteroid and the pieces were small enough, they might form a belt of rings around the Earth, like Saturn has.

I can now add another item to the list, which is that Philly wouldn't have been able to fly to France and back on her secret mission if there hadn't been a big enough moon for the Lysander pilots to navigate by. So all in all, the moon is pretty cool.

I'm still sort of wishing an asteroid would strike the Earth in the next 24 hours, though. That would mean the sailing camp would definitely have to be cancelled, and Mum probably wouldn't go on her writing course either.

Philly

It felt very strange to be back behind my desk at Bletchley Park again. My head was still full of images of the extraordinary team at Cadix and the chatter of Polish voices: Marian's patient tones as he showed me a method he was working on to break a new code; Henryk's uproarious laughter as he poured another round of drinks; Janina's gentle words of hope for a peaceful future for her unborn child as she watered her herb garden in the courtyard. It was all so vivid, and at the same time it felt like another slightly unreal world, a world overshadowed every minute of the day by the threat of deportation and execution.

Dilly Knox was absent when I was asked to report to the Cottage again. I briefed his trusted assistant, Mavis – the woman in the twinset and pearls – and a man who simply introduced himself as 'Commander Fleming, Naval Intelligence Division'.

I told them everything I'd managed to glean during my stay at Cadix and they took copious notes. I relayed Marian Rejewski's insistence on the importance of the police messages, building up that chilling picture of the deportations to camps in the east. And finally I passed on the message he'd given me on that last evening, stressing its importance: 'He says to look at the radio traffic in and out of a place called Peenemünde. Something is being built there. Something of great strategic significance. Large numbers of Polish workers have been sent to a factory there, they have it on good authority.'

Commander Fleming raised an eyebrow and nodded. 'That's helpful,' he said. 'Thank you, Miss Buchanan. We'll make sure this information gets through to those at the very top.'

As I left the Cottage, I asked Mavis, 'How is Mr Knox?'

She shook her head, her eyes filled with sadness. 'Not very good, I'm afraid. But he still insists on working. I'll be visiting him at his home tomorrow. He'll be very interested to hear everything you've brought back from your mission.'

'Please pass on my best wishes to him. If you think that's appropriate?'

She smiled. 'I will. He'll be glad to know you're home safely.'

Then the door shut behind me and I made my way back to Hut 8.

It was only years later, in the 1950s, when I read a book called *Casino Royale* about the escapades of a Secret Intelligence officer called James Bond, that I recognised the author's photograph. The man I'd met in the Cottage that day was 007's creator, Ian Fleming. And I couldn't help but wonder just how much inspiration for the characters of Vesper Lynd and Miss Moneypenny he'd drawn from his encounters with women like Mavis and me while he was working at Bletchley Park.

As the summer wore on, my work continued to keep me as busy as ever. Alan asked me to help work with him on a new project, working with a different team in a section code-named *Fish,* on a code which they called *Tunny*. This was a new method of coding employed by the German army, known as the Lorenz cipher. Lorenz was even more complex than Enigma – messages were coded using machines that had twelve rotors instead of Enigma's three or four – and while the *Fish* team at Bletchley were developing powerful machines to help break the code, Alan had devised a system of calculating mathematical probabilities to help shorten the process of working out the rotor sequences. We christened the new system *Turingery*. It reminded me a little of the methods the Polish team at Cadix were using, meticulously working out mathematical approaches to decoding the Morse-based radio messages they were intercepting there. I was glad to think the techniques the Poles had shared with me during my stay might have helped inspire his methods again. Alan's determination to solve every fresh challenge the German codes could throw at us continually impressed me and I could see how his colleagues held him in the highest esteem. He had a truly brilliant mind.

Our work was all-consuming, but on my precious days off I was able to see Ben a few times. Now that I knew better, I noticed that his own leave coincided with the two-week periods either side of the new moon, when the night skies were too dark for the Lysander missions to fly. I tried not to let on to him that I'd been to France, conscious that the details of that trip were so highly classified. But one hot August day we packed a picnic and walked along the canal and the river to Great Brickhill, where we stopped for a drink in the Old Red Lion. As we sat eating our fish-paste sandwiches, I couldn't resist saying, 'How is Jim Elliot these days?'

It took Ben a few moments to register and then he shot me a look of astonishment. 'How do you know Jim?' he asked. I made no reply, just took a sip from the glass of cider I'd been enjoying and smiled enigmatically. I could see the cogs turning in his mind as he worked it out. 'No,' said Ben. 'You didn't . . . ? I knew there'd been a special mission a few weeks back . . . That surely wasn't you, was it?'

'I'm afraid it's classified. If I told you, I'd have to kill you,' I joked.

He reached for my hand, shaking his head. 'What an astonishing woman you are, Philly Buchanan.'

I smiled and kissed him. 'And what an astonishing man you are, Ben Delaney. You and your Lizzies, flying in and out of Tangmere. It's quite an operation you Special Ops boys have going on there.'

He was quieter as we walked back along the river to my digs. When it was time for him to go, he held me for a long time beside the holly bush at the gate. 'You will take care, won't you,' he whispered, burying his face in my hair.

I tipped my head back to look right into his eyes. 'Don't worry, most of my days are spent sitting behind a very safe desk. But I promise I will,' I said. 'Just as you must. I couldn't bear to lose you, you know.'

'I'll always be yours, Philly. By the dark of the moon and the light of the sun, remember?'

I nodded. 'I'll always remember.'

And I stepped back and watched as he kicked the starter pedal of his motorbike and disappeared down the lane, raising his hand in a final salute. He didn't need to look back to see if I was watching. He knew I would be.

Summer became autumn and the leaves in the grounds of the Manor turned from red to gold, then tumbled to the earth, forming a thick carpet on the bank surrounding the lake. I was walking there after lunch one day when a soldier in a sergeant's uniform approached.

'Miss Buchanan.' He spoke tersely, unsmiling. 'They said I might find you here. Would you come with me, please?'

I followed him into the main house and down a corridor to an office. It was the room where I'd signed the Official Secrets Act on my first day at Bletchley Park. I glanced at the leather-topped desk, half expecting to see the revolver still lying there, but it had been replaced by a pile of papers, stacked tidily beside an inkwell and a blotter.

I didn't recognise the man sitting behind the desk, and he didn't introduce himself, but I could tell from the rows of gold braid on the sleeves of his jacket that he was a General. He peered at me over the top of his gold-rimmed spectacles and gestured to me to sit on the chair across the desk from where he sat. He glanced down, consulting the sheet of paper he held in his hands, then back up at me.

'Miss Buchanan,' he said. 'We have received a somewhat unusual request from our people in France. I understand you are familiar with the château where the French have given refuge to a team of Polish agents?' He paused, waiting for me to nod, then continued. 'We have need of your services once again. Our intelligence suggests the Germans may soon be taking over Vichy France as a result of . . . well, suffice it to say some significant developments. So it has become a matter of some importance now that the residents of Cadix leave as quickly as possible and we would like to offer them a new home in Britain. We've communicated this to our French counterparts, but unfortunately they do not share our sense of urgency. They want to hang on to the Poles, but we need them here in Britain. It has been suggested that a direct approach by you might be able to persuade them – the Frenchman known as Bolek, and the leaders of the Polish team – that they need to leave as quickly as possible.'

He paused, searching my face to make sure I understood the gravity of the situation. I returned his gaze steadily, giving a brief nod.

'They should make their way to Spain by whatever route possible and our people will meet them there, facilitating their transport out,' he continued. 'Could you do that, do you think? Would you be prepared to go back and deliver this message to them in person? It is vitally important.'

I didn't hesitate. 'Yes, sir,' I said.

'Very good. In that case, if you are prepared to leave right away, we have a car waiting.'

I was a little thrown by the immediacy of the arrangements. When he said it was urgent, he clearly meant it. But I stifled my qualms and said again, emphatically, 'Yes, sir.'

'You'll go tonight. Everything you need for the trip will be provided, and you'll be fully briefed. I think you know the drill by now.' He stood and extended his hand to shake mine, dismissing me. 'Thank you, Miss Buchanan. You'll find the sergeant waiting for you at the front door. He'll show you to the car.'

My day had begun like any other, but it ended with another journey to the airfield at Tangmere. The light was just beginning to fade as we drew up in front of the cottage and the moon was visible in the darkening sky. It was past its fullest, starting to wane. There would only be a few days left this month when the Lysanders could fly. But then if I was just going to deliver the message and persuade the Poles to pack up and leave as quickly as possible, I supposed it would all be over and done with quickly and I'd be collected in a day or two's time.

The door of the cottage opened, and Major Bertram beckoned me in. 'It's good to see you again, Miss Buchanan. Or should I say, Eveline,' he said. While his smile was warm, there was a tension behind his expression as he led me to the Ops Room and began my briefing.

The map was dotted with more pins than the last time I'd seen it, denoting an increase in the areas defended by flak cover. The corridor along which the planes could get through had definitely narrowed in the past months. The Captain noticed me scrutinising it. 'Yes,' he said. 'As you can see, the challenges haven't got any easier. But then I suppose that's why you're here. Things are hotting up, and not just across France.' He frowned. 'We haven't had the time I'd have liked to prepare for this mission, but we know it's important. You'll only have a day to liaise with the team at Cadix and we'll be back to pick you up the next night, before the moon window closes. We can bring two additional passengers on the return flight, so you may wish to ask the Poles to prioritise those who need to leave the soonest. The others will have to take their chances getting out via Spain, where it will be easier for us to extract them in greater numbers.'

I thought of Janina, along with Jakub and their unborn baby. Would they qualify as priorities? Or would it be more important to extract the group's leaders, like Marian, Henryk, Antoni . . . how would they decide?

Just then the door of the Ops Room opened, and Wing Commander Elliot walked in. 'Hello again,' he said, his tone matter-of-fact as he pulled out a chair and joined us at the table. Once more I was both disappointed and relieved that it wasn't Ben who'd be flying the mission. The map clearly showed how much more dangerous these flights were now. But then I realised it probably only meant Ben would be flying somewhere else over Europe. I imagined all the Special Duties pilots flying the Lizzies would be busier than ever these days.

Major Bertram handed me a thick envelope. 'There's money and papers in there,' he said. 'To help them get out of France. And here are the briefing documents for them, with details of an agent they should liaise with in Spain. If they can make it across the mountains from France into Spain, we can do the rest. I can't stress it too highly – although it probably goes without saying – if you're caught you must find a way to destroy this information. You understand that, don't you?'

I nodded, then glanced across at Commander Elliot. He, too, was looking at the map on the wall, a slight frown creasing his brow.

Major Bertram stood. 'All right then, Eveline.' He placed an emphasis on the name, reminding me of my role. 'If you go upstairs to the first room on the left, you'll find the things you need. Clothes, papers and so on. The ones you had last time. You won't need to take anything else, other than that.' He nodded to the envelope he'd given me. 'You'll be extracted tomorrow night. Thankfully, the weather is set fair so at least we have that on our side.'

'Right-o,' said Commander Elliot, getting to his feet in turn. 'I'll go and get our Lizzie checked over and ready for the off then. See you back here for supper and then we'll leave around ten-ish.'

In the bedroom upstairs, beneath the timbered eaves of the cottage, my fingers shook as I did up the buttons of the woollen jacket and tied my bootlaces. This mission felt horribly less well-prepared than my last, and the timing was tight. I pulled back a corner of the blackout and peeped out of the window. Over the wall, above the airfield, the waning moon was rising, just visible in the darkening sky. I settled the blind back into place and took one last look in the mirror. Eveline stared back at me, her face pinched and pale. But her expression was determined, and I gave her a little nod before I turned away, tucking the envelope into a leather satchel that had been provided with the clothes and going downstairs to try to force down a little supper. It was going to be a long night.

Finn

Very early in the morning of the Acclimatisation Day for the sailing course, Mum asked me if I'd like to go for another walk on the beach before breakfast. It was still dark, but we were both up because I hadn't been able to sleep very well and then I'd been sick. Mum came into my bedroom when she heard me trying to clean it up. It was all over my sheets and it smelled really bad.

She asked me if she could take my temperature. I said OK, because I was really hoping I did have a fever and then I wouldn't be able to do the course because I'd officially be ill. Mum would have to cancel her trip and stay in France and bring me Marmite sandwiches in bed (once the sheets had been washed) and that would make me feel better.

But she looked at the thermometer and said it was absolutely normal and that it must just be nerves. So I got dressed and then we went out of the gate and down the path through the dunes to the beach.

It was so early that there was no one else there, not even people taking their dogs for a walk. The moon was still quite bright and the waves were shushing on to the sand, leaving behind a few wisps of black seaweed and some little white shells (I counted 54 but then I stopped because I didn't want it to turn out to be an odd number which would make me feel even worse). It felt nice and calm to be walking along peacefully beside Mum in the darkness, with the breeze cooling my face, not saying anything.

When we got to the broken-down fence beside the rocks at the end of the beach, we turned around and started walking back. The moon was fading now and the sky was getting lighter, and we were walking back towards the house and our breakfasts and after that I would have to go with Dad to the harbour, so I didn't feel quite so calm. My stomach was empty, but it still gurgled and felt like there were waves churning around inside it.

'You're going to be fine this week, you know, Finn,' Mum said. The tone of her voice didn't sound quite as certain about that as her words did though. 'Dad will take good care of you. And you're such a good dinghy sailor. I think you'll enjoy learning how to sail the bigger boat. Being part of a crew.'

'I don't think you should go on your writing course,' I replied.

'Oh Finn,' she said, with a sort of sigh. 'It will be good for me to have a few days away. It's not for long. And you know I've really been looking forward to it for a long time. Besides, it's time for Philly to go home to England and it'll be good for her, as well, to have the company on the journey. I'll be back before you know it and then you can show me everything you've learned.'

I started concentrating on counting the shells along the tideline again, in twos to be on the safe side, but Mum interrupted me when I got to 22. 'It's good for us all to face challenges in life, you know. I feel nervous about my writing course, because everyone might think I'm not good enough or they might criticise my book. But I know I need to do it, because I'll learn a lot and it'll make me a better writer. I think you'll learn a lot from the sailing course too. And you know how much work Dad's put into organising it. I know you don't like new things, but we both have to brave this week and give it a go. Who knows, we might even make some new friends.'

I don't have Friends. But it reminded me of the Old Lady saying, 'My friends call me Philly', and I thought maybe she had become a Friend in a way after all, even though she's about 80 years older than me.

I bent down to pick up a double clamshell and handed it to Mum because she likes collecting them and putting them in a big glass jar which she keeps on the side of the bath in our house back in Scotland.

'Why, thank you, Finn,' she said and her whole face became a smile, so I knew she was pleased. She held up her right hand and did our starfish sign too. 'I'll keep this in my pocket when I'm away and it will remind me to be as brave as Philly was. Her life story is pretty amazing, isn't it? I think we can both learn a lot about courage from her. Imagine setting off in an aeroplane in the dead of night to go and deliver secret messages to that château! It must have been terrifying, but she did it not just once but twice. If she could do that, then you and I can do our courses this week, can't we?'

I decided not to point out that it had obviously not ended very well for Philly. I think I'm more likely to lose a leg or an arm or something on the sailing course than Mum is on her writing course, but I don't really want it to happen to either one of us. So I just said, 'Yes, she was very brave.'

Then we had come to the end of our walk and so we went back through the dunes to the house and put the breakfast things on the table. I made a promise to myself to try to be as brave as a secret agent being dropped into enemy territory. Actually, Enemy Territory is not a bad description for having to be on a boat with that other big kid. He is not a Friend.

Philly

The flight back to the south of France was a tense one. As we set off, I watched the moonlight shimmer on the dark waters of the English Channel, a path of gold unfurling beneath us. But soon we were approaching the dark huddle of the French coastline, and over the intercom I heard Commander Elliot swear under his breath as flak lit up the night ahead of us like some sinister firework display. He took evasive action to try to avoid it, veering further west. We were flying at such a low altitude I knew that the big 88-millimetre shells – targeted to defend against higher-flying bombers – would explode above us. But at our slow speed we could more easily be picked out by anti-aircraft batteries and hit by other lighter weapons. He managed to find a quieter patch and skirted round whichever port it was that the flak batteries were defending, trying to pick up a landmark or two again to get us back on track. After a tense few minutes, we began following the thread of a river and he gave me a thumbs up from the front cabin. We flew on through the night for several hours, but there was no way I could get any sleep. I knew the pilot would be balancing the need to get to the drop zone as quickly as possible with the risks of flying too close to any of the known danger areas. It would be a longer trip for him this time and he'd need to get in and out of there again as quickly as he could.

Further south, away from the northern cities, the darkness seemed a little more profound, and I began to relax just a tiny bit knowing we must be making good progress now towards Uzès. I glanced at my watch, tilting my wrist to read the time in the ray of moonlight filtering through the cabin roof. It was nearly 4 a.m. At last, Commander Elliot's voice came through the intercom once more. 'Almost there. Prepare for landing,' he said.

I tightened my safety harness, checking the satchel was still tucked beneath my seat, as the pitch of the engine slowed a little and we began to circle. I squinted out of the window, trying to catch a glimpse of the pale smudge of the lavender field.

And then suddenly, out of nowhere, came a noise like the sound of hailstones rattling against the side of the plane. The Lizzie bucked and lurched as a German fighter plane roared by, close enough for me to see the gleam of its silver paintwork and the stark black swastika on its tail fin in the moonlight. It must have been on its way somewhere else, though, because to my relief it didn't turn back to finish us off but disappeared upwards to resume its pursuit of perhaps a bigger, more important prey.

Up front, Commander Elliot sat upright, apparently unperturbed. The Lizzie's engine continued to slow as we descended towards the field, which I could make out ahead of us now.

'That was close! Where were we hit?' I shouted over the intercom.

There was no reply. But then I realised the sound of the engine had changed, overlain by a hollow whistling of the wind, and I saw the canopy had been pierced by a line of bullet holes. There was still no reply from Jim Elliot and, at first, I thought he was just concentrating on finding the marker lights beneath us. But then, to my horror, he slowly slipped sideways in his seat, and I saw the blood blossoming from his neck like a red rose opening its petals to the sun.

I think I screamed his name.

Time seemed to slow as the realisation that we were going to crash began to dawn. And then I heard Teddy's voice, as if in one of my troubled dreams, and he was telling me to move. 'Fly the plane, Philly,' he was saying. 'You have to try to fly the plane.'

I don't remember undoing the straps that held me, but I flung myself across the compartment and desperately attempted to squeeze myself through the gap between the reinforcing struts separating me from the cockpit. My jacket caught on the metal but I wrenched it free, buttons pinging on to the floor, and tried again to push myself through the gap alongside the fuel tank. The space was too tight though. I was trapped. And the unyielding steel of the tank was a horrible reminder that the bomber pilots at the base used to joke that Lysanders were basically flying incendiary devices – above all, these specially adapted ones with the additional tank welded on below.

The plane continued its ponderous descent. Surely the engine must stall? But somehow the prop kept on turning and I watched helplessly as the grey smudge of the lavender field grew closer. The plane slowed even more until it felt as if we hung in the sky like some helpless stringed puppet and with a grinding crunch the automatic wing flaps closed for landing. I could see the ground, tantalisingly close ahead of us. There were no torches marking the landing strip. If the *maquisards* had been there, they must have scattered at the sight of the German plane.

I knew if I stayed where I was, wedged between the reinforcing struts, I would surely be killed on impact – that is, if the exploding fuel tank didn't incinerate me first – so I wriggled backwards, manoeuvring on to the rear-facing passenger seat. I groped desperately for the straps, but in my panic I couldn't find them. Instead, I hunched over, hooking one leg around the metal leg of the chair to try to brace myself for the impact.

With another lurch, the fixed landing gear and heavy extra fuel tank on the underside of the plane collided with the trees. The dull roar of the labouring engine ceased suddenly as it stalled at last and instead my ears were filled with the screech of tearing metal. And then the world spun upside down as the Lysander's starboard wing dropped and the plane corkscrewed. My leg twisted with a sickening wrench as everything seemed to implode around me. And then my head collided with the canopy, and everything went black.

I think it was the pain that brought me round as the men pulled me from the wreckage. I screamed as they freed my leg from the jagged metal on which it was impaled. They were speaking French, their voices low and urgent, saying something about blood, too much blood. I remember looking up from the ground on which they'd laid me, among a crush of lavender beside the wreckage of the plane, and seeing the dying moon caught in the torn branches of the trees overhead. And then the pain surged through me once more, too much to bear, and I must have lost consciousness again.

I dreamed I was searching for something, although I couldn't quite remember what. I was stumbling through the woods, and I could hear sounds of muffled voices, coming and going through the trees, but couldn't make out what they were saying. Up ahead I could see a faint light, so I pushed on towards it, the effort almost more than I could manage, until I reached a clearing. The figure of a woman stood there in a dark-blue uniform, her blonde hair the colour of moonshine. She turned towards me and smiled.

'Amy!' I tried to say her name, but it caught in my chest. I staggered forward, wanting to reach her, but she shook her head, and her expression grew sorrowful.

She opened her mouth to speak and I strained to hear her words, which were little more than a whisper. They were from Ben's poem. '*The dark of the moon, in the night that we face, holds the promise that helps us get through.*' I felt myself falling as she turned and walked away. I longed to go with her, but it was the thought of Ben's words that was holding me back, keeping me pinned to the earth among the tumbled leaves on the forest floor. The mutter of voices came to me again from the trees, but I was too exhausted to move. The pain and the sadness were too much to bear. Then the voices faded, and oblivion drew me into its welcome embrace once more.

◆ ◆ ◆

I woke in a sort of twilight and looked up, expecting to see the trees overhead again. But instead of the darkening sky, there was a white plaster ceiling above a shuttered window. And instead of the leaves beneath me, there were smooth cotton sheets. A cool hand pressed against my brow. It felt hard to turn my head to look, it was too hot and heavy, my neck too stiff, too sore. Then the hand moved away, and Janina's face appeared above me, a worried smile crinkling the skin at the edges of her eyes.

'Eveline,' she said. '*Dzięki Bogu!* Thank God! We thought we'd lost you.'

She lifted my head and held a glass of water to my lips. I drank thirstily. My tongue felt too big for my mouth, and my voice cracked as I tried to find the words, fragments of memory returning . . .

'The plane crashed.'

She nodded.

'Need to hide it from the enemy . . .'

'Hush,' she said. 'It's been taken care of.'

'The pilot . . . ?'

She shook her head. 'He didn't make it. I'm sorry.'

'There was an envelope . . .' I said. Panic filled me as I remembered the money and papers for the Poles' escape. I struggled to try to sit up, but she pressed gently on my shoulder, making me lie still.

She smiled. 'Don't worry, we have it safe. Thank you for bringing it for us. Here, try to drink a little more.'

Something felt wrong. I frowned, concentrating. Everything ached. But there was a deeper, more intense pain somewhere, too.

'My leg . . .' I said.

'Hush,' she said again, gently wiping my face with a cool cloth. 'You were badly hurt in the crash. But we are taking care of you now. Try to sleep again. I am here. You are safe.'

The next time I swam upwards through the layers of sleep and troubled dreams, it must have been night-time. The room was dark and silent, the air thick with the smell of some sort of disinfectant. With an effort, I turned my head. Janina's husband, Jakub, appeared to be asleep in a chair beside the bed but he must have sensed my movement because he opened his eyes and smiled. 'Here,' he said, leaning forward to pour water from a jug into a glass and hold it to my lips. 'Drink a little.'

'Janina . . . ?' I asked once I'd swallowed a few sips and my tongue could work again.

'I'm doing the night shift so she can get some sleep.'

'The baby . . . ?'

'Is growing well. Kicking now. Going to be a strong one, like its *matka*.'

I licked my lips and swallowed, with an effort, trying to gather my scattered thoughts. 'How long have I been here?'

'Four days. You were badly injured in the crash, scarcely alive when the *maquisards* brought you here. We need to get you out as soon as you're strong enough, so you can get proper treatment. We've sent a message back to Britain. But you're too sick to travel at the moment. In any case, the moon is dying now, so it will be at least two weeks. They will come and get you as soon as they can.'

I felt there was something important I needed to tell him, something urgent. But my brain felt muddled, and I struggled to remember what it was. Then it came back to me. A wave of dizziness engulfed me as I tried to sit up, forcing me to fall back against the pillow. 'Jakub, you all need to get out of France now. Go immediately. That was what they sent me to tell you. To give you the papers you'll need and to tell you to go to Spain. The Germans will take control of the whole of France any day. It will be too dangerous for you all to stay here.'

He smiled again, a little sadly. 'This we already know,' he said. 'We hear the messages, can tell they are growing uneasy. But our French hosts continue to look after us and our work here is important. We cannot leave just yet.'

'We will take care of you in Britain. If you can get across the border into Spain, we'll get you out. It will be so much safer for all of you there. Think of your baby, Jakub!'

He nodded. 'We will go soon, don't worry. But for now we need to stay and keep on telling the Allies what is happening in the east. And we won't desert you.'

I began to protest again but he hushed me. 'Calm yourself, Eveline. I promise we will go soon. We'll talk to Bolek, because we'll need his help to get through France to the mountains. We have a little more time, I think. Once the British can come for you, then we will leave.'

When Jakub went off to refill the water jug, I gingerly raised my throbbing head from the pillow and lifted the sheet that covered my battered body. My right leg was swathed in bandages from ankle to thigh and around the shin a dark bloodstain oozed through the thick layers of wrapping. Another wave of weakness forced me to lie back again. I couldn't go anywhere even if I tried. I had to accept I was stuck there for at least the next couple of weeks.

The days passed slowly. I drifted in and out of sleep and Janina was there when I woke, trying to encourage me to drink the nourishing broth she'd made, or helping me clean myself with a bowl of water and a washcloth. I think the priest was there once or twice, holding my hand, praying at my bedside, although my mind was so muddled I wasn't sure if perhaps I dreamed that. A French doctor came to change the dressings on my leg. His visits were usually followed by muttered conversations with Janina, which I couldn't hear. They cared for me attentively, but I found it frustrating that I wasn't getting better any faster. I'd already been enough of a burden to my hosts. I wanted to be ready to walk to the lavender field and climb the ladder into the Lysander that would come for me as soon as the moon grew to fullness. But the pain and the weakness were ever present and so I swallowed down the pills the doctor gave me with gratitude, sinking back into the release of sleep.

I must have been there for about a week, existing in that limbo, drifting in and out of consciousness. But then something changed.

Amy appeared to me in a dream again, standing in that same clearing in a forest. But this time, instead of turning away, she smiled at me in the moonlight and beckoned me to follow her. I took a faltering step towards the trees, then another, unsure whether my injured leg could carry me. It hurt. But, somehow, I understood that if I followed Amy the pain would end . . .

All at once, Janina was shaking me awake, saying, 'Eveline! Eveline, wake up!' and the doctor was in the room. My body was burning with fever, but my fingers and toes felt icy cold. Janina held my hand while the doctor removed the bandages from my leg. A sickly stench filled the room, and I realised it came from my wounds. I watched Janina's face, saw her blanch. The doctor frowned. He said something to her and at first I thought he must be referring to the seven days that remained before I could be evacuated. But then he said the word again: '*Septicémie . . .*' My fever-muddled brain struggled to decode it. And then I understood. Sepsis had set in.

I understood the next thing he said as well. '*Nous devons amputer.*' We have to amputate. '*Sinon, elle mourra.*' Otherwise, she will die.

Finn

After the walk with Mum on the beach when we'd talked about being brave, she went upstairs to pack her case because she and Philly would be leaving that evening. We had to say our goodbyes, because they'd be gone by the time Dad and I got back. I didn't eat much breakfast. I was still feeling sick, because it was Acclimatisation Day, and I really didn't want to throw up again. Dad was very quiet on the drive to the harbour.

Everyone was there when we arrived, standing on the bit of beach beside the dinghies which were pulled up on the shore. The bigger boat was on a mooring on a pontoon at the end of the jetty. Dad took my ear defenders from me and left them in the car because he said it was Really Important for us to Set an Example and everyone needed to listen. Then we walked down to the beach.

'Good morning, everyone,' he said. 'It's great to see everyone here on time! Let's start with the Safety Briefing, shall we? Get that out of the way before we have a look at the boats.' He handed out the Safety sheets that he'd typed up. He'd said what a good idea it had been of mine to laminate them because then the seawater couldn't get in, so it was both helpful and practical.

The instructor started to talk about the life jackets we'd be wearing and he showed us how to put them on the right way, then let each of us do our own. I didn't like the way mine smelled a little bit like mould. It made my stomach feel queasy again.

Next, we had to put on our helmets. When I sail the dinghy, I just wear my cap. But this week we all have to wear helmets. When Dad told me about that, he said it was essential for Health and Safety. I said I wasn't going to. But he said it was a condition of the insurance, Kiddo, and so everyone had to, and I should take it up with my union representative if I wanted the rules to be changed. He was making a joke, but I didn't laugh because I was worried about the helmet being too tight and making my head hurt. Then Dad had said we could practise putting our helmets on before the course began so we could get used to them, and I wouldn't lose it on the Acclimatisation Day. He meant lose my temper, not the helmet. I still wished I could lose the helmet.

Once we all had our helmets on, Iain showed us a board with a plan of the boat on it. He explained how the areas that it was safe for us to be in had been marked out with coloured tape on the boat and these were shown on the plan. 'We'll get out on the water for the first time tomorrow, but for today we'll just be getting familiar with the safe areas on board and I'll show you the controls for steering and raising the sails.'

Then we all walked down the jetty and got on the boat.

We sat down on the benches on each side of the cockpit while Iain started to explain how the sails work. It was just like on the dinghy only instead of pulling on the sheets, which are the ropes, you use a winch with a detachable handle. The large boy was sitting opposite me. He started rocking again and that made the boat start rocking too. I felt sicker than ever. I wanted him to stop, but he didn't. Then the sick started coming up my throat and into my mouth, and I wanted to spit it out into the sea, but I was on the wrong side of the boat, alongside the pontoon, so I couldn't. The boy was watching me, and he started rocking even harder. I think he was doing it on purpose. I stood up and went over and stepped up on to the bench to be able to lean over and spit the sick into the water and he got up there too and pushed me, so I pushed him back and he went overboard.

Then there was too much noise, with screaming and shouting, and I had a meltdown and Dad grabbed me, so I bit his hand.

Afterwards, once we were all back on dry land, Iain said, 'What can we learn from what happened this morning?'

The mother of the large boy said we could learn that it was a bloody good thing we had our life jackets on, otherwise her son could have drowned. Then she said some other things about me, which were Not Nice. I didn't have my ear defenders so I couldn't shut them out. She also said they would be getting on the next plane home if her son was made to be on the boat with me again. Dad was apologising and saying, 'Don't worry, we'll make a new plan.' And then the Acclimatisation Day was over, and everyone could go back to their accommodation.

Dad didn't say a word on the drive home. We drove with the windows open and I didn't like how windy it was, making my hair flap in my eyes, but we had to do it because my T-shirt smelled of sick. At least I'd got my ear defenders on again though.

When we got back to the house, Mum was very surprised to see us because she'd thought she'd be gone before we got back. I went upstairs to have a shower and change my clothes and when I came back down the three adults were sitting at the kitchen table. Dad had his head in his hands, and he was clutching at his hair so it stood up in all directions. And Mum was saying, 'No Philly, we couldn't possibly ask you to do that.'

'I don't see why not,' she was saying, as I came into the room. 'It isn't as if I have anything in particular to get home for. Hello, Finn, we were just talking about making a new plan for this week. How would it be if I were to stay on while your mum goes on her writing course? Your dad needs to help with the sailing every day, so I could be here to look after you and we can do some more exploring together. If you feel like it, perhaps you can join in the dinghy sailing parts of the course later in the week. What do you think?'

I thought about it a bit and decided I would like that. I would have liked it even better if Mum could have stayed too, but I remembered what she'd said during our walk on the beach about how she really needed to go on her course. So I said, 'Yes. That would be an OK plan.'

Then the taxi arrived to take Mum to the airport and they had run out of time to discuss it further or to argue about it and so the decision was made.

As she got into the taxi, Mum showed me the double clamshell which she had in her pocket to remind her to be brave and we did the starfish sign. 'You'll be all right, won't you, Finn?' she said. 'Maybe it'll do us all good to have a bit of time apart. I'll phone every day. Be nice and helpful for Philly, won't you? And if she tells you more about her life during the war you can record it for me and let me know, OK?'

'I will,' I said.

So I carried Philly's suitcase back upstairs and sat on her bed while she unpacked everything again.

'Thank you for staying,' I said. 'If you like, I can make some labels for the chest of drawers and laminate them, so you know where everything is.'

Her red lips smiled. 'I'd love that,' she said. 'Sometimes I forget where I've put things, so it'll be a big help. I think we're both happy with the new plan, aren't we? Now, why don't you go and do a Sudoku on the porch and then we'll have some Marmite sandwiches for lunch?'

And that sounded pretty perfect to me.

◆ ◆ ◆

Later on, when Dad had gone back to Smooth Things Over at the sailing camp, and I was sticking the laminated labels on the drawers in Philly's room while she had a little lie-down on her bed, I asked her what had happened to the plane that crashed when she went back on her second secret mission to France, to tell the Polish cryptographers they needed to get out.

'The *maquisards* hitched it up to a team of oxen and dragged it into the empty sunflower field,' she said. 'It was the perfect cover. They burn the stalks at that time of the year, you see. So they drained out most of the fuel from the tanks, because it was a useful resource for them, and they set fire to what was left. They even waited to do it in broad daylight so the flames wouldn't show and draw too much attention to it. The police never suspected a thing. They buried the remnants in the woods.'

'So that is when you lost your leg in France?' I said.

And then she told me what had happened next. I recorded it for Mum, so she could put it in her book when she got back.

Philly

It was probably just as well I was so ill. I remember very little of what happened on those final days at the château. It would have been too dangerous to move me to a hospital, even if I'd been strong enough to make the journey – the sudden appearance of an injured British woman requiring urgent medical attention would have put the whole team at Cadix at risk of arrest, deportation or execution.

When I regained consciousness, it was Janina who told me they had operated. They'd set up a makeshift theatre in one of the bathrooms, and a surgeon who could be trusted to keep shtum had been summoned. With the assistance of Bolek, some chloroform had been procured to put me under for the amputation, as well as a precious supply of morphine, which kept me afloat as I swam in an ocean of pain in the days that followed. I drifted in and out of consciousness but there were no dreams, as far as I can remember, just a realisation every now and then, whenever I surfaced, that Janina was there. She'd talk to me, urging me to keep going, not to give up. But it was Ben's voice in my head that stopped me from making that walk into the trees.

'Hold on,' Janina said. 'They'll be coming for you soon, Eveline. The moon is growing again. Just a few more days and they'll be able to get through. And when we've got you out safely, we are going to leave too. We're going to head to Spain. Thanks to you, we'll be able to get to Britain now. And when we do, when all this is over, you and I will go and have that tea at The Ritz. You promised me, remember? Stay with me now. Stay with me.'

A tear trickled down my cheek. I was going to die in a place where no one knew my real name. My body would be buried in an anonymous grave – as, I assumed, Jim Elliot's must have been – with nothing to say who I really was.

I thought of Amy and Teddy. I tried to reassure myself that I'd be with them, the ones who had gone on before me. I remembered standing at Teddy's grave on the hill above the cold waters of the Firth of Tay, planting the white heather there, from the garden at my family home, how that had helped me still feel a connection with him. But Amy was lost forever, without a place where anyone could go to feel nearer to her. It would be the same for me. Once the Poles had left the château, who would there be to remember where I lay? The name Eveline would mean nothing to Ben or my family in Scotland, or anyone else who came afterwards to look for me.

I realised then how important it is for those who are left behind to have a place to go to remember those who've been lost; a place where we can feel that connection and honour our dead.

It was late, the room in darkness, when the pair of *maquisards* came with the stretcher. They lifted me on to it with such careful gentleness it brought more tears to my eyes. I was as weak as a wet paper bag. I was carried downstairs to where the Poles waited in the hallway. Each of them shook my hand and wished me luck, thanking me, saying, '*Powodzenia*, Eveline. *Dziękuję*.'

Janina waited by the door. She leaned over to hug me, the fullness of her belly making it awkward. Her face was as wet with tears as mine was. 'Remember,' she said. 'Tea at The Ritz. I'll see you there.'

'Come with me now,' I said, clinging to her hand.

She shook her head. 'There's no room in the plane. But we'll follow soon, I promise.'

Then I was carried through the woods to the edge of the lavender field, where more shadowy figures waited in the light of the half-moon. Moments later, I heard the unmistakable sound of a Lysander's engine in the distance and three of the Resistance fighters stepped forward with their torches to mark out the landing strip among the silver furrows. The plane landed, turned, rumbled back to where we stood. The prop blades glinted as they continued to turn in the moonlight, ready for a quick getaway.

I tried not to cry out in pain as the stretcher was manhandled up the ladder and hurriedly lifted into the passenger compartment, where a man was waiting. 'Hello,' he said. 'Very glad to meet you, Miss Buchanan. I'm an RAF medic, here to take care of you until we can get you to the hospital back home.'

The plane was already moving down the furrowed field, gaining speed, and then I felt the familiar surge as we broke free of the gravity that held us earthbound and the release as we lifted off into the night sky and were airborne.

As the medic busied himself, fixing up a makeshift drip and filling a syringe with some blessed pain relief for me, the pilot's voice came through the intercom.

And I wept again as I heard Ben say, 'It's all right, Philly. We've got you, now. I've got you.'

◆ ◆ ◆

Dawn was breaking when we landed at Tangmere, where an ambulance waited alongside the runway. Major Bertram was there, ready to help the medic lift me on to a trolley. But before they could do so, Ben had climbed down from the cockpit to gather me in his arms and hold me. Resting my head on his shoulder was the best medicine by far for all I'd been through. He came with me in the ambulance, never once leaving my side on the short journey to the hospital in nearby Chichester.

'Don't you have a plane to put away?' I said, smiling through my tears as I clung to his hand as if I'd never let go again.

Very gently, he brushed a strand of hair away from my eyes with his free hand, letting the palm rest alongside my cheek. 'Don't worry, our Lizzie's being taken care of,' he replied. 'And now I need to make sure you are too.' Then the ambulance was stopping, the back opening. But Ben kept hold of my hand the whole way as the trolley was wheeled along the corridor to the ward.

My rehabilitation took months. In spite of the makeshift conditions under which my leg had been amputated in France, they'd managed to do a pretty good job. The doctors repeatedly told me how lucky I was, that it was the care of the French surgeon and my Polish friends who'd saved my life. So, even on the days when I had to struggle through the pain and frustration of physiotherapy, and the indignity of trying to adapt to wearing a prosthesis, I was still grateful to be alive at all.

Once they'd cleaned up my wound and just as soon as I'd had a few days in the hospital to recover, Major Bertram came to see me. 'You've probably heard the news already,' he said. 'The Americans have invaded North Africa. In response, Germany has abolished the *zone libre* in France, occupying the whole of the country.'

'What news of the team in Cadix?' I asked.

'They got out. But it was cutting things a bit fine. At present, they've split up into smaller groups and are still on the French side of the Pyrenees, as far as we know. But at least they're a lot closer to Spain now. As soon as Bolek's people can arrange guides to take them through the mountains, they'll be making the next stage of their journeys. Things are pretty hot there just at the moment, as you can probably imagine. The Nazis have been clamping down hard on any Resistance activities, in retaliation for the invasion of Morocco and Algeria.'

'There was a woman called Janina who was about to have a baby,' I said. 'Is there any news of her?'

'Yes, there is,' he said. 'I remember seeing something about that in the intelligence report. She and her husband got as far as Toulouse when she went into labour. She's had a baby girl. Mother and daughter doing well. They're in a safe house, staying put for the time being until she and the baby are strong enough to attempt the journey through the mountains on foot.'

I felt a surge of conflicting emotions – joy that Janina and Jakub's baby had arrived safely, but concern that they weren't yet out of France, that there would inevitably be another delay, which would put them at greater risk.

'You did a great job, Miss Buchanan.' Major Bertram noticed my worried expression and tried to reassure me. 'Without the money and papers you managed to get to them, they wouldn't have got as far as they have. They're not home and dry yet, but at least they have a chance. Don't worry, the powers that be here are still doing everything they can to get them safely to Britain.'

Ben visited me at the hospital every day during the dark moon periods when he wasn't flying. He'd come down from the base on his motorbike and stay in one of the RAF cottages in Tangmere so he could be close by. He was there to push my wheelchair, to bundle me up in blankets so that we could go outdoors into the crisp winter air and I could lift my face to the weak sunshine. He was there to encourage me to take my first few steps without my crutches. And he was there to cheer and reward me with a hug on the day I managed to walk the length of the ward unaided.

I slept well during those fortnights. But I tossed and turned through the anxious nights either side of the full moon when he was away, continuing to fly the Lysander missions into France.

As the weeks went by, I slowly regained my strength and, as I did so, I thought more of Janina, Jakub and their newborn daughter. I hoped they were growing strong enough too to make the journey on foot into Spain, although I knew it was very unlikely they'd be able to carry their baby through the mountains in the middle of winter. There'd be deep snow on the high passes now. The route was fraught with danger at the best of times. But every day they remained in France increased the risk of them being arrested. I was desperate for news of them, but, although I repeatedly asked Ben to check with Major Bertram, there was no word yet.

It was January before any more news of the Poles finally came through. There were no details, but we heard two groups of four had left Toulouse on the fourteenth, and a party of others were expected to leave a week later. I breathed a small sigh of relief, praying that Janina and her baby daughter would be able to make the dangerous journey safely and that one day soon I'd hear they'd arrived in Britain.

One cold, bright day in February, during a new moon period, Ben and I were married in the church at Tangmere, right beside the airfield. Back in Dundee, my mother was now too infirm to make the trip and my brother Frank couldn't leave her or the factory, but they'd sent me some sprays of the white winter heather from Teddy's grave. My friend Jess came down from Bletchley and, to my delight, Agnieszka arrived in style in a Spitfire that she was delivering. She'd managed to wangle it with Miss Gower at White Waltham, she told me. All the Attagirls sent their congratulations, along with a case of champagne gleaned from heaven knows where. My long white dress disguised my wooden leg, and I managed to walk up the aisle on Major Bertram's arm with scarcely a limp. I carried a posy of holly and ivy, which I'd picked from the churchyard, with the sprigs of white heather tucked into it.

Ben smiled at me as he waited beneath the Gothic archway framing the altar, looking especially dashing in his uniform, and when he read the poem that had come to mean so much to us both there was a sudden flurry of handkerchiefs among the small congregation.

As he placed the ring on my finger, my wedding present to him glinted in the golden light streaming through the stained-glass window. I'd given it to him that morning – a signet ring engraved with his initials: BCD, those same letters that he'd written in my ATA logbook on the day we first met, more than three years before. On the inside of the band were inscribed the words from the poem: *I'll always be yours. P.* He'd laughed as he read them, saying, 'Great minds think alike!' Then he'd shown me the wedding band he'd had inscribed for me with the same words and his initials. He slipped the ring I'd given him on his little finger, saying, 'I'll never take it off. You'll be with me everywhere I fly.'

Some of the other Special Duties boys were there too and they formed a guard of honour for us as we emerged into the winter sunshine as man and wife, while a Spitfire roared overhead, just clearing the point of the steeple.

We didn't have far to go afterwards. Ben and I had been allocated one of the RAF cottages in the village as our married quarters, so we all walked there together for the wedding breakfast.

Ben would be able to continue his duties from our new home, and I would be taking on a new role. Major Bertram had asked me to join the team looking after the Resistance workers when they were brought over. I would help train them for their return to France, teaching them how to set up and use the radio transmitters they'd be taking back with them and briefing them on the use of the other equipment the Special Intelligence Service had developed for agents in the field.

On the day of our wedding, once the final guests had downed the last of the beer (the champagne having long since been polished off) and meandered a little unsteadily down the path from our little cottage, Ben scooped me into his arms – just as he'd done in the pale light of dawn when he'd flown the rescue mission to bring me back from Uzès – and carried me up the narrow stairs to our bedroom under the eaves. I felt self-conscious, suddenly, and I turned to stop him, burying my face in his shirt front. He reached out a finger and gently tilted my face upwards, looking into my eyes.

'Are you all right, Mrs Delaney?' he asked.

I nodded, then shook my head. 'My leg . . .' I said. Although he was used to seeing the stump of my knee, in the intimacy of that moment I became acutely aware of how ugly it looked. I felt unworthy of him.

'You have never looked more beautiful to me, Philly,' he whispered. 'I love you more than I ever thought possible, body and soul, exactly as you are. My courageous wife. *For the days without number, I'll always be yours.*'

'*By the dark of the moon and the light of the sun*,' I whispered back.

I reached over to turn out the lamp beside the bed. And then I smiled as he stilled my hand and we began to kiss again.

Finn

'What did they do with the bit of your leg they cut off?' I asked. I was more interested in that than in the romantic bits of Philly's story, but when she's remembering her Life Story she seems to like talking about them, so I just let her. I know Mum will like them too and will probably want to put them in her book. We were walking to the shops the next day, because Dad was off helping to run the sailing camp and we needed to buy some food for our lunches and suppers. There wasn't much in the fridge after Mum left.

'I never asked,' she replied. 'I think they probably buried it somewhere.' She tapped her false leg with her walking stick. 'There is a corner of southern France which is forever England. Or Scotland, I suppose, with just a bit of Poland thrown in for good measure.'

We walked up the lane, past the smallholding with the beehives and the donkeys in the orchard. 'That's where the old man from the cemetery lives,' I told her. 'Sometimes I see him there wearing his beekeeper's suit and a white hat with a veil.'

One of the donkeys wandered over to the fence when we got closer. Philly stopped to stroke its nose and feed it a handful of the greener grass that grows on this side of the fence. 'Do you want to give it some?' she asked, holding out another handful.

'No thank you,' I said. I don't think I'd like the feeling of the donkey's mouth on my hand. 'They're very old, these donkeys. They used to carry baskets of salt from the marshes.'

'They're in retirement. Like me,' she said.

We carried on up the lane for a bit. Then I said, 'Would you like to go back to the south of France and try to find your leg?'

She shook her head. 'I don't feel the need to do so. I did feel the need to track down Jim Elliot's grave, though, after the war. He was the Lysander pilot who was shot, remember? The *maquisards* had buried his body in the woods beside the sunflower field.'

'Like the remains of his plane,' I said. 'Is he still there?'

'No. He was given a proper burial in a military cemetery. His family wanted it. It's very important to do what we can to find the remains of those lost in the war. To bury them with the honour and dignity they deserve. I think it gives the families closure. We all need a place to go to feel that connection with those we've lost. Amy's disappearance made me realise that.'

'Do you have a place to go to feel a connection with her?' I asked.

'Not really,' she said. Her smile had gone. 'I always think of her, though, when I'm in a plane. Because we never managed to find her, it's as if she's still up there in the sky. So I suppose that's where I feel closest to her. Her spirit will always be flying free.'

We got to the shop, and I put on my ear defenders. 'Would you like to wait outside?' she asked, making a gesture so I'd understand. She was folding up her walking stick so she had both hands free to push one of the miniature-sized trolleys they have.

I nodded. Even though I'm meant to be helping her, the shop looked too crowded. 'Can you get a packet of Prince biscuits too, please? The chocolate ones.' They are the ones I like, and you can only get them in France.

When she came out, she had 2 pretty heavy carrier bags full of food. I took one and she carried the other, but it made her walk in a very lopsided way, even with her walking stick. Then I had a Good Idea. We were walking past the bike hire place and there was a tricycle there, but it wasn't a child's one, it was the size for an adult to ride. It had a basket on the front, big enough to fit one of the shopping bags.

'Do you think we could rent that?' I said. 'We could push it back with the shopping on it. You could even put your collapsible walking stick in the basket, if you like.'

Her smile came back again. 'Let's go and ask.'

The man in the bike place was very helpful. He said he could certainly rent Philly the trike and he'd give her a special rate for the week. So that solved our problem of carrying the shopping and as we walked back to the house, pushing the trike with the bags hanging on the handlebars, Philly said she might even be tempted to have a go at riding it.

'In that case,' I said, 'I can get my bike out of the shed and we can go on some expeditions.'

'I like that idea very much indeed,' she said. 'Let's give it a whirl.'

We tried it out in the lane, once we'd unpacked the shopping. She was pretty good at it, even with her false leg, and she smiled a lot and said, 'Not bad for a dinosaur.'

I said, 'Much better. A dinosaur couldn't ride a trike, not even a Coelophysis which was a biped and probably about the closest in size to a human being.' And then we had lunch and afterwards we sat on the porch, and I recorded some more of her Life Story.

Philly

Ben had returned from a mission a few nights before, the last one in that moon period, and now we had the luxury of two weeks together before he'd be off flying again. I tried to keep my anxiety from him, but he could tell something was up.

'What's happened?' he asked, as I cooked him breakfast in our cottage.

'There's been some news from Spain.' I set a plate of eggs and bacon on the table in front of him and sat down, pouring myself a cup of tea. 'It's still pretty sketchy, but none of it is good. Antoni, Gwido and Maksymilian were betrayed by their guide as they tried to cross the border. They're in the hands of the Nazis.'

'That's awful news,' Ben said, shaking his head. 'What about the others?'

'There's been no word of Janina and Jakub. As far as anyone knows, they're still hiding out in France. But Marian and Henryk did manage to make it through the mountains. They crossed the border safely, but then they were robbed by their guide, who took all their money. The Spanish security police arrested them. They're trapped there now, holed up in a Spanish jail, although I suppose that's better than being in German hands. Our people are working behind the scenes to try to get them released, but it's tricky with the Spanish.'

Ben set down his fork and knife and reached across the table to take my hand. 'I'm so sorry, Philly. Maybe there'll be better news soon, though. Don't give up hope.'

'I know,' I said. 'That's all we can do . . . hope and pray.'

I was kept busy during that time, helping train the latest Resistance fighters who'd been brought over, so I spent the days with them at the farmhouse in a village a few miles away where they were accommodated.

Major Bertram's wife, Barbara, was kindness personified. She'd welcome the agents arriving at Tangmere on the Lysander flights, no matter at what ungodly hour they appeared. She and Tony, along with their two young sons, cheerfully shared their four-bedroomed farmhouse with up to twenty guests at a time, somehow finding space for them.

As well as instructing the French agents on the skills they'd need to help operate makeshift landing strips in darkened fields, and set up and run new Resistance networks, we tried to make their time in England as homely as we could, knowing how hard it was for them to be away from their families in that time of war and knowing the risks they'd be facing on their return. Our 'guests' were always eager to help with the chores or bowl cricket balls for the Bertram boys on the lawn. I'd regained my strength by then and had got used to my wooden leg. When time and weather permitted, I'd take a couple of the visitors for walks down local lanes where we'd forage for food to help supplement the thinly stretched supplies. Our French visitors were often more adept than I was at spotting the supplies that grew in our natural larder. The Bertrams did a wonderful job of providing for them, but the full extent of the operations they were running had to be kept a close secret and so it was difficult to obtain extra rations without giving the game away. We put about the story that the house was a convalescent hostel for injured French officers who'd managed to get out of France, but I think some of the locals must have suspected a bit more was going on. Barbara's chickens provided an ample supply of eggs, and the local butcher would add a few extra sausages to our order whenever he had any to spare. In the farmhouse kitchen we would make hearty stews supplemented with vegetables from the gardens of neighbours, which were quietly offered up as gifts.

Some of our 'guests' were regular visitors. These were the leaders of the Resistance networks, who travelled back and forth carrying important intelligence. Others only came once. When they'd been given their instructions for how to identify suitable fields for use as landing sites, how to organise the operational side of things at their end and how to help a British Special Duties pilot land a plane with the use of nothing more than pocket torches, they would disappear back to France by the light of the moon, and we wouldn't see them again. They would either be successful, helping more agents be extracted from beneath the noses of the enemy, or they'd be denounced or discovered, captured and killed. It was a brutal time, and we were all too aware of the terrible risks they were taking.

The radio operators had the most dangerous job of all. Sometimes the awful news would filter back to us that one of them had been caught. I remember coming into the kitchen one morning to find Barbara sitting at the table with her head cradled in her hands. When she looked up, her face was wet with tears. She'd just heard that one of our recent guests had been shot. I recalled he'd been a quiet man, very conscientious as he practised operating a radio to improve his speeds before leaving us and going back to France. We'd discovered he was a farm labourer back in his home country, and he'd loved nothing better in his spare time than to tend the vegetable garden at the farmhouse. Barbara told me that because he'd been uncovered as a member of the Resistance, only his very close family could attend his funeral. If other members of the local community had gone, they'd have been arrested and possibly executed too. But they'd found a way to pay their respects to this neighbour who had given his life in resisting the enemy, because in the window of every house along the street where the coffin passed, a vase of flowers had been placed: field poppies, ox-eye daisies and cornflowers – the red, white and blue of the French flag.

On Easter Sunday, after we'd been to the morning service in the church, Ben and I climbed through ancient holloways leading up on to the tops of the Downs. Easter was late that year and the centuries-old pathways etched into the escarpment were already overhung with blossom, a lush carpet of wild garlic leaves releasing their pungent scent beneath our boots. He took my hand and helped me up the steeper sections where I struggled a little with my new leg. I was relieved when we reached the top, walking with easier strides across the close-cropped grass on the chalky ground. Up there, I held his hand again and told him that he was going to be a father. The wind wrapped its arms around us as we stood looking out across the low-lying fields below to where the sea flung handfuls of sequins into the spring sunshine, and my heart sang with the joy of that moment.

But then, all too soon, the moon entered its second quarter and Ben was off flying Lysander missions once again and I lay alone in our bed in the cottage, curling myself around the burgeoning curve of my belly, as I prayed for his safe return.

My work with the agents being taken to France continued to occupy my days. Alongside the French who'd be brought across for basic instruction were the more thoroughly trained British agents who were being inserted into the intelligence networks on that side of the Channel as well. One in particular remained with me. Her cover name was Madeleine, although on the afternoon before she left she confided in me that her real name was Noor and she was of Indian and American descent. She'd been in the WAAF before training to be a special agent, so she knew a bit about planes and was especially interested to see the Lysander that would be flying her to a field in northern France that night. From there, I knew from Major Bertram, she would be playing a dangerous role as a radio operator in one of the important 'circuits', as we called them, operating on the outskirts of Paris. She was instantly likeable, petite and self-effacing.

As I showed her around the village, she confided in me that her main concern was for her mother. 'She has no idea I'm doing this. I've asked them not to tell her if I go missing. They send messages to the families, you see. I've said only to tell her the truth if they know I've been killed. I don't think she could bear it otherwise, the not-knowing.'

I nodded, remembering Amy. Those days when we'd hoped for news . . . the not-knowing was indeed the hardest bit.

So, a couple of months later, I was horrified to hear that her particular network had been disrupted. The message had come through that most of her colleagues had either been arrested or had scattered. But the agent we knew as Madeleine remained at her wireless set all through the summer, doggedly continuing to transmit vital intelligence. Ben heard from his contacts that she'd been offered a place on a flight out but had refused to leave. She couldn't hold out indefinitely though. In mid-October, she was arrested, tortured and interrogated by the Gestapo at their Paris headquarters, and then sent to a camp. At that point, the messages about her stopped. And so the not-knowing began all over again . . . It was a grim pattern we were becoming all too used to. I thought of Noor's mother, back in London, and wondered what they were telling her, whether they were respecting her daughter's last wishes on leaving Britain to protect her from that dreadful limbo of hope while fearing the worst.

There was one bit of good news, though, among the distressing messages that trickled through. In July, I learned that Marian Rejewski and Henryk Zygalski had finally been freed from prison in Spain. They'd been extracted via Gibraltar and brought to Britain.

'I assume they've been assigned there to Bletchley Park with you?' I asked the colleague who phoned to tell me the news.

'No, they've been sent to a separate Polish cryptographic station in Hertfordshire, to work on deciphering German SS codes there. What a waste! Honestly, it's like using racehorses to pull a cart,' she grumbled.

'Well, at least they're safe,' I said. There was a pause. 'I don't suppose there's any news of the others?'

'No, nothing. I'll keep my ear to the ground, though. Promise I'll let you know if I hear anything.'

It was hard not to become too attached to the people we encountered. But we had to carry on, knowing how important the work was, and our routine, mapped out by the moon's phases, continued inexorably as the seasons passed.

By autumn, I was so huge I could hardly move. Our baby twins arrived on the first day of December, born beneath the fingernail sliver of a new moon. So Ben was there to hold them in his arms as we laughed and cried tears of joy, happy they were here safely and that our little family would be together for Christmas.

We named them Edward and Amy, for those two dear people who had each played their part in bringing us together.

The Lysander missions continued relentlessly through the grip of winter, although operations were dictated by the weather as well as the moon phase and we would regularly receive word at Tangmere that the plans for a particular night had been called off. I have to admit, I felt a pang of relief whenever that happened, knowing Ben would be safely grounded once again. When he was away, I was able to take the twins over to the Bertrams' house each day, where there were always plenty of willing helpers. The work I did there was a complete lifesaver for me, providing childcare as well as a most welcome distraction from worrying about my absent husband.

The war ground on and all we could do was pray for the safety of the agents we'd sent into the field and hope the Resistance circuits they'd established could continue to play their part in bringing the fighting to the earliest possible end. The intelligence being sent back was of vital importance, I knew. I still fretted about the fate of the ones who'd been sent to those terrible camps. Their faces haunted me: Noor, Gwido, Antoni, Maksymilian . . . what had become of them? And where were Janina, Jakub and their baby girl? So many people had become lost in the chaos and fracture of war.

Ben and I celebrated our first wedding anniversary quietly, toasting each other with glasses of cider and then falling thankfully into bed to catch a few hours of sleep before the twins woke again.

The next morning, as I bustled around the kitchen, I heard little Edward give the beginnings of a cry from upstairs and hurried to bring him downstairs before he could wake his sister. I sat back down at the table, feeding him while his daddy finished his own breakfast. The heavy cloud cover that had blanketed the south coast for the past few days was breaking up and it looked as if Ben would be flying again that night.

I don't think I had any sense of foreboding as he kissed me goodbye. No more so than at every other parting, at least. But I do remember drawing aside a corner of the blackout in the twins' bedroom as I walked little Amy up and down, trying to sing her back to sleep after feeding her in the wee small hours before the dawn. The full moon looked down on us, reminding me of a nursery rhyme my mother used to sing me when I was little. So I sang it to my daughter now.

I see the moon, the moon sees me . . .

Amy's dark lashes fluttered against the curve of her cheek as her eyes – the same sky-blue as her daddy's – closed. I let the blind fall again, plunging the room back into darkness, and laid her carefully back in her cot beside her sleeping brother.

I walked back to my room as quietly as my leg would allow, smiling as I thought of Ben. I thought of the way his eyes shone when he looked at me . . . Those first training flights with him when he'd been my instructor with his arm in a sling . . . That evening at the club, with the Attagirls, when I'd first worn that red lipstick . . . Our first kiss . . . I heard him reciting the words of our poem at our wedding, and it was such a vivid memory that I felt he was there with me as I slipped back under the bedclothes and turned out my bedside lamp.

He would probably be landing in France just about now. I hoped tonight's landing would be smooth, the handover quick and he'd be on his way back to us soon.

And I wondered whether he was thinking of me. Of us, his little family waiting for him back at home.

I knew straight away the next morning.

I was expecting Ben to walk into the kitchen, back from another long night's flying, ready for his breakfast and a few hours' sleep. But instead, there was a soft tapping on the back door and Major Bertram was standing there. He didn't need to say a thing. I slumped on to a kitchen chair.

'We don't think he was killed,' Tony said, reaching for my hand. 'Our contacts say the landing was compromised though. There were Germans waiting in the place of the *maquisards*. Someone in the network had betrayed them. The two agents and Ben were taken away. He's missing, Philly, not dead. And we're doing everything we can to find him and bring him back.'

And so it was that my own not-knowing began. A state of limbo, filled with despair and pain and what-ifs and empty hopes.

Upstairs, the babies began to cry. As if they could feel it as well.

Finn

Now that we had the bikes, Philly and I decided to go and explore some more cemeteries. We cycled all the way to Ars-en-Ré, near the salt marshes on the north side of the island, and Philly was very interested to see the war graves there, in a corner of the graveyard. There are 12, and it's easy to spot them because there's a big badge painted on the wall behind them with a crown and an eagle and the words PER ARDUA AD ASTRA, which means 'through adversity to the stars' in Latin. That's the emblem of the RAF and it's pretty cool.

She stopped in front of the very first headstone, which was for PILOT OFFICER JOHN PATRICK MUIRHEAD 100092, and reached out her hand to touch it. The inscription said he died on the 20th July 1942 and he was only 20 years old.

'I remember him,' said Philly. 'He was Scottish, a young lad from Stirling. See, it says it here on the stone. He was one of the many pilots who came through Tangmere – not flying Lysanders, but Wellington bombers.'

'Did you know he was going to be here?' I asked.

'Yes. I looked up all the war graves on the island before I came. Everything's online nowadays. I can show you when we get home if you like.'

'Look,' I said. 'There are two more from the same date.'

She nodded. 'More of the same crew. Their plane went down while they were on a mission in the Bay of Biscay. At that time, the Germans had made what they called the Atlantic Wall, a line of defences stretching all the way from the North Cape of Norway to France's border with Spain. These boys would have been on one of the missions to try to weaken it.'

I decided to make a rubbing of JOHN PATRICK MUIRHEAD. While I was doing it, Philly went and stood in front of another headstone in the next row. It said

AN AIRMAN
OF THE
1939 – 1945 WAR
FOUND 15 JANUARY 1943.

She put her hand on that headstone and stayed like that for a very long time, not saying a word. The sun glinted on her wedding ring, which she still wears even though Ben has been gone for more than 70 years.

I did some thinking while I finished taking my rubbings. It definitely wasn't her leg she was looking for because she thought that was probably buried in the south of France. And it wasn't the Poles from the château because she kept looking at British war graves more than any other nationalities. I made a deduction, which is what it's called when you rule out options to try to find an answer to a problem, just like in maths when you eliminate the common terms that you can on either side of an equation, to help you boil it down to what they're really looking for.

'Are you looking for Ben?' I said.

'Yes,' she replied. 'Still. After all these years.'

'So do you think there's a chance he could be buried on the island?'

'It's a slim one, but it's not out of the question. I've looked everywhere else and eliminated most of the other more likely possibilities over the years.'

'Do you think that's him?' I asked, pointing to the grave of the unknown airman.

She shook her head. 'The date's not far off, but it's still wrong again. You know, Finn, I've managed to find so many others. But not him.'

'There are some more war graves in the cemetery at Saint-Martin. We can go and look there tomorrow if you like.'

She laughed. 'I'm not sure trailing you around cemeteries looking at graves is exactly what your parents had in mind when they agreed to leave you in my care.'

'It's OK. I like cemeteries. They're peaceful. And we are getting fresh air, so Mum and Dad will be pleased about that. So it will be fine if we go to Saint-Martin tomorrow.' I repeated the bit about Saint-Martin because I'd noticed she hadn't said yes. I thought she might be giving up her search. She probably doesn't have as much persistence as I do. That's one thing Dad says I definitely have.

She still didn't reply, and she seemed a bit tired, so before we cycled home again, we went and sat down on a bench in the shade of a tree.

'What happened to the rest of the Poles after they left the château?' I asked.

'Well now, that's a very good question,' she said. 'As you know, Marian Rejewski and Henryk Zygalski made it to England. Gwido, Maksymilian and Antoni weren't so lucky though. We'd heard that the three of them were betrayed by their guide and captured by the Nazis as they tried to cross into Spain. The British Intelligence Services were still in touch with their French counterparts and heard from Bolek that the men had all been interrogated by the Gestapo. They'd realised that if they denied everything they'd simply be executed. So they confessed that they'd been working as codebreakers but managed to convince the Germans that they'd been beaten by the complexity of Enigma once the additional rotors had been implemented. They gave away just enough detail to save their lives, but still kept the secret of the French and British success.'

She sat up a bit straighter. 'You know, Finn, Winston Churchill said the Bletchley codebreakers were "the geese who laid the golden egg and never cackled". Do you understand what that means?'

I thought about it. I know the story about the goose and the golden eggs because it's in a book I used to read when I was younger. 'Yes, I think so,' I said. 'Even though you were doing something very important, you never talked about it?'

'Exactly. Well, Gwido, Maksymilian and Antoni never cackled either, even when they were put under the immense pressure of interrogation. Imagine having that presence of mind. They protected us all.'

'So after they'd been questioned, what happened to them next?'

She slumped against the back of the bench again. 'They were sent to a concentration camp called Sachsenhausen.'

I thought maybe she'd gone to sleep because she went quiet then and closed her eyes. But after a few moments she opened them again. 'Do you know about the concentration camps in the Second World War, Finn?'

'Yes. I did a project about them, even though Dad didn't really want me to. But I haven't heard of Sachsenhausen.'

She sighed. 'It was the first one created by Himmler when he was appointed Chief of the German Police. He used it as a model for those that followed, and it was especially brutal. Many political prisoners were sent there, especially from Poland and Russia. They were treated appallingly and many of them were executed. Those that survived were made to work in the brickworks there, and a munitions factory. But you know, Finn, even from there the Poles managed to get a few messages out. Some of the work they were forced to do made them realise the Germans were building something big, some sort of secret weapon. The metal cases they were working on were being sent to a place called Peenemünde, in the far north of Germany on the Baltic Sea. A team of Polish engineers who'd been interned in the camp were sent there to work on the project and they managed to smuggle out a message, via a Resistance network, telling the Allies to look closely at what was happening in that location.'

'And what *was* happening?'

'The Germans were developing a new weapon there. It was the first ever liquid-propellant rocket, called the V-2. It could be fired from Germany and hit Britain. A whole new way of waging war. The intelligence that had been smuggled out helped the Allies launch bombing raids against the facility at Peenemünde. And while they didn't manage to destroy it completely, they certainly hindered operations.'

We both sat quietly for a bit while I thought about that. Then I said, 'But you haven't told me yet what happened to Gwido and Maksymilian and Antoni. Were they still at Sachsenhausen?'

'Yes,' she said. 'And there were Allied bombing raids there as well. Antoni was killed in one of them.' She looked at me for a while. 'You know, Finn, I'm not sure these are appropriate topics of conversation. They are very hard to talk about.'

'I know,' I said. I repeated something Dad had said to me when I was doing my concentration camp project. 'Sometimes the world is a very hard place. Sometimes people do terrible things. But we need to know about them so we can try to make sure history doesn't repeat itself. We need to make sure they are never forgotten.'

She made a surprised expression, with wide eyes and raised eyebrows. 'You're absolutely right about that.'

'So Antoni was killed,' I said. 'That was very sad. Especially when he'd been so brave in the interrogations. But what about Gwido and Maksymilian?' I thought she was procrastinating, which is another word Dad uses quite often when I'm busy doing something and he wants me to do something else.

'Gwido Langer and Maksymilian Ciężki survived Sachsenhausen. The camp was eventually liberated by the Allies when the war ended, and they were brought to Great Britain to join their colleagues in the Polish Intelligence Service, which was still operating out of London at that time. But their return to safety and freedom at long last wasn't what it should have been. Bolek – the head of the French intelligence bureau – had made a report, you see. Fingers were being pointed at him for the Poles not getting out of France in time and he wanted to shift the blame elsewhere. So he said Gwido was the one who'd been indecisive and hadn't had the nerve to move. His report made Gwido, as Chief of the Polish Cipher Bureau, responsible for the deaths of those of his men who'd been lost. When Gwido and Maks arrived in London, they were given a chilly reception by their compatriots. And then they were sent, in some disgrace, to a signals station in Scotland, where more Polish servicemen were stationed.' She was quiet again for a few moments, then she went on.

'Maksymilian never made it home to Poland. He died in England in poverty, living on government assistance. Gwido died in Scotland a couple of years after arriving there, aged just fifty-three. I think his health had been badly affected by his interrogations and his time at Sachsenhausen. And he was consumed by a sense of betrayal, by shame and bitterness at how it had all turned out, feeling he and his team had been cast off by the French and British once they were no longer of use to them. He left word that he wanted to be buried with other Polish servicemen, in the corner of a cemetery in Scotland, because he didn't feel worthy of going home to Poland.'

She was quiet for a long time after that, and she closed her eyes again. So I didn't think I could ask her the other questions I had, about what happened to Janina and Jakub and their baby. I left her sitting there for a bit, in case she wanted to sleep, and went off to look at some more headstones. But when I was doing a rubbing of ARNAUD LEBLANC Le 6 Juin 1922, she came up behind me and said once I'd finished it was time we cycled home.

It was very hot on the ride home, because we'd stayed so long in the cemetery in Ars-en-Ré, and after we got back and had lunch Philly said she definitely needed a lie-down after all that exercise. I spent the afternoon in my room, laminating my new rubbings and typing up everything she'd told me about the Polish codebreakers because I knew Mum would be very interested to read it when she got back. She might even put it in her book and so I would have helped her a lot.

Then I looked up Sachsenhausen on the internet because I wanted to add a bit about it to my project on concentration camps. Philly wasn't exaggerating when she said it was especially brutal. More than 200,000 people were interned there between 1936 and 1945. As well as forcing them to work in factories and the local brickworks, the Nazis did experiments on them. They tried out drugs, which they hoped would make Hitler's troops fight harder. And they also had something called 'shoe testing detail'. They set out a track with different kinds of surfaces round the edge of the parade ground and prisoners had to march around it for days on end carrying heavy packs, wearing shoes with different materials making up the soles, testing which were the toughest so they could be made into boots for the German army. Some of them dropped dead from exhaustion. Overall, tens of thousands of the prisoners died, from starvation, bad treatment, disease, forced labour and medical experiments. I thought about Antoni and Gwido and Maksymilian who were there among those thousands of people and how brave they'd been.

And then I read about the extermination chambers. There was one they called the 'neck shot unit', which is pretty self-explanatory. But they decided it wasn't an efficient enough way of killing people so they built the first gas chambers there. It was completely horrible.

I stopped researching about Sachsenhausen then. It was too upsetting and was making me feel a bit sick. I knew what I'd learned would probably give me nightmares and I'd need to jump on the trampoline for a very long time.

We made fish fingers and boiled potatoes for supper and Philly let me count out my own peas from the packet to put into a separate pan of boiling water, so I knew it was an even number and didn't need to count them on my plate. It was a very good day, except for knowing about what went on at Sachsenhausen. I was glad Gwido and Maksymilian made it out of there alive when so many others, including Antoni, did not.

While we were eating our supper, I asked Philly if there could be any possibility that Ben had been sent to a concentration camp. 'Those were the first places I checked,' she said. 'The Red Cross compiled lists of people who'd been there. It was awful looking through them – there were so many names. So many people who'd had to endure those hellish places. I think even the ones who survived never really recovered. But Ben's name wasn't on any of the lists, so as far as was possible I could rule that out. Of course, it's still not impossible. Those lists could never be complete, and many families had to live with the not-knowing where their missing loved ones had ended up. But it seems unlikely Ben was sent to any of the main camps. I exhausted that line of investigation many years ago.'

I like having Philly looking after me. Dad was having his supper with the others at the sailing camp and Mum phoned to say she was really enjoying the writing course.

I think maybe Mum was right when she said it would do us all good to have some time apart, although it will be nice to have everyone back again.

Philly

I must admit, I'm quite enjoying my extra time on the island. Finn is an easy enough charge, even if he does ask a lot of questions. All that cycling too – who'd ever have imagined I'd be riding a bike again after all these years! Thank goodness the Île de Ré is as flat as a pancake. We make a very odd couple, I know, and we attract smiles and waves wherever we go, as well as shouts of encouragement from other cyclists as they go zipping past us on their much more serious bikes, clad in their Lycra shorts and their aerodynamic helmets.

The sea air and sunshine must be doing us both good. There's a bit more colour in Finn's cheeks and he seems to be sleeping a little better – at least, I haven't heard much midnight trampolining. I'm sleeping well enough too, although the questions he asks have stirred up ancient memories. Spending so much time in graveyards probably isn't helping either. It's brought the dead closer. I keep having vivid dreams of Ben and Amy, Gwido and Antoni, Noor and Violette. Full-moon dreams. They say it has an effect. Almost eight decades have gone by since I last saw any of them and yet they appear in my dreams as if it were yesterday. Every one of them so full of life. I have aged, where they have not. They wouldn't recognise me if they were to see me as I am today. An old woman, my body ravaged by the years. Better that than the alternative, though, as the saying goes.

I wonder whether that hobby of Finn's, making those rubbings of the epitaphs on people's headstones, is entirely healthy. But it serves my purposes well, the excuse to go looking in cemeteries. It's rather nice having someone to help me with my search. A lifetime of searching. A fool's errand, probably. Most people would have given up long ago. I've helped find so many others along the way, yet never found the one I've really been searching for down the years. Finn seems genuinely interested in hearing about my life as well though. He takes his task of recording my memories very seriously.

'I'm helping Mum write her book,' he told me as he set things up to record the next instalment. 'Then we can make some more money and Dad won't have to be so worried that we're spending too much, without him doing a proper job anymore because of looking after me.'

The expression on his pinched face makes my heart ache at times. What a funny combination he is of naivety and wisdom beyond his years. It must be hard for him making friends of his own age when he's simultaneously older and younger than them.

'Right then, are you ready? Chocks away, all systems go?' I asked. And that made him smile as he gave me the thumbs up and hit *record.*

In the wake of Ben's disappearance, I sleepwalked my way through the next few months in a state of shock. All I wanted to do was to crawl away into some dark cave and be alone with my grief. But I had to keep going, the twins gave me no choice. The Bertrams took me under their wing, both Tony and Barbara, and I spent every day I could at their farmhouse with my babies, where there were lots of extra pairs of hands only too willing to cuddle them and help with the endless routine of feeding them and changing their nappies. I suppose it was a welcome distraction for the French agents who'd been brought over, playing with the children in between their training sessions. Maybe for some of them it was a reminder of happier times with their own children back home.

I hated not knowing where Ben was. How he was. His German captors knew he was a pilot. Would they treat him with respect, or would they torture him? Would he be sent to a proper prisoner-of-war camp, or to one of those grim-sounding work camps somewhere in Germany or Poland? I couldn't get the thought of Noor out of my head and what we knew of what had happened to her. The passengers in Ben's plane had been three French agents being returned to work in one of the Resistance networks. Would they have been able to withstand interrogation and torture? Would the whole circuit have been compromised?

It was a bright April morning and I'd gone over to the farmhouse to help Barbara with the cooking. I'd had a sleepless night with both twins. They were fractious and unsettled, perhaps beginning to teethe or maybe just picking up on their mother's mood. I was relieved to be able to hand them over to Barbara's boys, who loved being given the responsibility of pushing the babies up and down the road in front of the house in a big pram. Tony's car pulled into the driveway. Barbara glanced up from the pastry she was rolling out and frowned. 'I though he was going to be busy over at the airfield all day today,' she said.

Through the window I saw him ruffle his sons' hair and bend down to smile at the twins, then he came into the house, calling my name. I hurried to meet him in the hall.

'Philly, there's some news. I wanted to come straight over and tell you. Here, let's go into the drawing room.'

I perched on the edge of the sofa, nervously wiping my hands on the hem of my apron. 'Ben . . . ?' I said, scarcely daring to hope.

'We brought back one of our agents this morning. In fact, you might remember her – her cover name is Louise.'

I nodded, recalling a pretty, dark-haired girl who spoke with a cockney accent. Her real name was Violette, she'd told me. Like me, she'd been given a poem to learn, which would be the basis for the codes she'd need to use to transmit messages from France. She'd needed a bit of extra help with her Morse code to get up to speed before her first deployment. We'd practised, using lines from her poem, which bore a striking similarity to mine. I wondered whether the original author had been the same for both.

Tony continued, 'Well, she was dropped in a few weeks ago but was caught by Vichy police and interrogated. She was released, though, and found her way to a local Resistance cell, who managed to get a message out. One of the Special Duties boys picked her up last night.'

He cleared his throat before going on. 'One of her contacts over there spoke of a British pilot who'd been captured by the Germans in the western area of the Loire, near Tours. It has to have been Ben. He was taken to Poitiers to be interrogated by the Gestapo but gave nothing away. He'd attempted to escape from the prison there, but was recaptured. When he was last seen, though, he was in good health.'

He stopped. My heart lurched with a jolt of simultaneous hope and despair.

'That's it?' I said, unable to keep the disappointment out of my voice. I'd hoped for more. I was always hoping for more.

'Yes. I appreciate it's not much, but at least we know for certain that he's still alive. And we've moved the focus of our search to the Poitiers area. There's a circuit operating there. We're asking them to try to get us more information. He's most probably being held in a prison in the area.'

I knew I should have been grateful that they were going to so much effort. Ben was just one of many who'd gone missing. Once I'd been able to swallow my disappointment that they hadn't found him yet, that he still wasn't coming home, I did give thanks for the news he was still alive. But if he was in the hands of the Gestapo, his future was uncertain. He was incarcerated somewhere. He could still be executed on a whim, or sent to the camps at any moment. The news had punctuated the not-knowing with a glimmer of hope, but the clouds of doubt and grief soon obscured it once again.

Like so many others, I clung on to the thinnest of hopes as the days turned to weeks and the weeks turned to months. I asked every French agent I met to listen out for any word of a British pilot with dark hair and blue eyes. They promised me they would, and I prayed that someday one of the coded messages trickling back to us through the ether might contain the news I'd been waiting for. But that message never came.

We became aware that something big was coming as spring turned to summer. The ground crews at the airfield were kept busy painting distinctive white stripes on to the wings and fuselages of Spitfires and Typhoons, as squadron after squadron passed through. They were called invasion stripes, designed to make Allied aircraft stand out during D-Day in the chaos of the onslaught from the air that would support the landings in Normandy.

One afternoon in early June, just before the D-Day landings, Tony Bertram told me they would be bringing back a very special pickup that night and he'd like me to be there when they landed. We were in the Ops Room at the cottage, preparing a French agent for his return and a British wireless operator for insertion into a network in the Corrèze. I was updating the map with the latest intelligence we had, showing the areas most heavily defended by flak and preparing the maps the Lysander pilot would be using to navigate. We needed to cut the maps into strips and stick them together to form a long roll that could be unfurled as the journey progressed, making it easier for the pilot to follow the safest route, then we'd add a much larger scale section at the end showing the landing site, helping pinpoint the darkened field where the *maquisards* would be waiting with their torches. I could picture it all so well, after my own 'visits'. But these days I always felt a pang of dread as I added the final, large-scale map, wondering whether this mission might end up being compromised as Ben's had been. Would the faint pinpricks of light guiding in the pilot be torches held by local members of the Resistance, I wondered, or might we be sending him into another trap where German soldiers lay in wait in the darkness?

I was at the airfield the next day in the early hours as the welcome party gathered – a more sizeable one than usual. We'd heard the pickup had been successful and only then had Major Bertram told me who it was they were bringing over. The Lysander landed, taxied, came to a standstill beside the hangar, and the three passengers were helped down the ladder.

The first wore a priest's robes, and I recognised the unnamed man who'd led me to the château on my arrival there, and who'd appeared at my bedside from time to time as I hovered between life and death.

The second was a woman, dressed in a tweed suit and a smart hat, carrying a handbag, as if she'd just popped out to the shops rather than escaped from the heart of Nazi-occupied France.

And the third was her husband – the man I'd known as Bolek. British Intelligence had finally brought their most important French connection across the Channel and back to England.

Gustave Bertrand stepped forward and shook my hand. 'Eveline,' he said. 'It's very good to see you again.'

My feelings towards him were a little mixed. I'd got the impression he was the one who'd been stalling the Polish team's escape from France, that British Intelligence wouldn't have sent me to deliver their message to the Poles if he'd heeded it in the first place. But then I remembered I owed my life to this man, who'd procured the chloroform that had enabled the French surgeon to operate on my leg. I knew, too, that he had looked after the Polish team, found a safe place for them and given them sanctuary when their lives were at risk. The British could have tried to bring them across earlier in the war as well but had simply taken their invaluable intelligence – which had helped Alan and Dilly get such a head start with their continuing work on decoding Enigma – and left the Poles in France. Nothing is ever black and white in life, especially in the world of secrets in which intelligence officers operate. I knew that as well as anyone. So I welcomed him and Madame Bertrand, and stayed with them in the cottage until the car arrived to take them to their new temporary home. They were to be living in Hertfordshire, close to the Polish intercept station where Marian Rejewski and Henryk Zygalski were now working. I never understood it all. I just knew that the complex links between British, French and Polish intelligence continued, that uneasy confederacy of convenience born out of the necessity of war.

In the aftermath of D-Day, more agents were to be dropped into France, building the momentum being gained by the Resistance circuits. I met Violette Szabo again, the agent known as Louise who'd reported the news of Ben. She was being dropped into France once more. We sat in the Operations Room in Tangmere Cottage drinking one cup of tea after another just to pass the time, as we waited for the message to come through giving the go-ahead for her flight that night. I asked her whether there were any more details she could give me about the sighting of Ben by her contact in the Resistance. She thought hard, then shook her head. 'All they said was he was in the prison in Poitiers. He'd tried to escape, apparently, but was caught. They interrogated him but he said nothing, other than telling them he was a British pilot, despite the fact that he was wearing civilian clothes.'

Even that snippet of information was a help. The Lysander pilots didn't wear their uniforms as the missions were so risky and it was always possible they'd need to go on the run. I was more certain than ever the man in the prison in Poitiers was him.

'I'll see what I can find out,' Violette promised. 'Maybe they'll have more news of him.'

Just then the phone rang, and Major Bertram answered it. Violette and I watched him expectantly. He replaced the receiver and shook his head. 'Sorry,' he said. '*C'est* off. It's a no-go for tonight. The weather's good enough, but the reception committee over there are calling it off because they say there are too many German patrols about. We'll have to rethink.'

In the end, Violette parachuted into France a couple of days later, leaving from another airfield. I waited to hear news of her – and hopefully of Ben – but when it finally came it was devastating. She had landed near Limoges and been dispatched southwards to liaise with a Resistance circuit in the Corrèze. The area was crawling with Germans, as the Panzer divisions swept northwards in the wake of the Normandy invasions, and the car she was travelling in had been stopped at an unexpected roadblock. The *maquisards* she was travelling with were killed and, despite fighting courageously, she was captured and taken for questioning, then deported to the camps in the east.

After that, I stopped asking the other French agents I met at the airfield to try to find out news of Ben for me. They already faced enough risks without feeling they needed to ask any other potentially leading questions. I only learned of the fates of Noor and Violette once the war had ended.

Noor Inayat Khan had been executed in Dachau alongside three other female agents. Her last word was reported to have been '*Liberté*'.

Violette Szabo's life ended in Ravensbrück concentration camp in February 1945, when she was executed alongside two other female SOE agents. I hoped she still repeated the poem to herself: she'd learned it so well, they could never take it from her no matter what else they did. And the words would have brought her a little light in that darkest of places.

◆ ◆ ◆

The twins were toddling by the time the war ended. They sat beneath festoons of bunting at one of the long trestle tables set up for the VE Day street party in our village, solemnly cramming slices of chocolate cake into their mouths. We'd made the cake with powdered egg and bulked it out with grated potato, but the addition of the last of our precious cocoa rations had transformed it into something miraculous as far as my babies were concerned.

With the war now over, I redoubled my efforts to try to find out what had happened to Ben. There was news – and shocking footage – of the liberation of the camps with names like Dachau and Auschwitz. I scanned the sunken faces on the newsreels, certain I'd recognise Ben if he was there among the living dead they found in those places. I spoke to people at the Red Cross, and I pestered everyone I could get hold of in the Air Force and in Military intelligence, using every contact I could think of. Even though I dreaded finding his name on one of the long, long lists of those who'd lost their lives, at least it would have given me the certainty of his death. It would have ended the not-knowing, given me a resolution to the story I would one day have to tell my children about their daddy.

Although it was hard to leave the cottage where I'd been so happy with Ben, especially through those dark-moon fortnights, and the village that had been such a source of support for me and my twins, I needed a job that would provide for the three of us. On one of her visits, bringing sweets for the children and the latest copy of *Picture Post* for me, Jess told me the Government Code and Cypher School had been renamed Government Communications Headquarters, shortened to GCHQ. The organisation was being moved from Bletchley Park to a temporary new home, and a new site was being developed on the outskirts of Cheltenham. She put in a word for me with her boss, and so it was that I returned to the world of Signals Intelligence, remaining there for much of the rest of my career as two of the world's superpowers became locked in the global arm wrestle we came to call the Cold War.

I moved with the twins to Cheltenham from Tangmere and, even though I recognised a few familiar faces at work, we still never spoke about our time at Bletchley Park. It was only in the 1970s, once enough time had passed and we were released from the promise we'd made when we'd signed the Official Secrets Act so long ago, that the work we did there began to become known.

Over the years, as I continued my search to find out what had become of Ben, I heard the stories of so many others. There were thousands of people who'd lost loved ones in the war and didn't know what had happened to them or where they might be buried. The stories I heard moved me and I suppose they brought me some sort of comfort, too, even if it was only in the knowledge that I wasn't alone. I was in the company of many others who had been left in this limbo of not-knowing. I realised that, even if I couldn't lay my beloved Ben to rest, perhaps I could help some of those other people find the ones they'd lost. And that was how eventually, after many years at GCHQ, I came to join the JCCC, the MOD's Joint Casualty and Compassionate Centre, an outfit also known more familiarly as the War Detectives.

Finn

I asked Philly to tell me more about being a War Detective. It sounded like a pretty cool job, and I wondered if it might be something I could do. Mum and Dad worry a lot about what I'll be able to do when I grow up, on account of me not being a Team Player. I'm not worried though. Since Philly's been here, I've thought of lots of things I could do. I could be a codebreaker at GCHQ because they still exist. I looked it up online and they have a whole section about applying to be an intern in maths and cryptography. I'd be good at keeping the Official Secrets Act too. I reckon I could make up some new ciphers that even a supercomputer would find difficult to crack. But I think I'd also like to be a War Detective because it involves having persistence and spending a lot of time looking at headstones in graveyards. I'm already pretty good at both those things.

Philly said she joined the War Detectives when she was ready to wind down a bit. 'I'd worked all my life at GCHQ, once the war had ended, and my twins had grown up and gone on to have careers and families of their own.' She told me she has grandchildren and she's even a great-granny, like Ella was to me.

The War Detectives work from an army base in Gloucestershire, so she didn't have to move house when she joined them. They are a team who search for missing servicemen and try to give them a proper burial. Mostly, they're dealing with soldiers who were killed in the First World War, which was also called the Great War but I don't know why because that was a really terrible one for losing people, which is not great at all. Philly says it was largely down to the way wars were fought then, and all the mud. Even now, human remains keep turning up in the fields of northern France and Belgium, which is where some of the biggest and longest battles were. When they do, if the remains are identified as being British because of things that are found with them, the War Detectives get involved. They can use DNA testing nowadays to try to identify the bodies. They also use a lot of deduction. For example, if they find a cap badge for a certain regiment then that gives them a starting point to work from. Then they can see whether there are any other bits of uniform left, like the stripes on a sleeve that show the rank of a soldier. And sometimes there are things like rings or photographs that help too. They have a big database of people who are still missing and relatives who are trying to track them down. It's not just Philly who's spent her life searching.

I did some googling. It's hard to estimate the number of deaths in the First World War, but they think it was about 20 million military personnel and another 20 million civilians who died of disease and starvation because of the famine caused by the war. Of the more than 1 million British servicemen who were killed, there are still about half a million missing. That's a lot of people to still be searching for.

'Not so many went missing in the Second World War,' Philly told me. 'The majority of the remains we were asked to try and identify from that time were from RAF crash sites, usually in the Netherlands and Germany. I found that especially hard, having worked with so many airmen myself in my time. It became very personal, trying to match up the remains with their families.

'Sometimes, too,' she said, 'we managed to put a name to an unknown burial, like some of the war graves we looked at in the cemeteries here. That usually happened when researchers or family members gathered some evidence pointing to a particular place and they'd submit it to the War Detectives who could then look into it further. We also had to rule out any other possible candidates who might be in a particular grave, you see, before we could officially say that a particular grave belonged to a particular person. It has to be able to be proven beyond doubt.'

All of this has to be done by research only, because the exhumation of war graves for the purposes of identification is strictly forbidden. Otherwise, as Philly says, you'd be digging people up right, left and centre and it would be chaos. But if they can successfully identify who an unknown grave belongs to, then they have a rededication service, with full military honours, and put a proper headstone in place with the person's name. They don't usually dig up the body and bring it home for a burial or cremation, though, even if that's what the family wants. 'The general rule is fought together, died together, buried together,' she explained.

Philly says it's all about giving people Closure, and even though she's been to a lot of rededication services, she's always found each one very moving because it meant an awful lot to the families to know where their loved ones were. I asked her what Closure means and she said it's about finding a resolution to something, a bit like the feeling we get when we work out a Sudoku or a Magic Square and everything fits into place at last. I understand that – I hate it when I can't work out a maths problem, it keeps me awake at night and I have to do some trampolining to try to stop thinking about it. As Philly said, there are few things worse than Unfinished Business.

Then Philly told me something else interesting that she did quite recently, even after she stopped working as a War Detective.

'You remember what I told you about Gwido Langer, the Polish Bureau Chief?' she said.

'Yes. He was buried in a cemetery in Perth, the city in Scotland, not Australia, because he was made to feel ashamed about not getting the other people in his team out of France earlier and losing some of them.'

She nodded. 'Yes, well remembered! Well, I met up with Maksymilian again at the unveiling of a memorial at Bletchley Park to commemorate the contribution the Polish codebreakers had made to cracking Enigma way back at the start of the war. It just has three names on it: Marian Rejewski, Henryk Zygalski and Jerzy Różycki. The others who had spent those years at Cadix, deciphering other coded messages and making sure they were sent to the Allies, still go unrecognised. But at least those three are now remembered at Bletchley, tucked into a corner of the grounds between the huts and the Cottage where I met Dilly Knox. Yes, Maks was there that day, for the unveiling, and we had time to talk afterwards. We spoke of Gwido Langer, and I told him I had visited Gwido's grave in the cemetery in Perth, where he lay with so many other Polish servicemen, and put a red and white wreath there. Maks told me Gwido's family in Poland really wanted people to know that the story wasn't as it had been made out to be. He had always tried to do his best for the whole team at the château, but they were so dependent on the French. The delay in getting out wasn't Gwido's fault. He'd been so courageous, too, when he was captured, interrogated and then sent to Sachsenhausen. He'd always kept the secret and protected not just his own team but the whole codebreaking operation for the Allies. It was a terrible injustice that he was laid to rest in the corner of a foreign graveyard where his family couldn't visit him easily.'

She paused, looking at me to make sure I was still listening, which of course I was. 'That conversation put the wheels in motion.

I was able to contact the powers that be in Britain, to help Gwido's family in their petition to have his body exhumed and brought home to Poland. And so, at last, in 2010 he was given a state funeral in his hometown of Cieszyn, with full military honours.'

She stopped again, and I could see she was remembering because it's important, so I didn't interrupt to ask her any questions.

'It was December and the snow was falling,' she said. 'Big wet flakes that bowed the branches of the cypresses lining the path through the graveyard. We walked behind the cavalcade of soldiers, one of them carrying a photo of Gwido, just as I remembered him from the château. So many people turned out to pay their respects: those of us who were left – his old comrades – but many young people too. We stood at the graveside as they played the Last Post and the snow fell faster, drawing a veil across the hills beyond the town. Once the army and his family had laid their wreaths on the grave, I left a bouquet of white roses and chrysanthemums, tied with a red and white ribbon.' She sighed. 'They know how to do things properly, the Polish military.'

'So did it give Gwido Langer's family Closure?' I asked her, because she'd finished talking.

She blinked, looking at me as if she'd forgotten I was there. Sometimes she seems to be remembering things so deeply that she does that. Her eyes go all misty.

'Why, yes Finn, I believe it did.'

'And now they have a place they can go, to remember him properly.'

She smiled and her eyes were brighter again. 'Exactly.'

And then we both said at precisely the same time, 'It's so important.' That made us laugh, and then it was time to make our Marmite sandwiches for lunch.

◆ ◆ ◆

When Dad came home after supper that evening, he said the sailing camp was going very well. 'Tomorrow is the last-but-one day, so would you like to come and do some dinghy sailing, Finn? The forecast is good, not too much wind so conditions should be perfect, and you can go out on your own if you prefer not to be with the others.'

I thought about it for a bit. Even just thinking about being with the other kids and the large boy's mother who had said those things about me made me feel a bit sick again. Then Philly said, very quietly, 'You know, I should love to get out on to the water again one day. It's been years since I was in a boat.'

'I could take you tomorrow, if you like,' I said. Because I knew she would sit still and not do anything upsetting.

'I'd love that.'

And so we made a plan to go in the car with Dad the next morning and Take Part in the sailing camp for 1 day, at least.

Philly

I have to pinch myself to believe I am really doing it. Me, in my nineties and minus a limb, being helped into a Laser dinghy and setting off into the Atlantic with Finn at the helm! I can see how much it means to Dan. He shot me such a look of gratitude last night when I said how much I'd like to sail again. I haven't been out on the water since once of my grandchildren insisted on taking me once, when we were on a family holiday in the Inner Hebrides. It must have been . . . well, I stopped trying to work it out in the end. Decades ago!

I can see what a success the sailing camp has been. The kids have obviously come on in leaps and bounds in terms of their confidence and the skills they've gained. I watched as they put on their life jackets and helmets and rigged the little fleet of Toppers and Lasers that Dan had managed to assemble for the day, and even though their expressions bore traces of the tension and anxiety that are such a big part of their daily lives, there were no dramas. Finn also looked tense as he prepared our Laser, and he steered well clear of the others, but at least he was there, joining in as best he could.

I was helped into the dinghy by Dan and Iain, feeling clumsy and awkward, already regretting this reckless folly, then I sat myself down in the well of the boat, trying to avoid the centreboard and keeping out of the way of the boom. I'm not exactly agile when it comes to tacking and jibing, but at least I can shift my weight a little from side to side when instructed to do so. I'm impressed to see how capable Finn is. He scoots back and forth as we zigzag our way out of the harbour mouth and into the open sea.

How exhilarating it is to feel the breeze catch the sail and the boat start to gather speed. I tilt my face to the sky and feel the years slip from my shoulders as I let the wind whisk away the tears that have begun leaking from my eyes. It's partly the dazzle of the sunlight on the waves, partly the emotion. I feel like I'm flying again. In my mind, I hear Teddy telling me to take the controls of the first training plane I ever went up in with him, flying out over the Firth of Forth and the rust-red spans of the rail bridge; I hear Amy's laugh as she exchanges a few words with one of the mechanics before swinging herself into the cockpit of an Oxford she'll be delivering; and I see Ben's face, looking just as he looked on the first day he took me up as my instructor, back in the days of my ATA training, his eyes smiling back at me, making my stomach loop the loop. They are all there with us as we fly out across the water, seabirds swooping and wheeling in an ever-changing formation of wingmen above the mast.

I dab at my leaky eyes and glance at Finn, making sure he isn't being made anxious by my reaction, but he's as fully focused on the task in hand as he always is, concentrating on reading the tell-tales, making sure the little strands of green and red cotton are streaming straight back evenly on either side of the sail.

The wind is with us as we sail out to the first marker buoy and tack to round it.

'That's Fort Boyard over there,' Finn says, pointing. 'They'll be going there with the big boat tomorrow.' If I squint, I can just make out a grey smudge on the horizon. I smile and nod as he pulls on the tiller, adjusting our new course towards the next buoy. I glance back to see the other boats following in our wake, and Dan and Iain not far off, holding back in the rescue boat. Like Finn, the other children's faces are a picture of focus and concentration, but the wind and the sun and the salt spray seem to have gently erased the tension and wariness from their expressions. *What a good thing you have done, Dan*, I think to myself. *What an achievement.*

By the time we return to the harbour, my body has seized up with the stiffness of unaccustomed activity. Dan and Iain have to haul me to my feet, and I limp over to perch on a low section of wall and attempt to regain a little of my dignity. I watch the children sort out the boats, with minimal instructions from the adults.

'Are you feeling OK, Philly?' Dan asks, approaching with Finn at his side once they've finished. 'It wasn't too much for you?'

'I'm absolutely fine,' I say. 'Finn, you were brilliant! Thank you for taking me out. I hope I wasn't too much of a hindrance.'

'No,' he says, his face deadpan. 'You were quite good ballast, actually.'

Dan draws a sharp intake of breath, and I can see he's about to take Finn to task. But I put my hand on his arm to stop him, and he smiles instead as I guffaw with laughter, saying, 'Glad to be of service in the ballast department any time, Skipper.'

'Are you sure you don't want to join the others for lunch?' Dan asks. We'd agreed the night before that we'd only stay for the morning session.

'No thank you,' Finn replies. 'We have to go home for our Marmite sandwiches and then Philly will need to have a post-prandial pause afterwards.'

He knows me so well now. To be honest, I'm more than ready to get back. All the excitement, and all those old emotions, have quite taken it out of me. Dan comes home to have lunch with us too. As I'm cutting the crusts off our sandwiches, Finn asks me, 'What is there to eat when you go for tea at The Ritz?'

I see his father glance at him in surprise, although of course I realise what he is really asking.

'Well, actually, I believe you have sandwiches quite like these ones. Only they probably have things like cucumber and smoked salmon in them, not Marmite. And then they'll bring you scones with jam and cream, and the most beautiful little cakes, decorated with fruit and rose petals. The tea will be served in silver teapots and poured into fine china cups. It's supposed to be an extravaganza. But I've never been.'

'So you never did meet Janina again,' he says, carrying our plates to the table and pulling up his chair.

'Sadly, no. I looked for her after the war ended, but I'm afraid her story was one like so many others. Through my contacts in Intelligence, I managed to find out what had happened. You'll recall their surname was Krakowski – a Jewish name. After the baby was born, they spent months hidden in the little village in the foothills of the Pyrenees. Suspicion and jealousy were rife, though, and all the more so once the Germans had taken over the whole country. Eventually, Janina and Jakub were betrayed by a French neighbour. The Gestapo came and arrested them, and they were sent away to the camps back east. It was ironic, really. They so wanted to go home to Poland and in the end they did – or, at least, to what had been their homeland before it was overrun by Hitler's army. I found their names on the Red Cross lists of people who'd been murdered in the gas chambers at Auschwitz. Jakub Krakowski. Janina Krakowska. They were killed a few days apart.'

'The baby too?'

I sigh. 'You know, Finn, the Nazis often didn't even bother recording the babies that were killed. Or maybe Janina and Jakub's tiny daughter died on the journey to the camp. The conditions would have been terrible, and many people did die en route, their names never recorded on any lists.'

Finn nods, then carries his plate over to the sink. 'Shall we have a Prince chocolate biscuit for pudding?' he says.

'You go ahead. I'm not very hungry. And now I definitely need to go and have a lie-down.' Those thoughts of Janina and Jakub weigh heavily on my mind, and I feel exhausted suddenly. 'Will you be OK on your own for a bit?'

'Of course. I'm going to do some maths.' He studies his biscuit, then takes a bite, starting to nibble around the edges before making any inroads into the chocolate in the middle. It's another one of those habits of his.

He pauses as I get to my feet, reaching for my stick. Then he adds, 'I'm sorry you never had tea at The Ritz, Philly. I'm sorry you didn't get Closure for Janina and Jakub and their baby either.'

What an old head that child has, and those young shoulders of his carry such a heavy load of anxiety, day in, day out.

Finn

In the afternoon, after we'd got back from the dinghy sailing, I was sitting on the porch when Philly came down from her rest. She had only eaten half of her sandwich at lunchtime and then said she needed to go and lie down on her bed for a while.

Dad had stayed to have lunch with us too. 'Are you sure you don't want to come back and do the afternoon session, Finn? You did so well this morning.'

I said no thank you and I would be OK doing some Sudokus for a while.

'You know, tomorrow is the last day of the camp and we're going to be doing the expedition to Fort Boyard. You could both come too, if you like.'

'I don't think so,' I said. 'Today was enough.'

'OK, well, you could just come and wave us off, if you prefer. I'd love it if you even did that. See how you feel in the morning.' Then Dad drove away in the car to get back to the harbour.

When Philly reappeared, I asked her, 'Have you had a long enough pause?'

'I feel like a new woman,' she said.

I looked at her. She was still just as old as she had been when she went upstairs. In fact, she was 1 hour and 12 minutes older. But I didn't say that, because Mum once told me talking to ladies about their age is another thing We Don't Do, after one of her friends said she'd be turning the big 4-0 soon and I said actually she looked a bit older than that, more like the big 4-5.

'In that case,' I said, 'shall we go out on the bikes and look at some more gravestones?'

'I think I'd better just stay here for the rest of the day, if you don't mind,' she replied. 'Even after a good rest, I'm still feeling a bit wiped out after our exciting morning.'

Then she said she'd been doing some thinking, after our sailing trip, and she'd reached the conclusion she was spending too much time chasing ghosts when she should really be concentrating on being in the land of the living while she still actually was. She said going out on the dinghy and cycling around the island with me had shown her that, and she thought we'd spent enough time in graveyards.

'But we haven't found Ben yet,' I said. 'It's Unfinished Business. You still haven't got Closure.'

She nodded and her eyes looked a bit cloudy again. 'Yes, but I don't think he'd want me to let however many months and years I have left on this Earth pass me by. There've been too many false hopes, too many dead ends, and they take their toll. When I was out on the dinghy today, I realised I've spent too much of my life living in the past. I want to share what time I have left with my family now, especially with my grandchildren and great-grandchildren, making happy memories like the ones we did today. There's been enough sadness without continually chasing after more of it.' Then she picked up her ancient iPad and opened it up.

'OK,' I said. 'Are you going to do a crossword now?'

'Yes,' she said. 'And then we can think about what we're going to cook for our supper. I don't know about you, but all that sea air has given me quite an appetite.' I knew that wasn't true because of her only eating half her sandwich at lunchtime, so I deduced that she was trying to be cheerful and change the subject. That made me think she was probably feeling quite sad about giving up her search really.

I haven't given up though. If I'm going to be a War Detective, perhaps my first successful case will be tracking down what happened to Ben. It will look good on my CV when I come to apply for the job.

So I went to my room and wrote out what we know so far. I thought if I treated it like working out a maths problem, I might be able to make some more progress towards finding a solution. Here's what I wrote . . .

Known factors:

We know Ben was captured. Last known to be in Poitiers early in 1944. He was in the prison there and he tried to escape. So they had to find somewhere safer to keep him.

Philly has looked in other possible places in that immediate area and there's no record of him there.

Philly has also eliminated concentration camps from her search – she checked all the Red Cross records, and he's not listed there.

Assumptions:

Ben was not executed at Poitiers. (The Resistance people would have found out.)

He was moved to a higher security prison.

During the war, it would have been easier for the Germans to move prisoners to the closest place.

Therefore, looking at the map of France, the highest security prisons within reach of Poitiers were the citadel in Saint-Martin-de-Ré and Fort Boyard.

Furthermore, we can eliminate Fort Boyard because the Germans didn't use it as a prison during the war, they just used it for target practice.

The Île de Ré didn't have a bridge joining it to the mainland back then, it could only be reached by a ferry, so it would have been a good place to bring prisoners if you wanted to make it hard for them to escape.

Hence, given assumptions (1), (2) and (3), and the factors listed above, we can hypothesise that Ben was brought to Saint-Martin.

And then I laminated it and went to tell Philly that I would like to cycle over to Saint-Martin tomorrow morning after all, to watch Dad and Iain and everyone else sail the bigger boat out of the harbour when they leave to go to Fort Boyard.

Philly

At first, I sleep deeply after the day out in the dinghy. Must have been all that sea air – Dan and Kendra are right! But I think, too, accepting that my search for Ben is over may have something to do with it.

I surface from the depths of my sleep in the wee small hours, though, to the sound of Finn jumping on the trampoline. I get out of bed and open the shutters. There he is, that beautiful boy in his pyjamas in the moonlight, leaping and bouncing. Freer than he ever can be in the unforgiving light of day. A ragged wisp of cloud half covers the face of the moon for a few moments, then dissolves, leaving the earth bathed in the soft, clear light, the moonbeams embracing the boy in a way that his loved ones cannot as he jumps and jumps. And in watching him, I feel a sort of weightlessness too, a shared sense of freedom, of fleeting liberation from the burden of getting through each day.

The moon is beginning to wane, relinquishing its fullness one sliver at a time in the inexorable cycle of light and dark. In its next iteration, it will be what is traditionally called a Hunter's moon. We're all said to be affected by that full moon. It's not just werewolves that feel some primeval instinct stir deep within, there's a wakefulness in every one of us – humans and animals alike – a restlessness making us long to prowl the earth on the nights when forests and hills are bathed in its soft glow. But now my hunting days are over. I wonder whether I'll sleep any better, or will that instinct to carry on seeking still keep flickering in some corner of my brain, whispering to me that I've been wrong to give up?

Letting go of my search has been a painful wrench, but perhaps a necessary one. If I can only come to terms with that, then maybe I can move on in my grief. That day in the cottage at Tangmere when they told me Ben was missing, something deep inside me became frozen. It's stayed that way ever since, I've carried it everywhere with me, that cold hard lump of loss. I always thought searching for him would be the answer to shifting it, but now I see that in fact it was the opposite. My obsessive searching kept the loss enshrined, cocooned it away, not allowing the light and warmth and love my family and friends have given me down the years to melt it. Until now. Giving up, letting go, accepting I will never find him and bring him home. It's taken a leap of faith – a trip in a little boat, with a child who sees the world through different eyes – to help me see that.

Finn's frankness, his raw honesty, his clarity of thought (once you understand the logic behind it) have been liberating. We so-called normal adults dissemble, creating elaborate constructs – manners and rules and evasions – as a means of protecting ourselves and others. Sometimes those constructs work, but sometimes they become like clouds covering the moon, obscuring the pure light of truth. And even though the truth can be tough to face, it can also set us free.

As the first rays of daylight begin to filter into the garden, overpowering the more subtle moonlight, Finn's jumping slows to a stop. Then he climbs off the trampoline and marches back inside, squaring his shoulders, ready to face yet another day in this strange world in which he lives, a world so filled with anxiety and perplexity, where truth is the only certainty he has.

◆ ◆ ◆

Dan is delighted that Finn has agreed to cycle over to Saint-Martin to watch the others sail off on their expedition to Fort Boyard. 'Are you sure you don't want to join us on the boat?' he says.

'No thank you,' Finn replies firmly, brooking no further discussion of the matter.

'OK. Well, maybe next year you'll feel more like it. The sailing camp's been such a success that the others want to come back again.'

Finn makes no reply, he just carries on methodically eating the crustless triangle of toast his father's made for him.

'That's great news, Dan,' I say, filling the silence. 'Fantastic. Kendra will be delighted to know that when she gets back tomorrow.'

He nods, then gets to his feet, gathering up car keys and a water bottle. 'Well, time I got off and rounded up the troops. There's a whole long list of checks we need to do this morning before we head out. I'll see you at the harbour.'

'See you there,' I echo, draining my coffee cup. 'Come on, Finn, we'd better get moving.'

It's a perfect day for their final sail. We cycle along the dusty tracks, skirting around the main road to avoid the traffic, passing vineyards and orchards and fields filled with wildflowers. As we cross through the centre of the island, I inhale the dry, spiced scent of the wild fennel growing in the verges. Little sulphur-coloured butterflies flutter about us, disturbed by the whirling of our wheels, and the light has that mellow, golden quality you get towards the end of summer, when the days begin to shorten almost imperceptibly, a softening around the edges that comes to all of us with age. And then the smell of the sea returns as we near the northern coastline. Before long, we are approaching the town, crossing the bridge over the dry moat where the summer-bleached grass has been cropped close by the grazing donkeys. Everywhere I look, I feel the sense of something ending – that feeling familiar to every schoolchild of a conclusion of the holidays and the beginning of a new term. Only for me, I hope this new beginning will herald a final few years (or however long might be left to me) of peace.

The harbour is busy, bustling with tourists as we wheel our bikes over the cobbles to the quayside. Finn stops for a moment to remove his cycle helmet and put on his ear defenders.

'All right?' I ask him as I take the helmet from him and put it in the basket on the handlebars of my trike, alongside my collapsible walking stick.

He nods determinedly, although his expression is pinched, his face twitching with the onslaught of sights and sounds and smells that his brain finds it impossible to filter.

The other children are already on board the yacht, sitting in their spots marked with tape, the engine ticking over. Dan catches sight of us and waves, then calls over, 'Do you want to cast us off?'

I point to the mooring lines for Finn's benefit, so he'll understand, and he unloops them from the bollards and throws the ropes to his dad.

As Iain manoeuvres the boat gingerly out of the marina, we walk to the end of the pier to give them a final wave as they slip past the lighthouse and out into the open sea.

'Right-o, what shall we do now?' I ask Finn. 'Do you want to go and get an ice cream before we cycle home?'

'I would like an ice cream,' he says, 'but first I'd like to cycle a bit further, to the beach past the citadel.'

I'm surprised. He's not usually very keen on spending time on beaches, unless it's after dark. But I'm certainly not going to object. It's a pleasant day and good for him to be enjoying being outdoors in the sunshine, so we mount our bikes again and cycle onwards, past the vast stone bulk of the fortress, the heavy prison gates firmly locked, to the other side of the fortifications and the stretch of sand beyond. We have the place to ourselves.

I sit on a bench above the beach, looking out across the curve of the bay to the rough, blocky rocks and the sea beyond. Shading my eyes against the sun, I think I can just pick out the sailing camp yacht, far off in the dazzle of the water. I tilt my head back to watch a pair of black-backed gulls as they swoop and scold against the blue of the sky, their shadows wheeling across the sand beneath them like ghostly fighter planes.

Finn wanders off to potter alongside the walls, paper and pencil in hand as he looks for more carved names to add to his collection of rubbings. His ear defenders are still in the basket on the trike's handlebars, but he seems OK. 'Don't go too far, Finn,' I call. He waves, then turns his attention back to the stones.

I feel bone-tired suddenly – the cumulation of the unaccustomed exercise and emotion I've experienced over the past days, I suppose – so I lean back and close my eyes, just for a few minutes . . .

I must have fallen asleep. Because the next thing I know, I'm being shaken awake rather brusquely.

'*Madame! Madame!*' a French voice is saying. I open my eyes to see a *gendarme* standing there. 'Madame, are you responsible for that child?' he asks. His tone is gruff with disapproval.

I look across to where he is pointing. Finn stands in front of the citadel gates, with another two policemen guarding him. Even from that distance, I can see he looks terrified. One of them reaches out to hold him by the arm and I shout, 'Don't touch him! *Ne le touchez pas!*'

And then all hell breaks loose.

Finn

After I bit the policeman and they arrested Philly for hitting the other one with her walking stick to stop him from grabbing me too, they kept us at the police station until late in the afternoon, when Dad came to get us.

Luckily, one of the policemen at the station spoke pretty good English, but it had still taken quite a lot of explaining, with the help of a FRENCH – ENGLISH dictionary, to work out what was going on, once everyone had calmed down.

Philly was brilliant. She demanded to know what they thought they were doing, arresting people who were simply minding their own business and enjoying the lovely holiday they were having on the island.

'This boy was spotted loitering close to the gates of the prison,' the *gendarme* said. 'And then he climbed down into the moat. He was behaving in a very suspicious manner. Do you not understand it's a prohibited area?'

'Don't be ridiculous,' Philly retorted. 'There's nothing there to say so. Tourists pass right by those gates the whole time. Show me the signs that say it's prohibited.'

'But, Madame, it may not exactly be advertised, precisely because of the tourists, but it's a high-security *prison*,' the man said again, emphasising the word. 'Surely you can understand, this is not a suitable place for anyone to be hanging around, let alone a child. And he was making notes on a piece of paper. He was picked up on the security cameras and, when asked what he was up to, he couldn't give a reasonable answer.'

'He was just looking at the names carved into the stones,' Philly said. 'Show him, Finn.'

I didn't really want to show them both of the rubbings I'd done because I had a hunch they were going to confiscate them, so I just pulled out from my pocket the one I'd done beside the gate, of BERNARD LEBLANC VI–IX–1859, and handed it over.

'You see,' said Philly. 'It's a hobby of his, taking rubbings of the names. He collects them.'

The man looked at the piece of paper and then back at me again and then he put it into a folder on his desk, along with some other notes he'd been taking of things like our full names, our dates of birth and the address of the house. My hunch had been correct, he didn't give it back.

'All right,' he said at last. 'I believe your story. But you must understand, a couple of inmates managed to escape two years ago – we can't risk that happening again, not with such high-risk prisoners in a residential area. That aside, there is also the matter of the biting of one of my colleagues. And your assault on another of them as well, Madame.'

'What do you mean, my assault! I merely reached out with my walking stick to try to prevent my young and terrified companion here from defending himself a second time when provoked in an entirely unjustifiable manner. I can't help it if your colleague got in the way when I was simply trying to protect him for his own good.'

There was quite a long pause then while the gendarme looked up some of the words Philly had used in the dictionary. Then he made some more notes, and he raised his eyebrows and scratched his head a lot while he was writing them.

All of this had taken quite a lot of time. Then the policeman asked for Dad's mobile number so they could call him to verify our story and take us home. But the phone was probably out of reach of any reception, and we explained he was on a boat, sailing to Fort Boyard, and that made the policeman raise his eyebrows and scratch his head again even more for a bit.

'OK,' he said at last. 'You'll have to wait here until he gets back then, so he can vouch for you.'

I wondered if they were going to lock us up in the cells, but Philly said they couldn't do that to me because I was a Minor. Instead, they let us sit in the office and one of the gendarmes went off and came back with ice creams for us, so they actually turned out to be kind in the end.

Dad was pretty upset when he came into the police station. Philly and the *gendarme* had to explain everything all over again, to reassure him that we weren't going to be prosecuted for a breach of the peace and GBH (which is what it's called when you bite a policeman). And then, at last, we were allowed to go home, as long as I promised not to take any more rubbings right beside the gates and never to climb down into the moat again.

I was happy to do that. Because I didn't need to look there again. I already had what I needed.

When we were safely home and we were sitting on the porch, I took the other piece of paper out of my pocket and showed Philly the name and date I'd found, carved into the stones beside the place where the donkeys were grazing. I hadn't even had a chance to laminate it yet.

Her eyes went really big, and she wrapped her arms around herself. Then her mouth went all wobbly and she let out a single big sob, and tears rolled down her cheeks as she read the words:

B.C. Delaney
22.8.1944

Philly

I cry when I read Ben's name on that piece of paper. And I have to fold my arms to stop myself from hugging Finn. Then I unfold them and reach over to touch the letters, carved by his own hand all those years ago. B.C. Delaney. My Ben. Found, at last. Or, at least, another piece of the jigsaw in the search for what happened to him. A big, important piece.

When, at last, I can speak again, I say, 'Finn, you are absolutely brilliant! Where did you find this?'

'In the moat, the grassy bit where the donkeys are. I went to look at the stones around the gates first. That's where I found BERNARD LEBLANC. But then I noticed there were some more stones with names carved on them down in the deeper bit and it seemed like the sort of place they might have let prisoners walk around for exercise in the past. It was probably fenced in then. I had to climb down, and it was pretty steep. I found Ben's name almost straight away and I'd just had time to do the rubbing when the police appeared. They made me climb back up, which was quite hard to do. I scraped my knees a bit. And then they said a whole load of things in French very loudly, which I didn't understand. So I pointed at you on the bench because I thought you could come and translate.'

'He was here,' I say. I'm still lost for words, really, taking it in. Tracing the letters of his name. He made his mark, left us a clue. Just like all those hundreds of other prisoners who'd carved their names into the stones over the centuries. 'How did you know where to look?'

'It was a hunch. I worked it out. I can show you, if you like. I made some assumptions and a hypothesis, and they turned out to be correct. I decided not to give up the search, even if you had.'

'Thank you, Finn. You're an absolute marvel.' I can't stop smiling through my tears.

'So now we have to make some more deductions and work out what happened next.'

That sobers me up pretty quickly. Knowing Ben had been held in that prison isn't good news. But then I suppose, knowing he'd been captured, there never was going to be any good news.

'Oh Finn, I think we can guess. He wasn't released, and the only other result of being imprisoned here would have been execution. Or death from starvation or disease.'

'Well, maybe there are prison records. We can ask the policemen we met.'

I consider that for a moment. 'I suppose you're right. There may be something . . .' All of a sudden, I'm not sure I want to know. Perhaps it is enough, having his name. Knowing I'm close to him here.

'You haven't got Closure yet,' Finn says. 'So we need to keep searching. At least now we have some definite new evidence to go on.'

I sigh. 'OK, we'll go back to the police station on Monday and ask if there's any way they can check the prison records from 1944. But my time is running out, you know, Finn.'

He nods. 'Mum is coming home tomorrow. But that doesn't mean you have to go home to England straight away. You can stay here with us for a bit while we search some more.'

I'm not sure that's exactly what I meant, but I smile and nod. Then I haul myself to my feet and head through to the kitchen to make some Marmite sandwiches, which are about all I can manage to cobble together for our supper.

◆ ◆ ◆

That evening, once I've given Finn his medication and seen him into his bed, I'm washing the plates and wiping down the surfaces in the kitchen when Dan returns. He'd gone back to Saint-Martin for the final supper with everyone from the sailing camp. It's been a great success, by all accounts.

'Thanks for doing that, Philly,' he says. 'In fact, thanks for everything. You've been an absolute wonder looking after Finn this week.'

'Hmm, yes,' I reply. 'Apart from getting us both arrested, of course.'

He laughs. 'Don't worry, it was a minor incident in the big scheme of things. And what a result, him finding Ben's name carved into the wall like that. It was worth risking being given a criminal record. I think even Kendra will agree.'

'She must be looking forward to coming home tomorrow,' I say.

He doesn't reply, just turns away and opens the kitchen cupboard where the booze is kept. 'Will you join me in a celebratory dram?' he asks, taking down a bottle of whisky.

'I'd love one.'

He pours generous measures into two glasses, and we go out to sit on the porch. The moonlight casts long shadows over the dunes, where the seagrass ripples gently in the night breeze.

We sip our drinks in silence, lost in our own thoughts. Mine are of Ben, picturing him here on the island. I wonder whether he could see the moon from the window of his cell in the prison, if it had one.

I wonder whether he would lift his face to let the sea wind caress it, thinking back to our walks on the Downs and those nights we spent together in our bedroom under the eaves of the cottage in Tangmere.

When Dan speaks, it pulls me out of my reverie. He sits slumped in his chair and his voice is low, the words so quiet that it takes a moment for them to register. 'I'm afraid I'll lose her, you know.'

I realise he's talking about Kendra. I'm not sure how to reply, so I don't. I just let him speak.

He takes another sip from his glass, swallows hard. 'It's a lot of pressure for her, being the breadwinner for the family now, while I take care of Finn. She has such a talent and I know she loves her writing, but it's still hard. I wonder whether one day she might just decide there's a far more glamorous life out there, go off on one of her writing trips and not come back.'

I shake my head. 'She would never do that. She'd never leave you and Finn. I know she doesn't have an easy job, but it looks to me like you have the hardest job of all. Kendra knows that too. She appreciates everything you've sacrificed in your own career to take care of Finn. There aren't many fathers who could do what you've done.'

He swallows again, and even in the darkened corner of the porch I can tell he's choking back his emotions.

'Thanks, Philly,' he says. 'I hope you're right. To be honest, it puts a strain on our marriage, all of this.'

'I can see that,' I say. 'It's so tough, day in, day out. I think the pair of you do a really good job, though. The demands of parenting an autistic child are relentless. But you've risen to the challenges of parenting Finn, and you've done it together. And I know you will both carry on doing so, simply because you have to. But you two are amazing parents and you have an amazing son. You manage to stay sane, to keep going, to meet every drama and crisis as it arises. I hope, as Finn gets older, the situation will evolve a bit. I hope perhaps you'll have a bit more time for yourselves. And for each other.'

He's silent again for a while. Then he sits up a bit straighter, turning towards me and squaring his shoulders. 'It helps a lot, having someone who sees it for what it is. We've become so cut off from the world we once knew that I think we lose the ability to do that, to see our situation through the eyes of someone sympathetic and understanding. There's so much judgement.'

'I know. But I suspect some of it is self-inflicted too.' I keep my tone gentle, not wanting my words to come across as more of that criticism. 'I think you'll find that those who understand your situation are completely in awe of what you do. After all, love is easy when it's easy. What really counts is how you are able to continue to love in the face of hardship, when the chips are down.'

He laughs softly. 'There are very many people who *don't* understand, though.'

'And why on earth would they matter then? That's their problem, not yours. It's up to them to look more carefully. Before you judge a man, walk a mile in his shoes, as the saying goes. There aren't many who could walk even a few yards in yours and Kendra's. Let alone write a book, or organise a successful sailing camp for a challenging group of youngsters.'

'Thank you for that. For everything. We're so grateful to you, Philly. You've made a real difference to all our lives in the short time you've been here. Finn's as well as mine and Kendra's.'

I raise my glass to him. 'You have my wholehearted admiration. All three of you.' Then I drain the remains of my whisky. 'And now, if you'll excuse me, Dan, I'll be off to my bed. It's been a most eventful day, one way and another.'

As I attempt to haul myself to my feet, he stands and offers me a hand. I take it. 'You know, Dan, one of the hardest things we all have to learn to do in life is to ask for help. And accept it when it's offered.

But helping one another is surely why we're put on this planet.' I give his hand an extra squeeze before I let it go, pressing home my point.

Then I make my way back into the house, leaving him there, sitting alone in the darkness. But, I hope, also giving him the gift that Ben gave me all those years ago. The gift of knowing that, no matter how dark the night, we are never really alone when we are loved.

'Well, you two certainly have been busy while I've been away,' Kendra says. Finn and I were sitting on the porch, waiting, when Dan pulled the car into the drive having been to pick her up from the airport. He'd clearly briefed her on the journey home about our little run-in with the *gendarmes*.

'How was the writing course?' I ask.

'It was great! I learned a lot and I've come up with several new ideas that I'm keen to get on with. But first I need to finish writing *your* story, Philly. I understand Finn's found some evidence that Ben was imprisoned here on the island.'

We have the rubbing of Ben's name ready to show her – neatly laminated, of course – and once we've told her the full story of how he'd worked out where to look, she and Dan both agree to come with us to the *Gendarmerie* the next morning. 'But we all need to be on our best behaviour,' she warns. 'No more getting arrested, OK?'

'OK, Mum,' Finn replies.

'Actually, I was talking to Philly,' she says.

Honestly, hearing that boy's laugh is one of the best things there is. And so is watching the expressions on his parents' faces as they relax their guard for once and join in.

Finn

The policemen were very interested to hear Philly's story and that we'd discovered Ben had been held captive in the citadel in 1944. We'd taken a photocopy of the rubbing of his name, just in case they confiscated that one too, but they handed it back to Mum after she showed it to them and explained what we were looking for.

The main *gendarme* went away and made some phone calls, but he came back shaking his head. 'I'm sorry, Madame. The Germans destroyed all the prison records from the 1940s as the war was ending, before they left the island. We have no way of tracing what became of your husband. All we know is that those prisoners of war who managed to survive were released once France was liberated. Any others, the ones who died while in custody, were buried in the cemetery here in Saint-Martin. Subsequently, the plots were properly marked as war graves.'

'We'll go and check there then,' said Mum. But Philly looked sad, and I knew it was because she'd already checked those war graves online and none of them had a date that might match up with Ben's being here.

We went to the cemetery anyway, because Mum said we might as well take a look as it was on our way home in any case. There are ten war graves in the Saint-Martin cemetery, and they are all airmen. One is unknown, but his date is 1941 – too early to be Ben.

One of the others had a date in August 1944, but his headstone said he was

> **J.W. HEAVNER**
> **PILOT**
> **ROYAL CANADIAN AIRFORCE**
> **12 AUGUST 1944**
> **AGE 21**
> **SON OF HARRY AND CLARE HEAVNER**
> **FLINT, MICH., U.S.A.**

So we knew it couldn't be Ben in that grave either, but I made a rubbing anyway. Then Mum said, 'Right, well, I think we've spent quite enough time in graveyards for one summer.' And we got in the car and went home.

Philly showed me how to look up the records on the Commonwealth War Graves database when we got back to the house, because after I'd laminated the rubbing of his headstone I wanted to find out a bit more about John W. Heavner. He'd been flying a plane called a Bristol Beaufighter, which was shot down by flak while attacking German shipping.

I wondered whether Ben had seen the plane fly over and heard the flak being fired. Maybe he had even been made to help dig the grave, because I could just imagine the Germans making prisoners do that sort of work.

Then I asked Philly if we could go through all the other records for war graves in cemeteries on the Île de Ré, just to double-check again now we had concrete evidence that Ben had definitely been here. She showed me how she'd searched the records. There were two more cemeteries on the island with war graves that we hadn't visited yet, but all the dates were wrong.

'What a lot of war graves there are, just on this one small island,' said Mum.

'I know,' said Philly. 'It just goes to show.'

Then we were all quiet for a bit, thinking about all those people who'd been killed in the war, the ones whose graves we knew about and the ones we didn't.

That evening, while we were having supper, Mum asked Philly what she'd like to do next. 'You're very welcome to stay longer if you'd like. But equally, we'll understand if you want to get back.'

'I'd love to stay longer, especially now we know Ben was actually here. But it's probably time I thought about getting myself home,' she said. 'Perhaps I could stay a couple more days and get a flight booked for one day next week. Whatever is most convenient for you.'

'We can't thank you enough,' said Dad. 'For taking such good care of Finn.'

She laughed. 'I think he took pretty good care of me. And Finn, you finding Ben's name has been more than I ever hoped for.'

I've given her the laminated copy of the original rubbing to keep for the rest of her life and to show to the family. And I've put the photocopy into my collection instead.

'Is there anything else you'd like to do before you leave?' Mum asked her.

She shook her head. But then she thought a moment and said, 'I think I'd like to go back to the cemetery up the lane one last time. I'll say my goodbyes to the island there. And that pot of white heather we put on the grave of the unknown airman probably needs watering, don't you think, Finn?'

I didn't say that the old man would have watered it, because I've seen him do that to the pot plants left on other graves. I wanted to go back to the cemetery with her, and Mum couldn't say no if it was what Philly wanted to do.

Philly

All four of us walk up the lane and along the road to the cemetery. It's my last day – again! – and a silent veil of sea mist has crept over the island in the night, adding to the feeling that this is an ending, a first suggestion of autumn as summer draws to a close. It's a little like being up in a plane again, I think, passing through the clouds before you break through the top into the sunlight above. The donkeys munch on fallen apples as we pass by, lifting their heads briefly before returning to their feast, and the fence around the orchard is festooned with spiders' webs, their gossamer filaments rendered visible by the hundreds of diamond droplets that the mist has strung along their lengths.

By the time we reach the graveyard gate, the sun has started to burn through, beginning to dissolve the blanket of white. Finn pushes open the door in the wall and we file in. We take our time, slowly walking the length of the cemetery to the far corner where the propeller blades mark the section of war graves. The remnants of the mist add to the muffled silence contained within the walls, broken only by the quiet crunch of the gravel underfoot. We have the place to ourselves, apart from the old boy with the rake who seems to spend most of his days there. Perhaps, like me, he's reached the age where he feels he has more in common with the dead than the living.

My pot of white heather is still here, just as I left it, slightly sunk into the gravel in front of the headstone for the unknown airman. I stoop to touch the surface of the soil with my fingertips and am surprised to find it well moistened. Perhaps the night mist has soaked it. Dan and Kendra step to one side, giving me space, reading the memorial plaques to the commando canoeists and those lost in the sinking of the RMS *Lancastria*. And, as usual, Finn wanders off, paper and pencil in hand, in search of more names to add to his collection.

I lean on my walking stick, lost in thoughts of Teddy (the flowers of the white heather bringing him to mind again), and wondering whether Ben ever felt the same sensation of the sun burning away the night's mist, perhaps while he carved his name into the stones beside the citadel. But then, all at once, the silence is disturbed by Finn's call.

'Philly! Come and look at this.'

He's over in the other corner, next to one of the ornate family graves. When I reach him, he points to a small stone alongside it, set low to the ground. It's chiselled with a single word: *Inconnu*. But what's odd about it is that someone has tucked a sprig of white heather into the ground in front of it. A sprig that appears to have been plucked from my own war grave offering.

Finn bends down and picks it up, handing it to me. And as I take it from him, a clattering sound makes me look over towards the wall. The old man has dropped his rake. He's simply standing there, watching us intently. Time seems to stand still, the mist-shrouded island holding its breath.

And then, slowly and very deliberately, the old man raises his hand and salutes.

His accent is thick and difficult to understand. Kendra's French is better than mine, so she's able to translate.

'He's asking whether we're looking for someone. A man who was on the island in 1944.'

Up until that point in the conversation, it could have been anyone. But then he says, 'A prisoner, who had been a British pilot.' And so I know. I can hardly take in his words at first, but then a certainty creeps over me, as if the sun is burning away the mists of doubt as well.

Finn is positively fizzing with excitement. 'We've found him, Philly! We've found Ben!'

'Do you think it really could be him?' asks Kendra.

I try to stay calm. From my time working as a War Detective, I've learned to proceed with caution. It's vital to examine every piece of evidence, to rule out all other possibilities before you can definitively confirm the identity of remains in an unknown grave. But I must confess, I feel it more and more strongly as I stand there. This is where Ben lies, where he's been through all these years of searching. I have to rein in that instinct though. Just because hope makes you long for something to be true doesn't make it so.

I look from Kendra's face to Finn's, their eyes filled with the same sense of hope that is making my heart beat faster. I recognise that feeling – I've seen it written on the faces of so many others down the years, all those other families longing for a conclusion to their own investigations. I've also seen hopes dashed. Often, I've had to disappoint people with the news that it wasn't their loved one who'd been found, or that we still didn't have enough evidence and couldn't conclusively say it was the one they were looking for. Those were the worst verdicts I had to deliver – knowing I was sentencing families to more years without a conclusion to their grief, no end to the not-knowing. So I remind myself again that we need to proceed with caution. It takes an effort, but I pull myself together and begin to formulate the questions we need to ask, the further evidence we need to gather.

The old man introduces himself as Philippe Bertaud – presumably a descendent of the many Bertauds whose names are inscribed on the graves that surround us in the little cemetery. When I tell him my name, he takes both my hands in his. He must be about my age, I think, and his face is deeply lined, weathered by a lifetime in the sun and the wind. His eyes are kind as he looks into mine. 'Madame Delaney,' he says. The words on his lips make my heart rate quicken again as I wonder whether mine is a name he's heard before. 'I have been waiting for you for many years. Come to my home and I will explain everything.'

We go there straight away, the five of us. Finn can hardly contain himself. He keeps running on ahead and then coming back to walk with us, impatient at the slowness of our pace. We turn in just before the orchard with the donkeys. They raise their broad heads to look at us again with their big, lustrous eyes, surprised at the return of this unexpected gaggle of people.

Monsieur Bertaud ushers us in through the door of his cottage and motions to us to take a seat at the table in his kitchen. Its surface is covered in a piece of oilcloth, old but well-scrubbed. He pulls up a chair for himself and then looks across directly at me.

'Please,' I say. 'What can you tell me about my husband?'

He rests his hands on the ancient oilcloth. I notice how gnarled they are, leathery with years of exposure to sun and wind, the joints of each finger as lumpy as oak galls. And then he tells us his story, which Kendra translates for Finn's benefit.

'I met the man in 1944. He was one of the prisoners of war *les Boches* had brought to the island, to be held in the citadel. At the time, I worked with my father in the salt pans, where he was the foreman. Each day, we went to rake the crystals into piles and skim the finer *fleur de sel* from the surface of the ponds. We loaded our baskets and put them on the back of the donkeys to bring them to the town. We were forced to deliver it all to the Germans, who needed it for their armies, and they paid us a pittance. Those were hard times.

'One day, two guards brought a contingent of about a dozen prisoners to the marshes. These men were to be made to work there as a punishment. The guards told us the men would help rake the salt and load the baskets, just as we did, but then they would be made to carry their full baskets on their backs, walking the miles back to Saint-Martin alongside the donkeys, used like beasts of burden. My father and I felt sorry for those poor wretches. They were malnourished, their ribs clearly visible through the tears in their shirts, stomachs distended with hunger. They were covered in sores and scratches, too, and the biting flies and mosquitoes soon added to those open wounds. The work was hard enough, without the added obligation to carry those heavy loads for miles at the end of a long day.' He pauses and shakes his head, remembering.

'The guards were vigilant at first, overseeing every move the men made. But as the weeks wore on, they grew bored of having to stand there among the marsh flies in the wind and the heat. So they would sometimes leave my father in charge and go off to the shade and shelter of a nearby blockhouse to smoke their cigarettes and play cards. Those times gave us the chance to speak to the men, to try to find out where they were from and how they'd ended up on the Île de Ré. We'd give them what food we could spare. Usually, it was no more than a crust of stale bread or a pear from the orchard, but they devoured those scraps as if they were a great feast.'

He raises his head and looks at me directly, his dark eyes as kindly as those of his donkeys. 'I remember your husband well, Madame. His head was shaven, as was the case with all the convicts, but I could see his hair must have been dark. And his eyes were clear and blue, *comme le ciel.* The colour of the sky above our heads and the sea out beyond the dunes.'

Finn can't contain his excitement at this point. 'You see, Philly,' he interjects. 'It was definitely him!'

I smile and nod at him. 'So far, so good,' I say, still forcing myself to stay calm, to try to think clearly and objectively. 'It still doesn't prove it's Ben in that grave though.' Then I gesture to Philippe to continue.

'I liked that man in particular. He had a spirit that couldn't be broken. He told us his name was Ben. He didn't tell us his surname, though. I suppose it was best we didn't know. He said he'd been a pilot, and so I asked him why he wasn't wearing a uniform – or at least what was left of one – like the other military prisoners. He told me he'd been involved in a special mission, so he'd worn civilian clothes in case he was captured. Which he was. But that meant they didn't believe he was just a pilot when they questioned him at the Gestapo headquarters in Poitiers. They accused him of being a spy. When he tried to escape from the prison there, that only made them all the more convinced. He said they'd given him what they called their special treatment, which definitely wouldn't have met any of the codes of conduct governing prisoners of war.'

I must have flinched then, imagining how Ben must have been tortured, because Philippe stops and says, 'I'm sorry, Madame. Perhaps I'm telling you too much?'

'No,' I say. 'I want to know the truth. It's very important. Please tell me everything you remember.'

'He told me, too, that he had a wife and twin babies back home in England, a son and a daughter. That his only wish was to escape and get back to them so he could also carry on doing his bit to bring the war to an end as quickly as possible. I remember how determined he was. I had the sense that nothing the Germans could do to him would break his resolve. No matter how heavy the baskets of salt he had to carry, he walked tall and held his head high.

'One day, when the Germans had disappeared off to the blockhouse for another cigarette break, Ben asked my father and me whether we could help him. He had a plan to get away. It was autumn by then, the days growing shorter, and coming up to a full moon, so the tides were stronger. He wanted to take a small boat and use the tide to help carry him out to sea. He said he thought he could row to Spain, if the wind was in the right direction. We told him that plan was madness, he'd never make it, and the Germans would surely execute him for trying. But then my father said we would help him, with a slightly different plan. We'd get him the boat and he could use the tide to carry him out into the ocean under cover of darkness, but only as far as one of the marker buoys for the lobster pots. The Germans allowed local fishermen to take their boats to sea, as long as they handed over their catch, just as we did our salt. What they didn't realise, though, was that out at sea under cover of darkness, the fishermen were running a line of communication for a Resistance network. They'd rendezvous with Spanish boats and hand over messages and letters, to be delivered to the Allies. My father said he could get word to his brother, who was one of the fishermen, and my uncle would pick Ben up, transferring him to a Spanish boat out at sea.'

He pauses again, making sure we are still listening. Four pairs of eyes are fixed on him with complete concentration, and I think Finn is so intent on the story he's almost forgotten to breathe.

'Please,' I say. 'Tell us.'

'We had a small rowing boat, which we used around the marshes, so the guards weren't suspicious when we pulled it up into the dunes alongside the salt pans one day. By then, the weather was turning. A cold wind began to blow from the north and the Germans grumbled even more about having to be on duty at the marsh. We chose a day when the moon was just past fullness, when the tide would begin to go out in the late afternoon just as dusk was falling. It was an overcast evening, too, dark clouds gathering, but that also suited our plan as the moonlight wouldn't illuminate the little boat as it was carried out into the Atlantic. We told Ben he'd be swept out beyond the lighthouse and there, once he was past the point, he'd find three creel floats, positioned in a triangle. He should row to them and wait for the fishing boat to pick him up. We knew it wouldn't be easy. He'd have to row hard to fight the tide and the waves, and with the night overcast he'd have only the beam from the lighthouse to help pick out the buoys. But if anyone could do it, it was him. We knew he had both the strength and the determination.

'As the working day was ending, Ben slipped away. We knew the guards would do a quick headcount from the shelter of their blockhouse, so I took off my overalls – I was wearing some old clothes underneath them, the same bleached-out colour as Ben's – and shouldered a basket of salt. Once they'd made sure the men were accounted for, it would be easier for us to conceal the fact that one man was missing as we led the others and our donkeys into town to deliver the salt. The Germans wouldn't bother counting again until the baskets had been dropped off and the prisoners were re-entering the prison, by which time Ben would be long gone.'

He stops again, swallowing hard, but this time he avoids my gaze, and his eyes fill with sadness.

'There was a storm brewing, as there so often is in that ocean out there beyond the dunes. It arrived sooner than we'd thought. My uncle still went out beyond the point in his fishing boat, but the conditions were wild. When he reached the marker buoys, there was no sign of Ben and the rowing boat. He waited as long as he could, then had to return to the harbour. Two days later, one of our neighbours told us a body had washed up on the beach at Le Bois-Plage.'

A great sob escapes from me then, a paroxysm of pain and grief released at last. I realise it's been trapped somewhere deep within me for decades, ever since the day I heard Ben had gone missing. The tears flow down my cheeks. I don't think I've ever been able to cry like this before. Kendra leans over and wraps her arms around me, supporting me, while the others sit in silence.

Once the squall of emotion has passed a little, Monsieur Bertaud reaches across the table to take my hand in his, before continuing. 'We recognised Ben straight away. But because he was in civilian clothing, we persuaded the *gendarmes* that it wasn't a matter for the Germans. We knew, you see, that if *les Boches* discovered it was a prisoner who'd escaped, he wouldn't have been given a proper burial. He would just have been thrown into one of the pits they used to dispose of such bodies. The man we'd got to know, who so wanted to get back to his wife and children, deserved better than that.

'They'd have asked a lot of questions of us, too, if they discovered we had gathered so much information about the prisoners and played a part in his escape. It wouldn't have been good for us, and it might even have jeopardised the whole Resistance network, of which my uncle was a part. Anonymity was safer and so we felt it was better to bury him as an unknown civilian. He was interred here in our local graveyard, in that grave marked *Inconnu*, where we could remember him. And where we could wait and hope for his family to come and find him some day.'

The silence sits heavily in the room when Philippe stops talking.

Finn breaks it, saying, 'There. I knew it was Ben. So, Philly, now do we have enough evidence? Can we ask the War Detectives to give him a proper burial, and you can have Closure?'

I take a deep breath, trying to take it all in, trying to make myself think clearly. 'It's certainly a strong case. But we would probably need something more, something to prove the man who's buried in that grave is incontrovertibly Ben. A body washed up on the beach . . . it happened often here, especially after a storm.'

Then Philippe gets to his feet and opens one of the kitchen cabinets, rummaging inside. He brings out a tin, which rattles as he pulls off the lid, and empties something into his hand. 'There was one more thing too, Madame. We took this from his body. He wore it beneath his shirt, tied around his neck on a length of cord.'

He holds out his closed fist and motions for me to open my own hand. And into my outstretched palm he drops the signet ring I gave to Ben on the day we were married. I hold it up to the dusty ray of light filtering in through the kitchen window and there are his initials. BCD. Just the way he'd written them, time after time, in my ATA logbook. And there, too, running along the inside of the band, are the words I'd had engraved for him: *I'll always be yours. P.*

As I hold the ring, clutching it tightly now, the memories flood back in, wrapping their arms around me as if they are Ben's arms, enfolding me again at last.

I remember the first time I saw him as he walked towards me outside an aircraft hangar, both of us rookies but determined to play our part in the war that had just begun. I remember dancing with him at the club and our first kiss at a darkened railway station, then how he stood and watched as the train pulled out. I remember Ben hanging on to my hand as if he'd never let it go again, in the back of an ambulance on the morning he brought me back from France, having flown all night to bring me home. I remember a day in February when I walked up the path to the door of the church in Tangmere to be married to the man who waited for me inside at the altar, turning to smile at me as I entered, his eyes as blue as the winter sky outside. I remember him holding Amy as a tiny baby, his face alight with wonder as he gazed down at her, while I stood next to him, holding Teddy, at their christening. I remember the dark nights and long years without him, never giving up the search to try and find him.

Tears spill down my cheeks again, a manifestation of the bewildering mixture of emotions that overflow from my heart, too much for my body to contain. The room is silent as I pull out a tissue and try to blot them away, but it is quickly soaked and still more tears come. Kendra hands me a hanky and I look up. Now it's my turn to be pinned beneath the scrutiny of four pairs of eyes.

It is Philippe Bertaud who breaks the silence this time. 'I never forgot him, Madame. I tended his grave. And I kept the ring. Just in case his wife or his children ever came looking.'

I look from Philippe to Dan to Kendra. And then I look at Finn. For once, his eyes meet mine and he doesn't flinch and drop his gaze.

I smile through my tears. And then I say, 'Well, Finn. I think at last we have our evidence, don't you?' I hold out my hand, unfurling my fingers, the ring gleaming softly in my palm. 'You've done it. You and Monsieur Bertaud have given me the final, definitive proof that now – at last – we've found Ben.'

Finn

We had to cancel Philly's flight home again. She said at this rate her family will start to think she's been kidnapped by us and is being held hostage on the island. But now she had some great news to tell them, about finding Ben. I think her twins must have been very pleased to know where their dad was, at long last.

There was a lot that had to be done officially to persuade everyone that it really was Ben in that grave. It wasn't just as easy as digging up the coffin and taking him back to England. First of all, we had to go back to tell the *gendarmes*. That took quite a lot of time. We showed them the evidence we'd gathered, which included the rubbing I'd done of Ben's name from the citadel walls that we'd shown them before to persuade them to look up the prison records from the war years. Of course, that reminded them that I'd been trespassing, and I was a bit worried they might have to arrest me all over again, but the main one just whistled through his teeth and said, 'Bravo, *jeune homme*,' so I knew they were going to let me off. Then everything had to be passed to the mayor and they had to speak to Philippe to get his testimony. And then it all had to be escalated to the Powers That Be, which meant a particular department in the French government. There was an awful lot of paperwork to fill in.

Philly got in touch with the War Detectives in Britain too, and they put some pressure on the French authorities when they seemed to be questioning things for a bit too long. Then there was even more paperwork. Mum and Dad helped. Philly went home, but we stayed on the island longer than we usually do to make sure no one could forget about Ben all over again.

Then we went home for Christmas and waited some more. But at last, in the spring, they decided they could dig up the coffin in the *Inconnu* grave and do a DNA test on the person who was buried there. They had taken DNA samples from Philly's twins to compare. The results came back 99.99 per cent probable that it really was Ben in the coffin. And as Dad said, that was enough certainty even for the French authorities.

I had assumed Ben would be taken back to England, but, in fact, that turned out not to be the case. Philly told me there's a rule about it for people who died in either of the World Wars: 'served together, died together, buried together'. So they are buried with their compatriots, in war graves in the country where they were killed.

'Are you disappointed you can't take him home with you?' I asked, when she came back in the spring.

'A bit,' she said. 'But it's a comfort knowing he'll have a proper grave here on the island. And that means there's somewhere for me to come and visit. Amy and Teddy too.'

'OK,' I said. 'And Philippe and I will take good care of it when you're not here.'

'Thank you, Finn. I know you will, and that means a lot to me.'

Her twins, Teddy and Amy, had come to the island with her this time. They were here for the ceremony, but they also wanted to meet Philippe and hear the stories of their dad and how he tried so hard to escape and get home to them all.

Philly stayed with us in the house, but Teddy and Amy stayed in a hotel, because otherwise it would have been a bit too cramped for everyone. They're nice. Teddy used to be a pilot in the RAF, flying planes like his mum and dad, and Amy was in the Foreign

Office, but they're both retired now and even have children and grandchildren of their own.

I took them to Philippe's house. I've been going there sometimes to help him with his bees. He says I make a good beekeeper because I can stay focused, even when we open up the hives and take out the frames holding the honeycomb to spin it and extract the honey. The bees buzz around us, but it's OK as we're wearing our white suits and hoods with netting on. I like wearing the suit. It makes me feel safe and cocooned, so I can stay calm. Sometimes I wear it around the house or to go to the market with Mum and Dad because it protects me from the noise and the people, just like it protects me from the bees. I'd like to wear it all the time. It would be good for going back to school in, but then I suppose the other kids would think I was even weirder.

Philippe's bees seem to trust him, and he says they never sting if you treat them with respect. He believes in doing it the old-fashioned way, only taking the honey that's left over after the winter so that the bees have had enough supplies to keep them going. In the spring, once the blossom on the trees in the orchard comes out, they can collect nectar and begin to make more, so we can take what's left as there's no risk of them starving.

We went with Philippe to the salt pans as well and he showed Philly's twins where their dad had worked. They all cried when they thought about Ben being bitten by flies and the salt getting into the sores on his legs. Philippe told them, too, that Ben had always been brave and dignified, that you could tell he was made of strong stuff, and that his love for his family kept him going even in the toughest times. That made them all cry again.

On the day before the ceremony, Philly asked me if I would take her out on the dinghy one last time. Amy and Teddy said they'd like to get out on to the water as well, so Dad took them all out in the bigger boat and we followed them in the Laser. That was a good day, because it wasn't too hot yet and the wind was just strong enough to make us go fast. When we got to the lagoon, Philly took a sprig of white heather from her pocket and let it float on the water. We let the boat drift for a few minutes, and stayed alongside the heather as the tide began to carry it towards the lighthouse. Philly shaded her eyes with her hand against the dazzle of the sunshine and watched the little sprig until it disappeared among the waves. She was holding on to the signet ring with Ben's initials, which she wears on a gold chain around her neck.

I sat still and kept quiet because I understood it was important to her to say that goodbye in her own way, in the place where Ben had got into a little rowing boat and headed out into the wildness of the sea one stormy night as he tried to get home to her again. Then a pair of kittiwakes swooped above the mast. They called to each other, their wings spread wide, and I thought they looked a bit like aeroplanes, flying in formation together. I saw Philly notice them as well, and her red lips turned upwards into a smile as she watched them fly away, soaring out over the ocean as the waves flung little drops of spray into the air around the bow of our boat.

And then I knew she had been able to Come to Terms with losing Ben, now she understood what had happened. She had found Closure and finished the Unfinished Business.

'Right then,' Philly said at last, turning to me when she'd finished thinking her thoughts about Ben and the kittiwakes. 'Are you ready to take me home, Skipper?'

We waved to the others, and I turned the dinghy so we had the wind behind us. It felt a bit like we were flying, too, as we headed back to the harbour.

When Dad came to tuck me in that night, he said, 'I'm very proud of you, you know, Finn. You're a competent sailor now. And you've done an incredible thing, helping Philly find Ben and bring him home.' He held up his hand and spread his fingers, making the starfish sign.

And then I did something I've never done before. I reached out my hand and held my palm right against his. And this time I didn't mind the touching. Because I knew Dad would get into a rowing boat and risk his life to try to get back to me and Mum if he was ever taken prisoner. I know that he loves me as much as Ben loved Philly and his children.

Philly

It's a winter's day when we gather at the churchyard gate in Tangmere. I'm quite overwhelmed at the turnout, not just my children and grandchildren, who surround me with their love, but the servicemen and women from the RAF, my former colleagues from the MOD's War Detectives team, volunteers from the military aviation museum next door, and of course Kendra, Dan and Finn, who have travelled down from Scotland to be here.

Ben's body lies in the cemetery on the island now, in a properly marked grave alongside the other servicemen, where we can go and visit him. The re-committal ceremony was beautifully done. But today we're also holding a memorial service for him here, in this church that holds so many of our memories. It's harder than I thought it would be, steeling myself to say my final goodbye to the love of my life, the husband I married in this same place so long ago.

Today, Ben waits for me at the altar again. But this time it's just a photo of him. His old RAF cap, which I've kept so carefully all these years, sits beside it, along with a bouquet with his family's handwritten cards tucked among the white lilies. A poppy wreath of remembrance is set beneath it. How proud he would have been of his children, who stand at my side, and how he would have loved his grandchildren and great-grandchildren who have all gathered with us to bear witness and pay their respects.

The RAF chaplain delivers the address and Teddy and Amy each do a reading. When Amy reads the poem Ben sent me, there's a flurry of handkerchiefs among the congregation. I glance across the aisle to where Finn sits between his parents. He's taken off his ear defenders to listen to the words. I hold up my hand, spreading my fingers wide like a starfish, and he returns the gesture, unsmiling, but connecting us in that moment across the distance that separates us.

Then the service draws to a close with one last hymn and we file out of the church in silence, passing between the RAF guards of honour who line the path. Apart from the crunch of boots on the gravel path, the only sound is the song of a mistle thrush, filling the churchyard with the promise of a spring yet to come.

Finn puts his sunglasses and ear defenders back on, squaring his shoulders, ill at ease in the crowd. Suddenly, as if out of nowhere, the air reverberates with an unexpected thunder of engines. I see Kendra glance down anxiously at Finn. No surprises! How will he react? Thankfully, though, his ear defenders do the job and he simply tilts his face to the winter sunshine, his eyes hidden behind his sunglasses, as a trio of planes appears above us, flying in formation. I look up in amazement, recognising the Spitfires. They circle overhead, each pilot tipping his wings in a salute, before they reform and then soar skywards, perfectly synchronised as they loop the loop, before roaring off into the distance. There's a ripple of applause, smiles on faces – including Finn's – and as the sound fades, a new sense of peace seems to settle in my heart. The relentless, life-long searcher within me has been laid to rest at last, too, now we know how Ben's story ends.

◆ ◆ ◆

Kendra, Dan and Finn come home to stay with me in Cheltenham for a few nights. We've arranged to take Finn round the Tangmere Museum, and then I have a big day out with a trip to Bletchley Park planned for them a couple of days later. I've discussed it in detail with Finn so there will be no surprises.

Dan goes out to get fish and chips for our supper and once we've finished (Finn having carefully selected exactly ten chips to put on the plate beside his haddock), he accompanies Finn upstairs to the bedroom that was once Teddy's. I know how hard it must be for Finn, sleeping in a strange house, but he's taken his medication and seems to be coping with it so far. I've shown him and Kendra how to open the back door and get out into the garden, just in case they need to go outdoors for a walk in the middle of the night.

As Dan settles Finn and reads him a few chapters of the book I've given him – my old copy of Amy Johnson's *Sky Roads of the World* – Kendra and I go through to the sitting room with cups of camomile tea. It's been a long day, but a good one. I think I'll sleep well, but still don't want to risk a cup of coffee at this late hour.

'Finn did so well today,' I say. 'I hope it wasn't too much for him.'

'He loved it! He's been talking non-stop about the Spitfires ever since.' Her face relaxes into a smile, broader than any I'd seen when I stayed with them in France those times. She seems a little less exhausted. Dan looks happier, too.

'And you?' I ask. 'How's the book going?'

'Really well. And I've got a contract to write another one too. So we're OK for the foreseeable future.'

'That's good news. And Finn's starting at the new school next term?'

She nods. 'Fingers crossed. He's already given it his seal of approval, though. It's a far better environment for him, I think. Specialist staff, great facilities. He and Dan have begun covering some of the curriculum topics to help ease him in. No surprises!'

She's silent for a moment, then says quietly, 'Dan and I are better as well. We've managed to find a little bit more time for each other. Last summer, having you there with us in France, it helped us both see things differently.' She looks up, fixing me with her beautiful sea-green eyes as she tucks a strand of hair back from her face. I can see there's more she wants to say, so I say nothing, giving her the space to find the words.

'Philly, you know what it is to spend your life searching for someone, so I think you get it. Ever since Finn was born, I feel as if Dan and I have spent our lives searching for our son. We never had the child we'd thought we would – all our preconceptions and expectations turned out to be wrong. He turned out to be someone entirely different. And so we've had to set aside our own ideas of how life should be – of how a child should be – and search for ways to engage with him, to keep him safe, to teach him what he needs to know in order to be able to navigate his way through this world. Hopefully, too, to be able to support himself when we're no longer here to do it for him. It's exhausting and unremitting. But, like you, we will never give up that search.'

I let her words sink in. Then I say, 'And that, my dear, is surely the definition of unconditional love. You once told me some people think you and Dan are bad parents. Well, I think you're two of the best parents I've ever met. You've sacrificed so much in your own lives, in order to be with Finn in his. No matter how hard it is, you will always be there at his side. That's nothing short of heroic, so don't let anyone tell you otherwise or make you feel as if you're failing. I've seen how you meet the relentless challenges you face every day with grace and humour and imagination, while still managing to remain true to your own values of kindness and humanity and creativity. Summoning up the endless energy to parent an autistic child day in, day out, is a testament to your love for your son.'

'Thank you, Philly,' she says. 'You've helped us a lot, you know.'

I laugh. 'Not as much as you've helped me, my dear. My family too. We owe a great debt of gratitude to the persistence of that wonderful son of yours.'

Dan comes into the room, joining Kendra on the sofa and putting an arm around her, pulling her close. 'Finn's dropped off. He has the book beside his bed in case he wakes up in the middle of the night.' He grins at me. 'Thanks for that, Philly. It's not exactly the easiest of reads, is it? A bit dated now, but the detailed facts and figures about all those routes she flew are right up his street! I've promised him we can do a project on them when we get home.' Kendra rests her head on her husband's shoulder for a moment and he drops a light kiss on to her hair.

As I watch them, I think about their son as he sleeps upstairs, exhausted after another long day filled with challenges that the rest of us can't fully understand. I think about the summer we spent together, how I began to learn a little more about this brave family, to see how extraordinary they all are.

'You know,' I muse, 'it's not always the bright light of day that shows us the truth. It has been the dark of the moon that's come to mean more to me, as my perspective has changed over the course of my life. In the short time I had with Ben, instead of looking forward to the sunlit days and moonlit nights, I came to love the darkness. The times in between. Those were the times when he wasn't flying, you see. The times we had together. I think I always knew I needed to treasure them because they wouldn't last.'

The two of them wait, expecting me to say more. But I leave it at that. They will understand, one day, that their extraordinary son – whose mind is as mysterious and unknowable as the far side of the moon – has a brilliance all of his own. He will shine, in his own way, when the sun and the Earth align to allow him to do so.

To be able to see it, it just depends on where you're standing.

'Well,' I say, hauling myself up with the help of my stick, 'I think I'll retire too now. Sleep well, my dears.'

I leave them sitting there together hand in hand, pondering my words, encircled by the halo of light cast by the lamp, the shadows dark beyond them, as I make my way slowly upstairs to bed.

Finn

The museum at Tangmere was really interesting. Philly knows all the volunteers there and they were very helpful. We went early so it wasn't too crowded. I really liked the Typhoon simulator, and I managed to land it. You have to stay very focused. Dad crashed. Philly bounced but managed to take off again quickly. 'I've lost my touch,' she said. 'But still, not bad for an ancient Attagirl.'

There was a Lysander in the museum, but it's one that was built for a film, not a real one, which is a shame. I think I'd have liked to have tried going up in one. There were some displays about some of the Lysander pilots who flew their missions from the airfield, and about the farmhouse at Bignor where Philly helped out with the French agents who came over. There was a bit about Violette Szabo and her poem code too.

We took a walk up on to the South Downs and there were good views down across the airfield and out to the English Channel. It was quite windy up there, but I took off my ear defenders when we got to the top because I wanted to listen to Philly's stories about being there with Ben during the dark moon periods. Then we went back to her house, and I spent the afternoon laminating the leaflets I picked up at the museum and checking the plans for tomorrow, making sure everything is in place. Mum and I had organised a Big Surprise because even though I don't enjoy them, I think

Philly does. And if I'm the one organising the surprise then it isn't a surprise to me.

That night, at bedtime, Mum and I read some more of Amy Johnson's book, about the dangerous South Atlantic crossing. She never flew that route, but her husband, Jim Mollison, did. Amelia Earhart had also flown that route in her Lockheed 10-E Electra as part of her attempt to fly around the world, but she went missing later on, somewhere in the Pacific Ocean in 1937. So that's another person for me to try to find one day.

At the end of the chapter, Amy Johnson says, '*I envy not clothes, jewels and luxuries, but experiences lived through, dangers survived, difficulties overcome. Perhaps some day, when the route is opened to passengers – a day not far-distant – I may see these smiling South Atlantic skies and these flooding sheets of torrential rain in the safety and comfort of a huge flying-boat, but it can never be the same as a lone flight against the elements, with not only nature but the whole world against you crying "Fool!"*' So it turns out even she must have felt like she was a Mentalist sometimes, which, as Philly says, just goes to show how wrong people can be. I've copied out the section and laminated it so I can keep it as a reminder.

I felt sleepy, so we put the book aside and then I pressed my hand against Mum's as we did our starfish sign. I really don't mind the touching feeling anymore, in fact it's quite reassuring.

'All set for another big day tomorrow?' Mum said.

'Do you think they'll be able to do the Marmite sandwiches?' I asked.

She smiled. 'Well, it's The Ritz. So I think they can do pretty much anything.' And then she turned out the light and I went to sleep.

Philly

We drive up to London. The traffic is terrible, of course, and there's the congestion charge and the parking on top of that, but Dan takes it all in his stride. I sit in front, so I can stretch out my leg in comfort, and Kendra and Finn are in the back. I glance in the mirror to watch Finn's face. He's wearing his ear defenders, and an expression of resolute determination, but I can still see the tension around his eyes. I only hope whatever it is they've organised is going to be worth it. I wouldn't want it to end in another disaster after they've gone to so much trouble. All they've told me is there's some big surprise. Which is a surprise in its own right. I can see how much it means to him, though, so I go along with it.

We walk through Green Park beneath the bare branches of the trees, and turn in at a set of grey stone arches, straight up to the main door of The Ritz, where Finn turns to me with a look of triumph.

'Oh, my goodness,' I say, feeling somewhat overcome. 'Are we here for tea?'

'Yes. It's another bit of Unfinished Business, so we are going to help you finish it today.'

'Well, this really IS a wonderful surprise, Finn.'

A top-hatted doorman ushers us inside with a flourish, not batting an eyelid even though we can't look much like his usual clientele: an old woman with her walking stick and a young lad wearing ear defenders and now – even though it's a dull London day – his sunglasses as well, which he's put on in order to help him face this ordeal.

At the Palm Court we're shown to a table in one corner, tucked behind a large potted plant and facing away from the mirrored end wall. Finn sits with his back to the room. He sheds the sunglasses but keeps his ear defenders firmly clamped to his head, shutting out the babble of chatter and the clinking of cutlery on china. The room is already filling up, even though we've come for the earliest sitting. I look around, taking it all in, from the crisp white tablecloths to the white-and-gold pillars and the ornately gilded dome of the ceiling above where we're sitting. A piano tinkles discreetly in the background at the far end of the room.

Kendra excuses herself, saying, 'I'll just go and find the Ladies.' I turn my attention back to our table. There seems to be an extra place set, which I suppose must be a mistake, despite all of Finn's meticulous planning.

But then Kendra returns, and Dan is getting to his feet, pulling out chairs, and I realise they've invited an extra guest. The woman pulls off the red scarf covering her hair and undoes the buttons of her overcoat. Then she says, 'Finn, it's so good to meet you in person at last,' holding up her hand and mouthing the words clearly so he'll understand. Her accent is French, but there's something else beneath it. It takes me a moment and then I identify it: a faint twang of Polish.

'Philly,' says Kendra. 'May we introduce you to Eveline Espelet? Also known as Dr Ewelina Krakowska. This is Janina and Jakub's daughter.'

And then there are exclamations and tears, and laughter and more tears as she enfolds me in a warm embrace, before taking her seat at the table.

Once the emotions have died down a little, Finn tells me how he managed to track her down in another miracle of persistence and determination. 'It was through a maths blog. She was invited on as a guest because she's Professor of Mathematics at the Sorbonne which is a university in Paris.'

'I've heard of it,' I say, nodding.

'Her specialist field is Partial Differential Equations,' he says. 'Seeing her name was a coincidence, but I remembered you said Janina's surname was Krakowska, so I recognised it straight away. And then I realised Ewelina is the Polish version of Eveline, which was your code name in France. So I came up with a hypothesis that this could be Janina and Jakub's missing daughter and I sent her a message and the hypothesis turned out to be correct.'

A waiter hovers, but Dan asks him to give us a little more time as we have much to catch up on, and Ewelina tells me her story.

'I grew up in a tiny village in the Pyrenees, believing my name to be Eveline Espelet and my parents to be French. When I reached my teens, and I was old enough to know such things, they told me my real parents had been a Polish couple to whom they had given sanctuary during the war. A neighbour had denounced them to the Gestapo and they'd been arrested one night. But there was just time to hide me. The French couple who'd taken us in passed me off as their child in order to save me. They kept me safe as my real parents were taken away to their deaths. All I have of them is this headscarf of my mother's, and my name. They called me Ewelina, the Polish version of the French name Eveline. My adopted parents told me they'd said it had been the name of a dear friend of theirs. I was named in honour of another brave soul who had tried to help them.'

Her words make me cry all over again. Once I've blotted the tears from my face, I raise my hand towards Finn across the table, spreading my fingers wide. 'You truly are a remarkable boy,' I say.

He looks at me, his expression serious. 'Are you happy or sad, Philly? Now you are having tea at The Ritz with Janina's daughter?'

'Bless your soul, my dear, I am utterly happy. Absolutely stunned by your brilliant surprise, but totally and utterly happy.'

I really don't think it can get any better. But then the waiter reappears and sets down towering stands of cakes and scones in front of us. And with a final flourish, he puts a smaller plate down before Finn, saying, 'Your special dietary requirement, sir. Marmite sandwiches, as ordered.' And my joy is complete.

Finn

Ewelina met us at Bletchley Park the next day. She was very interested to see the memorial to the Polish cryptographers and to hear all about Philly's experiences working there, which had led to her meeting Jakub and Janina at the château in France. She laid two red roses on the plinth, one for each of her parents.

Ewelina was wearing her red scarf and Philly was wearing a black jacket with a little gold and blue brooch on the lapel. She saw me noticing it and she showed it to me. 'It's my Bletchley Park commemorative badge,' she said. It had the letters GC&CS at the top, for the Government Code and Cypher School, and the dates 1939–1945. As we were going round the rest of the Park, I spotted another lady wearing one so I knew she must have been there during the war as well. I pointed her out to Philly but she said she didn't recognise her, but as there had been about 9,000 people who had worked at Bletchley Park and its outposts it was statistically unlikely that they would have known each other.

Philly showed us the Hut where she'd worked with Alan Turing and the Cottage where she met Dilly Knox. There was even an old-fashioned car in the stable block, just like the one she'd been driven down to Tangmere in. We walked through the rooms in the main house, and she swore she could still smell the over-boiled cabbage in the dining room, but I think she was imagining things. It just smelled of dusty carpets and old wood panelling to me.

In one of the other buildings there was a display which was all about Enigma machines and the origins of supercomputers, which I found very interesting. Then it got a bit busy and suddenly there were too many people, and we had to go outside quite quickly because I started feeling panicky.

'Let's go and see the lake,' Philly said. We walked away from the crowds and stood on the grass under the trees on the far side. 'We used to come and sit out here in our lunch breaks if the sun was shining,' Philly said. 'Not Alan, he'd stay at his desk, whatever the weather. But some of the others. And occasionally I'd meet Jess here, if we were both doing a day shift and our lunch hours coincided.'

'What a lot of extraordinary people there must have been,' said Mum. 'I had no idea there were so many thousands who worked here. It makes it all the more remarkable that none of the secrets ever leaked out.'

'I don't think we realised how extraordinary it really was, at the time,' said Philly. She was leaning on her walking stick with one hand, while the fingers of the other were touching her commemorative Bletchley Park badge. 'But you're right. It was a place filled with brilliance. People like Alan and Dilly, obviously, but all the others who played their part as well. We may have been hidden away in our own little universe, but there were thousands of stars here, secretly shining in the darkness of war. Each of us determined to make a difference and bring it to an end as quickly as we possibly could.'

She was quiet for a few moments. The winter sunlight slanted through the bare branches of the trees and shimmered across the surface of the water, glinting on Ben's signet ring where it hung on the chain around her neck.

I thought about the film we'd gone to see at the open-air cinema in France the summer before. And then a line from it popped into my head. 'Do you remember what Keira Knightley said to Benedict Cumberbatch at the end of *The Imitation Game*? That sometimes it's the people no one imagines anything of who do the things no one can imagine.'

She looked at me and her red lips turned upwards into a smile. 'I do indeed,' she said. Then she unpinned the Bletchley Park brooch from the lapel of her jacket, and she held it out to me. 'I want you to have this, Finn. Because you have done things I never could have imagined. Finding Ben for me. And Ewelina.'

I took it from her and put it in my pocket. I remembered to say thank you as well. I wasn't going to wear it, because obviously I hadn't actually worked at Bletchley Park, but I decided I'd take it home and put it in the special drawer where I keep my most treasured possessions. The photocopied rubbing of Ben's name is in there. And I'm going to laminate the menu from our tea at The Ritz and keep it there too.

'I'd like to go home now,' I said. And so we all walked back to the car park. Ewelina said she'd give Philly a lift to the station to catch her train and we all said goodbye. Mum and Dad had booked us a room in a Travelodge for the night. But when we got into our car, I said again, 'I'd really like to go home now.'

They looked at each other and nodded. 'Me too,' said Dad. 'Let's just go then.' And so he turned the car towards the motorway.

It was completely dark by the time we crossed the border into Scotland. Mum was fast asleep in the back and I was sitting in front with Dad. He said it was like he was the Pilot and I was the Navigator, although we have Satnav so I didn't really have to do any map-reading. Instead, I was watching the lit-up signs flash past us and counting the emergency telephones along the side of the motorway. I thought it might be useful to know where the nearest one was, in case we broke down and then discovered that Dad's phone had run out of battery. In the distances between the signs and the phones, the road was lit only by the car's headlamps and the moon which was shining in the sky towards the west. It reminded me about something Philly had said to me one day when we were sitting on the porch at the house in France and I'd been telling her about Synchronous Tidal Locking and the moon never turning its back on the Earth. I told her, 'There isn't a dark side of the moon, you know. It's more accurate to call it the far side, because it does receive sunlight at certain times. It's just that we never see it.'

And then she said, 'I think people are like that, Finn. There's the face they show and then the side they keep hidden. It's the less obvious side that can be the most intriguing.'

'I'm not very good at understanding the side people show,' I said. 'So I don't think I'll be any good at understanding the dark side.'

She shook her head. 'No, I don't think that's the case. I think you are better at it than you imagine because you aren't dazzled by the light of the obvious in the way that other people are. Like the stars, which are always shining, but we can't see them in the daytime because the light of the sun blots them out. You see the truth, though, because you look at life through a lens of logic and persistence.'

We passed another emergency phone – the 122nd since I'd started counting them – and I thought about how people can get lost. It made me feel a bit panicky but then I held the Bletchley Park badge in my pocket tightly and I looked at Dad's face, lit up by the glow from the dashboard, and I felt calmer. So then I went back to that thought. People can get lost. And some might never be able to be found, like Amy Johnson and Amelia Earhart. But if you're very persistent and you use logic, sometimes you can be the person who finds even the ones that other people have given up on.

They are out there, waiting to be found. Just because you can't see them, it doesn't mean they're not there. You don't always have to see things to still believe in them.

Like gravity.

Like truth.

Like the stars in daytime.

Like the far side of the moon.

Like Ewelina.

Like Ben.

Q.E.D.

AUTHOR'S NOTES AND ACKNOWLEDGEMENTS

The Dark of the Moon is one of a trio of books telling the stories of three school friends – the 'Three Musketeers' – whom Philly refers to when she first arrives on the island to stay with Kendra, Dan and Finn. Philly, Ella and Bea were three ordinary young women whose lives were changed by the onset of the Second World War. If you'd like to know more, you can read Ella's story (and meet Kendra, Dan and Finn too) in *Sea of Memories*, and Beatrice's story in *The Cypress Maze*. However, each book can also be read as a stand-alone novel in its own right.

There are many fascinating books about the ATA, the Bletchley Park codebreakers and the courage of the Special Operations Executive agents who operated in Europe, all doing their bit to help hasten the end of the Second World War. Just a few of these are listed here for readers who may wish to delve deeper . . .

Contact! Britain! – An American Woman Ferry Pilot's Life During WWII, by Nancy Miller Livingston Stratford.

No More Secrets – My Part in Codebreaking at Bletchley Park and the Pentagon, by Betty Webb.

Dilly: The Man Who Broke Enigmas, by Mavis Batey.

Between Silk and Cyanide – A Code Maker's War 1941–45, by Leo Marks.

Mission France – The True History of the Women of SOE, by Kate Vigurs.

Resistance – The Underground War in Europe, 1939–45, by Halik Kochanski.

Amy Johnson's book, *Sky Roads of the World*, details her pioneering flights, which would later open up the world to commercial air travel, made before she joined the Air Transport Auxiliary to assist the war effort. Her obituary in *The Woman Engineer* magazine, written by the society's president, Caroline Haslett, in 1941 sums up not just her aeronautical achievements but also who she was as a person: *All the world knows of the Amy Johnson who flew solo to Australia ten years ago, but it is perhaps those who knew her more closely who were able to appreciate her gifts and abilities, the generosity of her mind, her modesty over real achievement, her unquenchable spirit which, with her keen wit and boundless humour, must have carried her through times of tedium as well as of horrific experience. Whatever Amy did she did it with zest and relish.*

The Lysander missions, dropping off and picking up agents deep behind enemy lines, are commemorated at the Tangmere Military Aviation Museum, near Chichester. Just some of the incredible stories of those who ran these clandestine operations are told in the following books:

We Landed By Moonlight – The Secret RAF Landings in France 1940–1944, by Hugh Verity.

Lysander Pilot – Secret Operations with 161 Squadron, by James Atterby McCairns.

French Resistance in Sussex – by Barbara Bertram (detailing her experiences of hosting agents in her home).

A House for Spies – SIS Operations into Occupied France from a Sussex Farmhouse, by Edward Wake-Waller.

Dermot Turing's book *X, Y and Z – The Real Story of How Enigma was Broken* examines the Polish contribution to breaking Enigma, crediting them with handing over their findings to Alan Turing and his colleagues at a secret meeting outside Paris in 1939 on the eve of the British entry into the war. Without this collaboration, the Bletchley Park codebreakers wouldn't have been able to make such rapid progress, building on the vital work of the team of Polish cryptanalysts.

Only as recently as the year 2000 was the Anglo-Polish Historical Committee established, made up of historians and official experts from both countries, to identify and evaluate surviving records that would show the extent of the contribution made by Polish Intelligence to the Allied victory in the Second World War. Their reports make lengthy and fascinating reading. In a paper entitled *Cryptographic Co-operation – Enigma*, the record is set straight, emphasising the fact that among all the Poles who knew about Enigma not a single one turned out to be a Soviet or German agent. The Polish cryptanalysts, even when facing the threat of death, heroically kept the secret.

In my own attempt to retain historical accuracy, I always try to stick to the truth as far as possible and have therefore mentioned many of the real Polish cryptanalysts by name. However, Janina and Jakub and their daughter, Ewelina, are fictional characters. They are based on a real Polish couple who did serve in Château Cadix as cryptographers, Henryk Paszkowski (a Polish and French language specialist), and his wife, Janina Paszkowska (a cipher clerk). Janina was pregnant when they fled to try to escape to Britain via Spain, but they became stranded in France, near Toulouse, when the baby arrived in 1943. All my attempts to try to find out what happened to them drew a blank. Perhaps if anyone knows, they will tell me.

Poem codes were used by the SOE as a relatively simple means of allowing agents to communicate with Britain from mainland Europe. The poem that Ben gives to Philly is one I have written myself. It was inspired, however, by the poem known as *The Life That I Have* (or sometimes simply *Yours*), given to Violette Szabo by one of her SOE 'minders', Leo Marks, and made famous in the film *Carve Her Name With Pride*.

For helping me with my research into Autism and Autistic Spectrum Disorders, I'm deeply grateful to Pamela Griffin for sparing the time to talk to me (as if she wasn't busy enough already), and to Finnan, without whom the laminating machine might not have made an appearance.

I'm also grateful to my friends Derek Smith and Margaret Whitten who pointed me in the direction of several different sources of information. I found two books especially useful:

George and Sam – by Charlotte Moore (a bravely down-to-earth and moving account of parenting autistic sons).

Stim: An Autistic Anthology, compiled by Lizzie Huxley-Jones, and particularly Robert Shepherd's story *Becoming Less*, which references the Selkie myth.

Autism Afloat is a purely fictitious organisation. But the idea to run a sailing camp was inspired by seeing a yacht belonging to Autism on the Water, a Scottish-based organisation started by autistic sailor Murray MacDonald. The charity aims to increase awareness of the autistic spectrum through sailing and boating. More information can be found on their website here: www.autismonthewater.net.

Thanks, as well, to the many friends who took an interest and helped me in the writing of this novel:

John and Rachel Stapleton – for introducing me to Tangmere Museum as well as the Manor at Bignor, and the stories of the SOE Lysander operations to and from France.

Mala Saye – for coming with me to visit Bletchley Park, helping to explain the bits my brain just couldn't comprehend, and checking my maths.

The wonderful team of volunteers at the Tangmere Military Aviation Museum, and in particular Sheryl Green for checking certain technical details of the Lysander. Sheryl's website – www.courageindisguise.co.uk – outlines some of the talks she gives, conveying her passion for wartime history.

Fiona Ritchie and Ruth Brown of the Dunkeld & Birnam Archive (www.historicdunkeld.org.uk), who shared their experience of working with the MOD's War Detectives to identify and commemorate a local soldier killed during the First World War, who had lain in an unknown grave for over a century. Thanks to their combined efforts, 2nd Lieutenant David Bell's final resting place is now known and has been properly re-dedicated.

My unending gratitude goes out to the Lake Union team at Amazon Publishing – especially Sammia Hamer, Nicole Wagner, Eoin Purcell, Sana Chebaro and Bekah Graham – as well as editors *par excellence* Mike Jones, Jenni Davis and Swati Gamble, and to Emma Rogers, who designs the beautiful covers for my books.

My brilliant agent, Madeleine Milburn, and her team are all superstars, working tirelessly to make sure my books find their way into the hands of readers the whole world over. I am so grateful, too, to every single one of those readers (and that means YOU!), for supporting my books and for all the wonderful reviews.

And lastly, love to all the other family and friends who support me in so many ways, big and small, every single day.

ABOUT THE AUTHOR

Fiona Valpy spent seven years living in France, before returning to live in Scotland. Her love for both of these countries, their people and their histories, has found its way into the books she's written.

She draws inspiration from the stories of strong women, especially during the years of the Second Word War, and her meticulous historical research enriches her writing with an evocative sense of time and place.

An acclaimed Number 1 bestselling author, Fiona Valpy's books have been translated into thirty languages worldwide.

Follow the Author on Amazon

If you enjoyed this book, follow Fiona Valpy on Amazon to be notified when the author releases a new book!
To do this, please follow these instructions:

Desktop:

1) Search for the author's name on Amazon or in the Amazon App.
2) Click on the author's name to arrive on their Amazon page.
3) Click the 'Follow' button.

Mobile and Tablet:

1) Search for the author's name on Amazon or in the Amazon App.
2) Click on one of the author's books.
3) Click on the author's name to arrive on their Amazon page.
4) Click the 'Follow' button.

Kindle eReader and Kindle App:

If you enjoyed this book on a Kindle eReader or in the Kindle App, you will find the author 'Follow' button after the last page.